Unbridled

Unbridled

K. L. McKain

HODDER CHILDREN'S BOOKS

First published in Great Britain in 2026 by Hodder & Stoughton Limited

1 3 5 7 9 10 8 6 4 2

Text copyright © K. L. McKain, 2026
Cover illustration copyright © Kim Ekdahl, 2026

The moral right of the author has been asserted.

*All characters and events in this publication, other than those clearly
in the public domain, are fictitious and any resemblance to
real persons, living or dead, is purely coincidental.*

All rights reserved.
No part of this publication may be reproduced, stored in
a retrieval system, or transmitted, in any form or by any means, without
the prior permission in writing of the publisher, nor be otherwise circulated
in any form of binding or cover other than that in which it is published
and without a similar condition including this condition being
imposed on the subsequent purchaser.

A CIP catalogue record for this book is available from the British Library.

ISBN 978 1 444 98383 8

Typeset in 10.88/14.35 Adobe Garamond Pro by Six Red Marbles UK, Thetford, Norfolk
Printed and bound in Great Britain by Clays Ltd, Elcograf S.p.A.

The paper and board used in this book are made from wood from responsible sources.

Hodder Children's Books
An imprint of
Hachette Children's Group
Part of Hodder & Stoughton Limited
Carmelite House
50 Victoria Embankment
London EC4Y 0DZ

The authorised representative in the EEA is Hachette Ireland,
8 Castlecourt Centre, Dublin 15, D15 XTP3, Ireland (email: info@hbgi.ie)

An Hachette UK Company
www.hachette.co.uk

www.hachettechildrens.co.uk

To Captain and Sparks – thank you
for teaching me about connection

Chapter One

Carrie

'Ow, my frickin' feet!'

Carrie Brent's shoes were killing her already. Three-inch heels were *not* for walking down country lanes and muddy tracks, but they were all she had that went with the dress – her usual high-tops weren't going to cut it.

The dress had come from the back of her wardrobe, bought a couple of years ago for Auntie Gemma's wedding. Floral and floaty, it wasn't her usual sort of thing, and she'd had to stop herself from putting leggings under it, at least, if not jeans. But this was what you wore to the polo, right? That's what the girls in the pictures of polo games on the Langdon Estate, where she was headed, were wearing. Yep, she'd done her research online.

Carrie didn't give a toss about polo. Or fashion. But she had a deep, burning passion for horses.

There weren't many in South London, although she sometimes saw people riding out on Dulwich Common. She always tried to jog the same way, just to be near them.

Now, here she was. About to enter horse paradise. It was only a tenner, just a weekend game, not the Guillards Cup or anything, but it was all she had – the last of her seventeenth birthday money from Auntie Sue. So, no drinks – she hadn't wanted to ask Mum for anything.

Her mind was pulled back to their recent move. It was strange, with Mum and Dad. Obviously, all of them knew why they'd really left London. And she knew not to ask for anything other than the basics – sixth-form lunch money, deodorant, that kind of thing. Definitely not spending money. But they never talked about it. Every time she asked outright, she got the same old bluster about a better way of life, greater sense of community and a slower pace. She wondered if people *actually spoke* to one another in other families.

She shook her head. Today was about being under a stunning blue sky, admiring the summer dresses and designer handbags, revelling in the smells of the fresh air, grass, sunshine, expensive perfume and, best of all, *horses*. Play hadn't yet begun, but some ponies were tied up nearby, all tacked up and ready to go. Just the sight of them made her heart soar.

As did spotting the VIP area. Carrie took it as a challenge. *Operation Free Booze.*

She made a beeline towards it, head high, swishing her hips, past jewellery and boutique stands and groups of hobnobbing socialites. She was taking care to walk on the balls of her feet and keep her heels out of the grass, so she didn't get stuck. She'd got the dress right, but the shoes very wrong.

Blagging a glass of champagne was pretty easy, thanks to the low level of the white link fence and a shy teenage waiter with a silver tray who clearly liked busty, tanned girls in pretty dresses. Carrie sipped her fizz as she stood watching the game about to begin, holding the stem – well, she did know *some* things, even if it *was* only from watching *Made in Chelsea*. Two girls about her age – a tall, slim blonde and a buxom brunette – turned to look, and she stood up straighter and pushed her shoulders back, pretending not to notice. The brunette nodded towards her shoes and smirked.

Carrie checked her phone in what she hoped was a 'my friends will be here any moment, in their Rolls Royce, probably' kind of way, trying to look glamorous and at ease, like she fit in. That would have been a lot easier without the bloody heels. She virtually had to stand on tiptoes to stop them from sinking into the ground and her calves were already killing her.

And then – bam. The horses worked their magic. She forgot about being by herself. Forgot about the stupid heels. Forgot everything but a chestnut mare and a bay gelding pounding down the middle of the field. Her heart pounded with them as, at a fast canter, one tried to barge the other out of the way, urged on by their riders. They moved so fluidly, and there was something about them cantering along together, flowing, majestic and determined, that took her breath away. Like, *actually*.

'Stunning, aren't they?'

A middle-aged woman was standing beside her, smiling. She was dressed head to toe in designer gear, but not at all flashy, with sensible, solid wedges on. She looked like she owned at least three Labradors and probably had a husband called Henry and a London flat to save having to get the train back after the theatre.

Carrie shut down her overactive imagination. 'They're so beautiful,' she gushed.

'And at top speed they go about thirty-five miles an hour.'

'Wow!'

'Do you ride?'

'No, but I'd love to.'

The woman smiled. 'You should go and see if Terrence is around at the stables.' She gestured over to the smart-looking stable-yard to the right of the polo fields. 'Lovely old boy. He'll let you know about the different classes and so on. You can do beginner's polo training right here, on a Saturday.'

Carrie's knees went weak at the thought. *Bliss. Heaven.* It would definitely cost more than a tenner, though – and she didn't even have that any more. Still, she said, 'Thanks, I will. In fact, I think I'll go and look for him right now.' Maybe he'd have a job going. *Bliss. Heaven. And pay.*

'It's terribly good fun,' said the woman. Then, with a final smile, she turned back to the game and was soon absorbed again.

With a last lingering look at the horses on the field, Carrie tiptoed, and then pretty much limped, over to the imposing Georgian stable block, with its high archway and huge clock. She ducked her head into the office. No Terrence. No anyone. A couple of gorgeous horses had their heads stuck out over stable doors and there was the sound of contented munching on hay from stalls further along the row. Breathing in the sublime horse smell, she felt like her heart would burst with contentment.

She crossed the yard over to a beautiful bay pony with soft eyes, who stood watching her. She stroked his nose and he snickered softly. She laughed and thought she'd die of happiness as she felt the soft breath from his nose on her cheek. 'You're a gorgeous lad,' she told him, soft and singsong. 'These bloody shoes though! If I could just . . .'

She looked around. She didn't want anyone to see her standing there in her bare feet, but she had to get them off. What if her calves seized up like Yasmina's had in Year Eleven PE? She'd rolled around the sports hall screaming in front of the whole class, and that wouldn't be a good look if Terrence, or anyone else, showed up.

She thought about hiding in the stable with the beautiful horse, but he was untethered and, lovely as he seemed, she didn't feel confident enough being that close. And who knew what she could step in barefoot. Ew.

She limped down the row until she found an empty stable and slipped inside. Fortunately, it seemed to be used for storage, and there were a few hay bales. She collapsed on them and pulled the killer heels off, sighing in relief. Then she caught sight of something out of the corner of her eye . . .

Polo boots.

Really, really, really nice polo boots.

Could I?

She walked over, relishing the cool, swept paving bricks under her sore feet, and picked one up.

Just to try them. Just for a minute . . .

The leather was like butter against her calves.

'What are you doing in here?'

She whirled round and blinked at the stable doorway. There stood a figure in the light – a tall, muscular, young, hot guy . . . who looked furious. With her.

She tried to style it out even though she wanted to die of embarrassment. 'Erm nothing, just, well—'

That failed.

'You can't just wander in here. These horses are worth a fortune!'

She made herself meet his gaze, defiant, and was annoyed to feel a wave of desire ripple through her body. 'You don't have to look at me like that, you know,' she snapped, surprising even herself. 'I've got just as much right to be here as you.'

For some reason, this made him laugh. 'Apart from the fact that you're a little trespasser.' His eyes flickered to the boots and seemed to linger on the exposed skin above her knee. 'And a thief.'

Her mind raced, but she forced herself to smile – she needed to get him on side. 'If I'm a trespasser, what does that make you?'

His face hardened. 'I *belong* here,' he said. He looked her up and down and snorted loudly. '*You*, very obviously, *do not*.'

She adjusted her dress to cover her calves then inwardly swore at herself. Why did she care what this arrogant posh boy thought of her?

He came into the stall and closed the door behind him, tension rolling off him in waves. She shivered with fear but also . . . desire.

Was she imagining it, or did he feel the heat too? She dared herself to step closer to him and the energy between them intensified. She told herself to get a grip – she could end up going home with a police caution instead of a job at this rate.

But his breathing had quickened, his muscles tautened and, when she'd closed the gap between them, he hadn't stepped back.

'I don't have to answer to you,' she said slowly. She could just walk out of here, but then it really *would* be stealing, and her shoes were . . .

Carrie glanced towards them, stuck with mud, probably ruined, peeking out from behind a hay bale. The boy followed her glance and clocked them. She braced herself for anger, accusation . . . But to her surprise he laughed, loud and sudden. There was something free about it, joyous. His whole face changed. It startled her and disarmed her all at once. It was then that she noticed his vibrant green eyes.

'Who wears three-inch heels to the polo?' he said, with a wide grin. Sparks danced in his eyes. He really was incredibly good looking, and those powerful shoulders . . . *Oh my days*.

'So, why are you in here?' he asked, leaning back against the whitewashed wall and looking at her with amusement. The confidence of him. It took her breath away. Not a flicker of self-doubt. She smiled, slow and easy. Enjoying herself, feeling like she was in a movie.

'I love horses. Like, *totally love* them.' It just came out. The straight-up truth, just like that, as she tugged off the boots. Then she added, 'Who do you have to shag to get a job around here?'

'Well, that would be me.'

She looked up sharply. 'You're not . . . You're *not*, are you? The Langdon Estate heir?'

He gave the slightest nod.

Carrie was horrified. 'You do know I was joking, right?'

He laughed and she instantly relaxed. 'Of course. And for the record, I would never misuse my position of power like that.' He looked into her eyes with a sizzling intensity and a lazy grin. 'Anyone not currently employed by the estate, though . . . well, that's a different matter.'

He may have been posh as caviar and crème brûlée, but he was hot as a chilli pepper, and possibly even a bit of a player. Maybe he just hadn't met his match yet . . .

Carrie held out her hand. 'Carrie Brent.'

His large hand engulfed her own as he shook it, and that same smouldering heat was back, making her breath catch in her chest. 'It's a pleasure to make your acquaintance, Miss Brent. Freddie Langdon.'

She smiled. 'You too.' Pause. *Let go of his hand, you idiot.*

'I have to go, but come back another time and meet Kerala.' His eyes sparkled with mischief. 'Seeing as you *totally love horses*. The poor girl's injured and she'd love the company.'

Carrie's heart cantered at a million miles per hour. 'I'd love to. Thanks.' Finally, reluctantly, they broke hands.

He threw her a flirty look. 'Now, get my bloody boots off and allow me to escort you back to the game.'

Chapter Two
Luella

'And then in the half-pass, if we just get a little more uphill, and rounder in the frame and a bit more through . . . and when did I get in the habit of talking to myself?'

Luella smiled as she strode along the busy, Saturday-morning Henlake high street. She knew the answer – since she'd stepped up two levels and entered the Dressage Nationals at advanced medium level.

The plan was to qualify for the Prix St George. Training with Donald Fergerson, the best dressage coach in the country, was going well, but it was only once every six weeks, when he was seeing clients in her area. She had weekly sessions with Jenna, the coach who'd got her this far, but it didn't feel *enough*. They just weren't making the progress she'd hoped for. She loved Charlie – her beautiful dapple-grey Connemara whose full name was Ragdoll Charlotte's Web – to the moon and back, but they were lacking a connection that would win it.

She smiled to herself. She had a plan to help with that. *A secret plan.* The smile widened. A *secret plan* involving someone *rather special.*

'What's up with you, grinning like a Cheshire cat?'

Luella whirled around, recognising the deep, easy-going voice of Hugo Haggquist. He was sitting outside Elodie's Patisserie with the world's tiniest, strongest coffee, a chocolate éclair and, of course, Simeon Carmichael.

'Hugo! Sims!' She air-kissed them both, her smile strained as she tried to squash down the horrible, sick feeling in her stomach. 'Well played on Wednesday, you both. That ride-off heading for goal got pretty tasty, Hugo . . .'

The boys didn't notice her discomfort, thank goodness. Hugo laughed heartily. 'I kept my line, just about. If it had been against the Balfour team, well, maybe I would have pushed the bounds of safety a bit harder . . .'

Sims laughed too and sipped his huge latte. 'If Barnaby Balfour had been out on the field, you'd have had that ball off him like a shot.'

Hugo wiggled his eyebrows. 'Nothing wrong with a bit of rivalry.'

'You're doing really well, though,' said Luella encouragingly. 'You've had an excellent start to the season. Both of you. Maybe you'll even get a crack at the Guillards Cup. Lord L hasn't picked the team yet, has he?'

Sims shrugged easily. 'We'll see. A lot of competition from the pros for that.'

'And you?' asked Hugo. 'Dressage going well?'

'Good, thanks. Charlie's on form and I'm doing my best to keep learning and improving.' The churning in Luella's stomach intensified. They sounded like distant cousins, catching up at a family barbecue. When, not so long ago, they'd all been such close friends . . .

Before she could stop herself, her eyes lingered on their drinks. There was a moment, a beat, but no *'Why don't you join us?'*

'Good on you,' said Sims. 'Well, best of luck with it.' Worse – that was code for *'Bye-bye, then.'*

'Thanks, you too. I'm looking forward to seeing you play in the charity game. Only three weeks to go now.'

Hugo nudged Sims's arm. 'We'll see those Balfours off, that's for sure,' he said.

'That's for *sure*,' Sims echoed.

Luella instantly envied their easy friendship. 'You're such dorks,' she said. 'See you later.' They were busy laughing, doing stupid impressions and pushing each other, and only Hugo raised a lazy hand in her direction.

As she strode away, she let herself imagine for one moment that Freddie was on his way and she was calling Bex to remind her, because they were all meeting at Brown's like they used to. In the big booth at the back, by the old church window, ordering champagne and chips in the middle of the afternoon because . . . well, why not?

She shook the image out of her head, checked the time and grimaced. She was late, and no one kept Bex Chapman-Foster waiting.

'Vile. Gross. Great-Aunt Harriet would wear this one, and she virtually *shaves*. Urgh, I'd rather die,' Bex pronounced.

Luella shifted uncomfortably from foot to foot in the smart boutique. She wished that her best friend wouldn't say what she thought about the dresses quite so loudly as she flicked through the rack. The owner was only over by the desk, after all. Miming blowing her brains out wasn't great either.

Luella's heart was still racing from seeing the boys. That beat . . . that awkward pause – it was tormenting her.

'I wish things would go back to normal with Sims and Hugo,' she said, as Bex held up a beautiful blue silk halter-neck dress and pulled a face like it was a saggy feed bag. 'I'd look vile in this,' she announced.

'You'd look sensational – try it on,' said Luella automatically. As she had done for years now.

Bex smiled. 'Thanks, darling. Maybe I will.' She tossed it on the 'maybe' pile she was building on a mauve crushed velvet sofa, and Luella noticed the boutique owner flinch slightly. She'd never say anything, though, of course. What Bex's mother spent in this place in a year probably kept the owner's children at St Jerome's. And paid for violin lessons on top.

Luella tried again. 'It's such a shame the old gang broke up. We were all such good friends, for, well, almost five years, really, since that water sports summer camp . . .'

Bex looked up sharply and fixed her with a piercing glare. 'If there's anything less attractive than *this dress*, it's hankering after the past. Nostalgia is very tedious, Lulu. Look forward, chin up, keep moving on. Friendships come and go. You won't get very far in this world by banging on about how you wish things were different.'

'I guess . . .' A sudden, overwhelming feeling washed over her. It surged through her chest and took her breath away. It had been coming and going for a few months, usually when she was with Bex. And, finally, she knew what it was.

Loneliness.

'God knows what Hugo and Sims fell out about, but since they made up, they're closer than ever, so now there's no room for *you*,' Bex pronounced.

Ouch.

'And Freddie's busy learning the ropes on the estate now – it's not *personal*.' Bex said *personal* with a sneer, as if Luella having emotions was a hideous embarrassment. 'Anyway, you've got me, what more could you want?'

Luella sighed and steadied her breathing. How could being with her best friend, the best friend she'd had since pre-prep, when they'd shared their lunches at school play rehearsals, make her feel lonely?

Her mind wandered. Bex's lunches had always been leftover party sushi while Luella's had been sturdy cheese sandwiches lovingly made by her old nanny Petra. Bex had been a star in the play, literally – a twinkling, shining star with two songs and a dance solo. Luella had been a tree. She was tall, even then, so they had just given her a couple of big branches to hold, added some green crêpe paper, et voilà.

'Lulu? You're missing my pearls of wisdom – and unlike everyone else you don't even have to go on Insta to get them.'

'Sorry . . . I've got a lot on my mind.'

'What, *A levels*? Easy. *Boys*?' Bex snorted. 'No, definitely not.'

Luella wondered what that was supposed to mean, but she didn't rise to it. 'Dressage Nationals, of course.'

Bex blinked at her, as if it were the first she'd heard of it. In fact, Luella and Charlie had been training for months.

'Charlie will be fine, and so will you.' Bex fluffed up her glossy deep-brown hair and sighed dramatically. 'Oh my God, are you having some kind of late-teen crisis? Cheer up, it's not good for my image, having you moping about. It's a total buzzkill.'

Luella forced herself to smile. 'Yeah.' She pulled a dress from the rack – rich purple, tight-fitting, gathered silk. She turned it to show Bex, said, 'This will look amazing on you,' and immediately hated herself for it.

'You know, it would,' said Bex. She threw it on the pile and then gathered all the dresses up in her arms. 'Time to try these monstrosities on, see if we can salvage something from the wreckage. Take some shots of me, Lulu, won't you? No, some video, and use the filters I like.'

'Sure, no problem.' Luella fished out Bex's phone from her designer bag and each time Bex emerged from the fitting room, she filmed her looking fabulous in a different outfit.

'Write "shopping with my bestie" on it in one of the fonts in my brand kit and upload it for me, would you, darling?' Bex said as she swished away one last time.

Eventually, Bex appeared in her own clothes, with five dresses clutched to her chest. The rest lay in a heap on the floor of the fitting room.

The owner rang up Bex's purchases while they made chit-chat about St Barts and let the cash register speak for itself, rather than announcing the shocking total. Bex handed over a credit card while waxing lyrical about Laurent's seafood shack (seafood luxury dining room, more like) and hardly even blinked when the card wouldn't go through the first time.

The second time she tried putting in her PIN, but no.

The third time she stopped her monologue about the ceviche. She laughed. 'Oh, for goodness' sake! Let's try another.'

When that one didn't go through either, they all agreed that it must be some problem with the card machine. The problem magically resolved itself when Luella paid with her Amex though.

As they headed out of the boutique, Luella felt a sudden surge of indignation. Like a sudden itch, it nagged away at her until she just had to scratch. 'You could thank me, you know,' she snapped.

Bex snorted, her shopping bags swishing in time with her slinky hips as she swayed along. 'You want to talk about money? How vulgar.'

Luella noted the irony. Bex *loved* talking about money, and scheming about different ways to make lots and lots of it. 'I just want you to say thank you.'

Bex laughed. '*Thank you!* Is that better?' She stopped and peered at Luella. 'Are you coming on, or something?'

Luella forced herself to smile. Even though she was, and always had been, intensely loyal to Bex, she found herself making a list in her head. *Brittle. Ruthless. Possessive. Defensive.* Things her best friend was becoming more and more each day.

She thought again of her secret, and how Bex most definitely would not approve, and, for only the second time that day, a real smile lit up her face.

Chapter Three

Bex

'That's not actually on the menu.'

Bex gave the anxious young waitress a death stare until she withered. 'I'll see what I can do.'

Bex sighed and pulled her phone and laptop from her custom Louis Vuitton tote. Time to get on with some work. Her personal brand wasn't going to build itself, after all. As she replied to her fans' – sorry, *followers*' – comments and hearted anything that wasn't outright offensive, she thought back to her morning of shopping with Luella.

She was sure it wouldn't be long before her beautiful, talented, rich and clever friend was thanking her. There was no point having the whole package if you went through life with a face like a wet weekend. *Someone* had to tell Luella to get a grip, sort herself out, find her positive mindset and get rocking and rolling again. They used to have so much fun together. Pubs and clubs and cafés and brasseries. Gossip and boys and horses and fun.

Of course, having a fabulous gang to hang out with had all been part of it, and had made everything extra shiny. But if Hugo, Sims and Freddie had gone in other directions in the last few months, that was up to them. Luella shouldn't fall behind in life because of it. Daddy was always talking about the danger of that. Life was a race, after all.

Bex knew exactly where life was a race *to*. Her own highly exclusive livery yard, It-girl status, fame as the hot, young face of British polo, her own perfume brand (far better than that awful stench she was photographed promoting last night) and coupled-up bliss with Freddie Langdon.

The race of life was more of a marathon than a sprint, and she wasn't committing to Freddie and securing all his connections, wealth and status just yet. She was keeping him warm, with a night together here and there while they both had their fun, but they were endgame.

The fresh new generation in polo needed a king and queen, after all. And as for a kingdom, well, they didn't come much bigger, or better, than the Langdon Estate. All that money was wasted on Lady L – she only spent it on wellies, organic tea made of twigs, and Labradors. And it was a shame about all that recycling and water saving and going on about nightjars, whatever *they* were. For old people, Lord and Lady L were surprisingly eco-friendly. When Bex finally married Freddie, she planned to bring a touch of sophistication back to the Langdon family brand.

So, yeah. Bex knew she had to look after Luella, and make sure they both made it to the finish line with all the money, status, horses and designer handbags they could possibly want.

Her skinny latte arrived, with a double shot – the night before had been a late one, at the launch of that dreadful perfume on Bond Street followed by VIP treatment at Cirque Le Soir.

She smiled at a social media comment referring to her as 'Sexy Bexy', and when she called her agent about a sponsorship deal with Ralph Lauren, she lifted her voice a little louder, loving the attention from people at the nearby tables. *Civilians*, Liz Hurley had famously called them. Bex thought this was a good way of describing most people. People who didn't *get it*, and people who didn't *have it*. The 'it'. The shine. The Bex Factor.

She dived into a couple of polo club Instagram accounts and dropped nice, sportsmanlike things about other players here and there – all part of her brand. Then, she read about an Argentine pro coming to stay with the Balfours for the rest of the season, to play in their team and bring his smart, South American training methods with him. She didn't think much of it – she wasn't interested in another vain male polo player who spent more time looking in the mirror than she did. Freddie was hot, but he was *effortlessly* hot, which was far sexier.

Her green salad arrived, with a double helping of chicken breast and no dressing, exactly as she'd ordered. 'See? Not that difficult, was it?'

The waitress blushed and fled.

As Bex ate, she politely turned down a couple of dates from friends of friends on her WhatsApp and blocked a dick pic sender who had slid into her DMs. God, those were enough to put you off your side of edamame beans – they didn't even use the good filters.

After lunch she'd go and see Freddie. It had been a while since they'd had any fun together and it was time she reminded him where his priorities lay. With her.

Driving across the Langdon Estate, knackering her Lotus's suspension, was always a thrill – especially as Bex loved to spend the time imagining what it would be like when she owned everything she saw, with Freddie.

She screeched into the stable-yard, stealing the disabled space. That was another Langdon obsession, accessibility and legal requirements and all that.

Freddie was striding towards her. He was waving, so she waved back, making sure her leg did the sexy Marilyn Monroe thing as she got out. As he got closer, she realised he was still waving – *at the car*. 'You can't park there. You know that, Bex!'

She smiled demurely. 'No one disabled ever comes here, Fredders,' she said smoothly.

'That's not the point, they might,' Freddie said sternly. 'And don't call me Fredders.'

She swished over and threw her arms around him. 'I love it when you're cross. You're all sexy and masterful.'

She was rewarded as she watched him become noticeably flustered. He soon gathered himself, though, and peeled her off him. 'Why do you drive that silly little thing up here, anyway?'

'There's no way I'm swapping my Lotus for a big, stodgy old Land Rover,' she said archly. 'I'm not dead yet, you know. I'm very much alive. And young. And' – she leaned in close and lowered her voice – 'we should go for a private ride.'

That was their secret code, and it got Freddie all hot under the collar. But he soon recovered. Much quicker than usual, annoyingly. 'Move your car and then come and see me in the office. I need a word with you. In private.'

She gave him a provocative look. 'Oh, sounds intriguing,' she teased. *'A word in private.'* Maybe that was a new code. Luckily, she always wore a matching bra and knickers set – which was her take on feeling good on the inside. Sod green smoothies. It was hot pink today, lace and satin, French couture.

Lucky future Lord Langdon.

Bex followed Freddie towards the office, after pointedly *not* moving her car. They'd played this game before and her defiance was all part of the flirting.

She caught sight of Gordo and Bomba – her two beloved polo ponies – in the yard and allowed her hard exterior to melt a little. Along with Estrella and Blanca, they'd got her to the position she was in now – poised to play for the Langdon team in the Guillards Cup, the jewel in the crown of the season's tournaments. One of the grooms, Heather, was grooming Bomba, while another, Beatrice, was putting brush boots on Gordo, ready to take him and the others up to do sets. Bex's facial expression returned to its natural state – as sharp as diamonds – and they stopped chatting instantly, focusing instead on their tasks.

Freddie would make a great husband, when the time came, Bex thought, as she returned her attention to the strong shoulders rippling under his checked shirt. He was a bit too country squire for the London scene so perhaps she'd date a rock star or a rapper for a while first, to round out her image and make her look street and savvy. And to keep Freddie on his toes.

'Bex, we have to talk,' Freddie said, his voice serious as she stepped into the yard office. He didn't even offer her coffee from the electric jug warming on the table. Charming. 'Dad was going to take this up with you, but I said I would, as a friend.' He hesitated and Bex kissed her teeth at that word. *Friend.* 'The payment for April didn't go through as usual, so your father gave us his new card details, but when Robert tried charging the outstanding April payment and the May payment to it, it was declined.'

Bex's stomach lurched, as she thought back to the boutique. But there couldn't be anything wrong. Not *really* wrong. 'It must be an admin mistake,' she said. 'Probably the card company making an error. You know how they are.'

'Hmm.' Freddie didn't agree – but at least he didn't push the point further. 'Well, I said I'd let you know first, so you can quietly sort it out, without this going any further.'

Bex turned up her slow, flirty smile again. 'I will. I *really* appreciate it.' She let her top slide slightly off her shoulder invitingly.

Freddie glanced up at the wall clock, a hideous monstrosity painted with two pheasants, for goodness' sake. That would be the first thing to go when she took over the place. 'I've got a meeting in a few minutes.'

'Sure. I have to go too. Busy, busy.' She leaned in and kissed him on the cheek, her lips brushing his ear as she breathed, 'Let's go for that ride soon.' Then she turned and swished out of the office.

'Oh – Bex, one more thing . . .'

She smiled to herself then turned back, fixing him with a smouldering gaze. 'Yes?'

'You need to be nicer to the grooms. We've had complaints.'

She held her fury in. *I bet it was that little ratbag Matilda*, she thought. 'I can't help it if they don't do things to my standards,' she said sweetly, but the edge was there in her voice. 'They should up their game, or you should provide better training. Maybe I'll get my own grooms, that might be best. I'll think about it.'

Freddie simply nodded. 'As you wish.' His voice had a slight edge too. 'All our staff must be treated with respect.'

'Of course. There must have been some misunderstanding,' she said smoothly. 'I'll talk to them and we'll straighten it out.'

If he could play it cool, so could she. She left without a backward glance.

Bex was still smarting over her encounter with Freddie as she stood in her kitchen, staring into the vast American fridge.

Her mother appeared in the doorway, leaning against it slightly, and they both ignored the obvious fact that she was drunk. 'Bex, my angel, come and have Pimm's in the garden. The Gregsons are here, they'd love to see you.'

Bex groaned. 'Urgh, the Gregsons are so boring.'

'I know,' her mother said, reaching across her to pull a bottle of champagne from the fridge. 'Come and save me, darling. They're talking with your father about hedge funds. I think I might die.'

Bex rolled her eyes and turned back to the fridge. It was full of champagne, smoked salmon blinis and little prawn vol-au-vents, but no actual meals. 'Why is there nothing to eat? Where's Carlotta?'

'Oh, she's gone,' said her mother, looking edgy. 'She was offered a job in Maui, so we had to let her go and spread her wings, darling. You know, we only ever wanted the best for her.'

Bex blinked at her. No housekeeper? 'But who's going to *shop*, and *cook*?'

Her mother wobbled in the doorway and flashed her a bright smile. She looked slightly psychotic. '*We* are! We can go to Waitrose. It'll be fun, darling!'

Bex shuddered, but at least it would be a way to spend time together – something they never really did. Until they found someone to replace Carlotta, anyway.

As her mother tottered off with the champagne, Bex's mind shifted to her upcoming photo shoot. It was going to be in the drawing room, for an It-girl's blog – all about her success on the polo field, as well as her plans for the future.

She wandered through the hall and into the vast room. A revamp had been planned for the previous autumn, but it had been delayed. Apparently the designer had had some trouble getting the right marble from Italy to match the cracked fireplace. The curtains needed updating – they were sun-faded on one side – and she'd have to replace that portrait of ugly old Great-Uncle Albert with something modern. Urgh – the carpet would have to go too, whether the designer was ready or not.

She strolled over to the far side of the room and idly raised the roll-up on her great-great-grandfather's desk. She was surprised to see papers there, clogging the pigeonholes. No one ever really used them – that's why she used to hide sweets in them when she was a child, and vodka when she was a bit older.

She pulled out a sheaf of them and flicked through, her heart banging in her chest. Here was the April invoice from the Langdon Estate. And her summer term invoice for school, and – here – a polite reminder from the Tennis Club . . .

Her mouth went dry, and her hands began to shake. What the hell was going on?

Chapter Four

Carrie

On this beautiful Saturday morning in late June, as Carrie breathed in the fresh air, rich with the magical scent of horses, fresh hay and, OK, *poo*, she couldn't have been happier. She had secured a job at the Langdon Estate *without* any help from Freddie Langdon himself, and over the last couple of weeks she'd worked hard, learned quickly and, even though she was just a lowly stable hand, the grooms still spoke to her when they gathered round the coffee pot for a break.

It was only eleven, but she'd been there since seven and most of the heavy work was done – at least until the afternoon round of skipping out stables and refilling hay nets. She finished sweeping the yard and then it was time for her favourite job, grooming, with her favourite horse, Blaze.

Blaze was Freddie's chestnut eight-year-old Argentine polo pony.

Carrie worked her comb through his knotted tail and dreamed of cantering through the hills and fields round Yetbourne, with some kind of magical riding ability, since she'd never had a lesson in her life. Carrie and Blaze were just jumping a crystal-clear stream in her imagination when Freddie leaned against the stable door. 'If you get a chance this afternoon, can you go over to the Balfours and get our ultrasound machine back? They borrowed it last Sunday when the vet's was closed, and I want it back before they sell it to make a quick buck.'

Carrie smiled to herself. He wasn't one for easing into a conversation. 'Sure,' she said. 'I'll ride my bike over when I've finished with Blaze.'

She wrestled with the tangles in Blaze's tail, very, *very* aware of Freddie's presence, the feel of him and his intoxicating scent of horses, aftershave and washing powder. 'Do you really think they'd sell your stuff?'

He laughed easily. 'No, probably not.'

'I mean, I know your families are rivals.' Direct as ever, she asked, 'What's *that* all about?'

Freddie took a deep breath and let it out slowly. 'That's a long story – the best way of putting it is that we don't share the same values.'

'Like, what?'

He looked a little surprised at her pressing him.

'I find the best thing to do if you have something to say is to just say it,' Carrie said.

'Me too, actually,' said Freddie. 'OK, well, let's just say they aren't as committed to their staff as we are at the Langdon Estate, or the welfare of the horses, or the land, or sustainability, and probably not even the law . . .' He paused. 'Actually, the topic of what's wrong with the Balfours is quite an enjoyable one. I could go on, but I won't waste my breath.'

Blaze snickered gently and nuzzled Carrie's hand.

'You're good with him,' he said. 'Not everyone gets him.'

She smiled. 'Thanks.' There was still that sizzle between them, but she reined in her urge to flirt, now that they worked together. She hoped he was struggling to resist just as much as her, though. Hoped the fact he couldn't get with her made him want her more. Hoped he could still feel the air prickling like electricity around them.

Freddie stroked Blaze's nose, and Blaze whinnied contentedly.

'So are you,' she replied, looking at him from under her lashes.

He cleared his throat. *Hopefully banishing out-of-bounds thoughts.* 'Kerala's off the bute now and the bloody box rest should be over soon,' he said.

'That's great!' Carrie's heart leaped. She loved spending time with Kerala, a beautiful bay mare who had a superficial flexor tendon strain and was confined to her stable. 'She'll be so excited to get out.'

'Maybe a bit *too* excited,' said Freddie. 'I wondered if you'd like to walk her up the lane with me, when it's time. Just in case two pairs of hands are better than one.'

'I'd love to,' she said, grinning. Then tried to look less like a thrilled Labrador puppy. Alone together . . .

'I've noticed you sticking around to keep Kerala company, even when your shift is over.'

'Yeah, well . . . I worry she's bored.'

'It's good of you.' He stroked Blaze's nose. 'This one's quite young still but he has a lot of promise.'

Like me, thought Carrie. 'Do you think he'll ever be a star like Willow?' she asked. Willow was Freddie's best polo pony, a beautiful grey mare whom he always brought out for the final chukka, the last period of play. Carrie knew that he'd had lots of offers from other polo clubs to buy her, but he'd never part with her – they were a team.

'Maybe. Time will tell.'

'He won't win any trophies with these knots,' Carrie said, as she wiggled the comb back and forth, where it was stuck fast in Blaze's tail.

'Here, let me.'

Before she could tell him she was perfectly capable of brushing hair, Freddie closed his hand over hers. Sparks leaped at his touch and coursed through her body. She couldn't look at him. She couldn't even speak.

'Like this, see? Turn the comb a bit sideways.'

'Uh-huh.' That was all she could manage. *His hand is on my hand.*

She risked a glance and they shared a brief look – the kind of look that whispers *'Kiss me'* and makes the hairs on your neck stand on end. She desperately wanted to lean in. But desperately wanted to keep her job, too. *He probably does this with all the girls*, she told herself. *It probably means nothing.*

Freddie seemed to get a hold on himself then and lifted his hand away, running it through his artfully tousled chestnut hair. 'Speaking of troublesome, I'm having a bit of an issue with Blaze here,' he said, a little hurriedly. Was she imagining it, or was his voice a little heavy, thick with desire for her, too? *Wishful thinking*, she told herself. *The conditioner spray probably got into his chest.* 'He's skittish and freaks out easily.'

Carrie stole a glance at him, then picked up a curry-comb and started working over Blaze's back – as well as getting out any leftover winter coat, it was good for his muscles. 'Oh, really? I've never found that. But then, all I've done is walk him up to the exercise fields occasionally and groom him in the main yard.' She looked up, caught Freddie's gaze this time and smiled. 'I mean, I haven't tried to ride him at thirty miles an hour with a crowd cheering, horses galloping at him, mallets swinging and a ball flying about, so I wouldn't know.'

'Well, feel free to take him out, walk him round, handle him more.'

Carrie's heart soared. *Really?! Horse heaven, here I come!* She managed to keep some kind of cool and said, 'Thanks, I will.'

Freddie smiled. 'Great. Like I said, you're good with him. Don't start off by waving foil balloons in his face. Go steady, but anything you can do to get him used to shining things, flapping things, rustling things, moving things – you know, all the usual –'

Carrie *didn't* know but she nodded anyway. *Hello again, Google.*

'– would be great. God, horses are a bloody nightmare. Who'd have them?!'

Me! thought Carrie. *Me, me, me! All day long!* She shrugged, playful. 'Toffs like you, I guess.'

Just then, Freddie's two Labradors, Bucket and Crumble, came running up to them and Blaze startled backwards. Carrie soothed him and then made a fuss of the dogs. Freddie, however, waved a welly-clad leg in the air to send them away. 'Get on!' He turned to Carrie. 'Or dogs. Total pain in the arse as well. Always hungry, always in the way and always disappearing off when you take them out on a hack.'

Carrie's chest seared for a moment with longing, and not for Freddie Langdon, for a change. It was out of her mouth before she could stop it. 'I wouldn't know.'

'What, about the perils of riding with dogs?'

'About the perils of riding at all. Although, I don't think it would be perilous, I think it would be paradise.'

Freddie stared at her, as if she'd said that she'd got through the last seventeen years without *breathing*. 'You've never ridden? How ridiculous!'

Carrie screwed up her nose and shoved his shoulder, playfully. 'Hey! Not many stables in South London. If we're talking about ridiculous, let's talk about your wellies, or your fogey old man shirt, or your . . . face!'

Freddie laughed at that – loud and easy, like he had in the stable that first time they'd met. She wanted to be annoyed with him, the overprivileged tosspot, calling her ridiculous. But she had to laugh too. 'Posho!' She pushed him again, raising one eyebrow, biting her lip. He caught her wrist and their eyes locked. 'Hey!' she protested.

'OK, I accept that I have a – what did you call it – a "fogey old man shirt", but what's wrong with my face?!' he demanded, not letting go, his eyes sparkling as he held her gaze.

Her breath caught in her throat. 'It's annoyingly handsome. I hate that classic good-looking thing. So boring.'

He smirked and they breathed together for a moment, losing themselves in each other's eyes. The vibe deepened and before Carrie could think, she began to lean in . . .

'Freddie!' cried a voice so posh it could have cut glass. Bex sashayed round the corner in spotless riding gear, with the willowy blonde friend Carrie had seen at the polo in tow. She'd been working there long enough to know who Bex was now – the grooms had been complaining about her since day one. Carrie hated the way she treated them, and she hated the way she acted like she owned Freddie too.

Freddie stiffened, and his whole manner changed. 'Bex! Luella. Hi. We were just . . .' He looked helplessly at Carrie, lost for words, still holding her wrist.

'I thought maybe I sprained it,' she said quickly. 'But it's probably OK.'

Luella smiled at this lame excuse, but Bex ignored her completely. 'Let's have a coffee in the office,' she said imperiously to Freddie, giving him a full-on, lash-heavy flirty look and touching his shoulder. 'We have business to attend to.'

Freddie raised an eyebrow. 'What kind of business?'

Carrie felt her hackles rise. He'd better not be flirting with that snooty, mean, annoyingly perfectly turned-out girl. Not that she had any right to feel that way. Did she? She was sure he'd felt it too – that the flame between them was now a roaring inferno. And had they been about to . . . kiss?

No one said anything for a moment. Blaze broke the tension by lifting his tail and doing a splattery poo on the concrete by her feet. *Thanks, mate.*

'*Private* business, which we can discuss in the office,' said Bex then. 'About *settling up*.'

Not for the first time, Carrie wondered how much it cost Bex to have her horses here – what she would earn in a year probably couldn't even cover a month for one horse on basic livery. Her dream of owning a horse vanished further into the distance. And so did her dream of kissing Freddie as he led Bex towards the office without even a goodbye.

'Wow, for a minute there I thought she was going to lift her leg and pee on him.' Carrie laughed, turning her attention to the other girl.

She only stared. 'I beg your pardon?'

Carrie demonstrated a comedy leg-lift. 'You know, like a dog, marking her territory.'

'Oh, I see!' she said, snorting with laughter, then composing herself.

Carrie smirked. 'Seriously, she might as well have done the "I'm watching you" eyes thing at me.'

The other girl visibly relaxed. 'We haven't been introduced. I'm Luella.' She held out her hand. 'Nice to meet you.'

Carrie wiped her sweaty palm on her shorts and shook it, beaming. 'Carrie.' Even though Luella was besties with the world's meanest, poshest polo princess, and obviously loyal, Carrie had a feeling that the two of them were going to get along just fine.

Chapter Five

Luella

Kit was standing behind Luella, his hands over hers on the stick and string, and she was finding it very difficult to concentrate. She was supposed to be keeping Charlie going round the circle at an even pace using the energy projecting out from her navel.

Feeling his arms brush hers every time he moved the stick slightly, showing her how to direct her focus, was sending her energy all over the place. Charlie was lurching, and the circle was more like a rugby ball. It didn't help that the afternoon sun warmed them both, making Kit's scent swim in the air around her.

'Charlie's a bit jazzy today,' he commented.

'Hmmm... Maybe it's the weather.' She cringed. Kit must have thought she was the worst natural horsewoman in the world.

Still, he persevered. He'd been helping her with her connection and communication with Charlie for a couple of weeks now, so they'd spent, what . . . eight sessions together? *Don't pretend to have to think about it. You counted down the hours to each one and replayed them every night afterwards.*

Kit was one of the stable hands at the Balfour Estate. The tenth generation of Pearces to work there. His mum and dad were employed full time and even his grandfather still pottered about in the gardens. They all lived together in a beautiful centuries-old cottage on the estate, which had been part of their wages for generations. Kit had told her all about it, on their breaks.

She also knew he liked pancakes, but with jam, not maple syrup. She knew he'd believed in Father Christmas until he was twelve. And she knew he'd once nursed an injured fox cub back to health and released it into the wild. Which melted her heart and only made her fancy him even more.

He was known around Yetbourne as the strong, silent type, but it seemed that, with Luella, everything came flooding out. He also knew about her irrational fear of big boats (on the horizon, but especially in the dock) and about how one day she'd looked at a packet of cornflakes and finally grasped that cornflakes weren't just a thing on their own, but were actually *flakes* of *corn*, which had blown her ten-year-old mind. He'd almost wet himself laughing, and when they stopped training to eat their sandwiches together, he'd say things like 'OMG, cheese spread! It's actually *made* of cheese!'

But mainly it was about the horses. Luella loved that Kit had the same passion for them as she did. He was a great rider and polo player, too, and she'd encouraged him to ask Jasper Balfour about riding for Team Balfour in the upcoming charity polo match at the Langdon Estate. He'd told her he'd think about it, but, if he got a chance like that, who knew where it could lead?

As Charlie circled round them in a nice springy trot, Luella allowed herself to lean back into Kit's chest a little, just to see, just to test the water. He didn't leap away or anything, so she took it as a good sign and let herself breathe in the smell of him and feel the heat of his body against hers. She let the shift of weight in his hips move hers, as a strong feeling of want overwhelmed her. He stayed right there, leaning his weight forward to meet hers. A conversation between their bodies. *What if she turned in his arms right now and . . .*

What would it be like to kiss him?

At that moment, Charlie broke off the circle and trotted right into the middle, where they were standing.

'No, cheeky, get out there!' cried Luella.

Kit laughed and stepped backwards, and Luella breathed in sharply, resisting the urge to turn and tuck herself under his arm. 'It's not her fault,' he said, stroking Charlie's nose. 'You took your focus completely off her, so she came in.'

Luella felt her cheeks flush and busied herself with adjusting Charlie's rope head collar, which was perfectly fine. 'Well, you were distracting me with your . . .' She faltered.

Kit half-smiled, and she blushed again. 'With my what?'

'With your . . .' *Your hands, your hips, the intoxicating scent of your aftershave as I leaned into your chest.* She panicked. '. . . your smell!'

'What? How could I distract you with my *smell*?!' Kit sniffed his armpits comically.

'Trust me, you—'

'Hello! Anyone around?!'

They both startled at the voice, coming from behind the barn. Kit pulled Luella into a bush. She fell into his chest and stayed there for longer than necessary, savouring the feel of him against her once more.

'No one ever comes down here,' he said, with a groan that vibrated against her back. Their training area was right at the far edge of the Balfour Estate, far from the yard and all the hustle and bustle. It was shielded by the tall barn, which was rarely used. It wasn't exactly secret, but no one had found them yet. Until now. 'Keep quiet, they might go away,' Kit whispered, his lips on her ear, making her shiver with desire.

She leaned into him again and stifled a giggle. 'We can't exactly hide *Charlie*.'

Kit seemed in no hurry to leave the close confines of the bush either. 'They might think she's grazing, from a distance.'

Clearly not, with the lead rope and the rucksacks, and they both knew it, but Luella let it slide and pressed herself tight to him until she could feel his heartbeat.

'Guys, get out of the bush. I'm not blind!' came the voice.

They stepped out, Kit delicately plucking a leaf from Luella's hair.

It was the girl she'd met at Langdon's the same day she'd paid two months' worth of Bex's bills with barely a *thank you*. 'Hi!' Carrie called.

'Carrie, hi! Sorry, we thought you might be a Balfour. This is Kit.'

Carrie rode up to them on her bike, looking a little out of breath. 'I'm a bit lost,' she told them. 'I'm trying to get to the yard to get our ultrasound machine back, but I thought I'd come through the back lanes to save cycling on the main road. And then I saw the little gate in the hedge.'

'Sure, I'll get it for you,' Kit said, looking much more relaxed now they hadn't been caught. 'I know where it is. You don't want to go up there with that lot.'

'Oh, OK, thanks – that would be great.'

He jumped on the quad bike nearby and roared off. The two girls, and Charlie, watched him go.

'I bet he offered just to have an excuse to bomb that thing around,' said Carrie. 'I wish Lord L would let me on one of ours.' Barely a pause. 'Is he your boyfriend? *Cute.*'

Luella squeezed her eyes shut and shook her head. 'No, he's not. He's helping me and Charlie – we've got the Dressage Nationals coming up and he's teaching us natural horsemanship. It's all about connection and communication and energy and stuff. It helps get the horse thinking, too, rather than just running round in a panic or switching off.'

'Sounds interesting,' said Carrie. 'In fact, it sounds like the perfect thing for Blaze, one of Freddie's polo ponies. He's asked me to try and desensitise him – apparently he's a bit flighty on the field.'

'I'm sure it would help,' said Luella. 'Kit's amazing.'

Carrie was on her like a shot. 'I saw you flirting.'

Luella flushed. 'We weren't!'

'Totally were. Before you tried to hide in that bush. I only called out to be polite. And just now I could hardly breathe, the air was so choked with sexual chemistry.'

Luella grinned. 'I could say the same thing to you. I've never seen Freddie look as happy and relaxed as he was with you.'

Carrie glowed, but she didn't reply to that. 'Nice setup you've got here,' she said playfully instead. 'Very cosy.' She put her bike down, walked up to Charlie and made a fuss of her, stroking her neck and running her fingers through her mane. 'And who is this beautiful girl?'

'Carrie, meet Charlie.'

Charlie made them both laugh by snickering loudly.

'I think she likes you!'

Carrie smiled warmly. 'Do you keep her here?'

Luella shook her head. 'No. I wouldn't go to Balfours if they were the last stables on earth. She's kept at our stables at home. I'm Team Langdon, through and through. Oh—'

Carrie gave her a questioning look.

'It's just, could you keep this to yourself? My and Kit's meetings are secret. Bex wouldn't approve.'

Carrie rolled her eyes. 'Fine.'

'No, seriously,' Luella insisted. 'Kit doesn't like the Balfour family knowing his business either. He says it's bad enough them being their bosses and owning his family's home – he doesn't want them to know what he does in his spare time as well.'

Carrie softened. 'Your secret is safe with me. Oh, but can I tell Freddie, though?'

Luella sighed, but she was still smiling. 'Fine, but swear him to secrecy.'

There was an awkward silence, and then she couldn't seem to help herself. 'So, Bex – she doesn't seem like much of a friend, ordering you around like she did at the Langdons', and being so judgy about Kit.'

Luella looked startled. 'Well, she—'

Carrie read the change in energy right away, as did Charlie, who looked up sharply from munching the grass beside them. 'Sorry,' she said. 'Sometimes I speak before I think. Well, most of the time, actually.'

'No, it's OK. You're right – Bex has changed, lately. She's always been ambitious, and a bit of a snob and very, you know, *vain*. But now she's—' Her eyes filled with tears and her words came out in a rush. 'A bitch.'

They both laughed in shock.

'Gosh, sorry! I don't know where that came from! Don't tell her I said that!'

'Seems like that's been waiting to come out for a while,' Carrie said. She held up her hand. 'Don't worry, course I won't tell her. I won't be having anything to do with her after the evil look she gave me earlier. She's tried to order me around on the yard a few times, but Terrence says I answer to him not her, so I just keep out of the way. You know, because I have to watch my big mouth.' She paused and, for a moment, Luella noticed a fleeting look of vulnerability cross her face. 'What's the deal with her and Freddie anyway?' She asked it like she didn't care. A little *too* much like she didn't care, in Luella's opinion.

'They have history,' she said. 'Bex is convinced they'll end up together – in fact, she's banking on it.'

They both let the word *banking* slide by.

'But he's single, right?' asked Carrie.

Luella warmed to her even more, when she saw how hard she was trying not to look bothered either way. Clearly, there was a sensitive soul under the robust exterior.

'From what I know,' she said. 'Not that we talk much now. We used to be really good friends – me, Bex, Freddie, Hugo and Sims, but not any more.'

Carrie gave her a sympathetic look. 'I feel you. I really thought I'd stay close with my old friends when I moved, but it's like they've forgotten I exist.'

'I'm sorry,' said Luella. 'That must be really—'

Carrie shrugged and cut her off. 'It is what it is. Anyway, I'm too busy shovelling horse poo to care too much. And, as for you, ask Kit out!'

Luella squealed. 'No!'

'Why not?' Carrie pressed. 'Who cares what Bex thinks?'

For a moment, Luella revelled in the excitement that bubbled up inside her. Then she squashed it down. *She* cared. Sad as it was, *she* cared what Bex thought.

They heard the roar of the quad bike and Kit rounded the corner. Just at that moment, a girl rode up from the bridleway and trotted her horse across the field towards them. Luella frowned and as Kit parked the bike beside them he sighed and said, 'Looks like someone else *does* know about the secret gate in the hedge.'

The girl came cantering across the field, whooping and cheering. Luella leaned close to Carrie. 'Felicity Balfour, youngest Balfour child.'

'Hi, Felicity,' said Kit, as she halted dramatically straight from canter a couple of metres away. He didn't sound like himself at all, but stiff and formal. 'Luella just saw me here and popped over to say hi.' He reached out to pat her beautiful bay hunter. 'How is Major Tom?'

'He's great, thanks, Kitster, and so am I. Hi, Lulu! Lovely to see you.'

Luella baulked at the childhood nickname – she was growing out of *Lulu*. And *Kitster*??

'Hi, I'm Carrie,' said Carrie.

'Hey, Carrie.' She turned to Kit. 'I need to measure Major T up for a new rug,' she said, without taking her eyes off him. 'Would you come and help me? I'd really appreciate it.' Then she let out a high-pitched strangled giggle and fluttered her eyelashes like she was trying to take off. 'The sale ends today so I need to order it, and I want to show Daddy I can be good with money too, like he is.'

Carrie and Luella exchanged a glance, eyebrows raised. *Did Felicity have a crush on Kit?*

Kit looked torn. 'You go on,' said Luella, reassuringly. 'I was just about to leave anyway.'

'Sure. OK. Thanks,' he muttered. They didn't hug, as they usually did. It felt a bit weird, too intimate, with other people around. Carrie and Luella watched Kit roar away on the quad bike and the younger girl set off at a canter behind him, waving to Luella as she went.

'I know he hates being at their beck and call,' she told Carrie. 'But she's a Balfour, what can he do? And she's OK. The only one of them who is. I feel sorry for her, being born into that viper's nest of a family.'

'It must be difficult,' said Carrie. 'I'd be telling them to stuff it and getting in trouble all the time.'

Luella sighed. 'He hates how they behave to the staff and, sometimes, the horses, But there isn't a lot he can do about it. Ten generations of his family have worked on the estate. Everything's tied up with it – his home, his parents' jobs, and his grandfather lives with them too.'

Carrie gave her a sly smile. 'The two of you seem very close.'

Luella shrugged, but she felt a warm glow inside. 'I've always known *of* him, you know, seen him around. But now, yeah – we talk. A lot. And—' She felt silent, not wanting to say too much, in case she was delusional, but . . .

'He likes you. It's obvious,' said Carrie.

Luella lit up like a beacon. She knew she looked goofy, but she didn't care. 'You think so?'

'Totally.'

Carrie was kind, and fun. Luella felt both empowered and relaxed with her, and she wanted to get to know her better – *sod Bex*. For a moment, she felt like her old self again.

She'd been a bit of a mouse lately. Bex wasn't doing her self-esteem any good at all. A new friend, a new way of connecting with Charlie . . . maybe even a new boyfriend? Life was really looking up.

She smiled at Carrie. 'I have a feeling you're going to shake things up around here.'

Carrie smiled back. 'I know I am.'

Chapter Six

Bex

'This is absolutely unacceptable!' Bex screamed.

'Careful! That's Prada!' cried her mother.

Bex gave a hollow laugh. 'Get your priorities right!'

It turned out that handbags fly across kitchens pretty well.

Her father cleared his throat and smoothed down his tie. He was finally back from his 'business trip'. 'Control yourself, darling,' he said wearily.

She grabbed the stack of bills off the counter again and shoved them in his face. 'What the hell is going on with all these?!'

Not meeting her gaze, he poured another Scotch. 'Don't be so dramatic, Bexy,' he said. 'It's a small blip. A few deals gone south. You know what it's like for me, running the company. You have to speculate to accumulate and sometimes it doesn't go your way, but you've got to have skin in the game.'

Bex gaped at him. 'I have literally no idea what you're talking about,' she said. 'So, are you saying everything's fine?'

He swayed his glass in the air and took a long swig from it, draining it to the rocks. 'Absolutely.'

Bex felt like she could breathe again. She glanced at her mum, but her face was unreadable. 'So, these are paid now? It was just an oversight at the Langdons'?'

'How vulgar that they sent a reminder after only a month,' said her mother. 'They've got no sense of decorum.'

'I completely agree,' said her father. 'Everything is built on relationships in our circles, and business is mixed with pleasure. It's the way. We all know when a chap needs a few more weeks for some payments to come in. We let it slide. It's just how we do things.'

'Of course, dear,' said her mother. 'I mean, for goodness' sake. It was only a few thousand.'

Bex felt like she was tripping. The Langdons had bills to pay, like everyone else, and they were running a business. 'So, the payments came in, and everything's been sorted now?' she pressed.

'I told you – a few deals didn't come off, darling. Nothing to do with me, or the company. Bad timing, and that stupid affordable housing scheme slowing things down.'

'So, they're *not* paid? And I can't repay Luella what I owe her. And . . .' She hardly dared ask. 'School? That's sorted, surely. I mean, that's absolutely essential.' Bex felt her heart pounding in her ears.

A look passed between her parents, sliding through the silence. Bex sat down heavily on the cream leather bar-stool at the vast marble kitchen island and put her head in her hands. 'Fuck.'

'They haven't even got back to me yet, about overcharging for the ski trip. I've emailed three times,' said her mother. 'The women in that school office are hopeless. Until we get a new, correct bill I won't even *look* at it.'

That's it, they're delusional, Bex thought. She'd always loved being an only child, but just then, she passionately wished for a brother or sister to help her through this shitshow. The truth flooded in, the truth she hadn't been wanting to admit. The declined credit card transactions. The delayed interior design revamp. The cancelled Easter holiday thanks to the double-booking at the same place they always went to in St Barts. (Of course, her mother wouldn't think of going anywhere else, slumming it in a regular five-star hotel.) The money was gone. And Carlotta.

'You lied to me about Carlotta,' she said to parental silence. She lifted her head from the cool marble counter. Maybe that would be sold out from under her soon. The rage bubbling up in her couldn't have been expressed if she'd thrown a hundred handbags. It came out in a cold hiss. 'I can't go to that local sixth-form dive. They probably have metal detectors on the way in, and sharps bins in the loos. Oh my God.' She stood up, pushed her shoulders back, lifted her chin and fixed them both, one after the other, with a piercing look of contempt. 'Get this sorted. *Now*.'

Her father met her eye. 'We'll have to sell two of your ponies,' he said, without any emotion. 'Larkin's Polo will take them – I've talked to my old pal Jonty there. You'll need to decide which ones.'

Bex's insides turned to mush, and she could hardly breathe, but she didn't show it. 'No. Fucking. Way,' she said, holding his stare. 'This is *your* mess. My ponies are going nowhere.' With that, she spun on her heel and marched out of the room, letting out a loud shriek of fury about her parents as she ran up the stairs to her room. She'd enjoy sticking them in a nursing home one day.

She thought for a moment about calling Luella. But she felt strangely embarrassed. Even though it wasn't her fault and she knew that Lulu would be kind, she couldn't risk the news getting out. And she wouldn't be able to *take* Luella being kind. It would break her.

She couldn't break right now. She had to be strong, for her ponies. Her beautiful Bomba and Gordo, Estrella and Blanca. The pain seared her like a hot knife. There was no way in hell she was choosing between them, and no way in hell they were going to be sold, any of them. *End of.*

She downed a couple of shots of vodka from her vintage drinks trolley, and formulated her battle plan. *For her ponies, her future and her parents, even if they didn't deserve it.*

1) Play on the Langdon team in the Guillards Cup
2) Win (obviously)
3) Secure all the endorsement deals, launch a very expensive coaching programme for wannabe It-girls and get her father a big business deal with Lord L
4) Get Carlotta back so they could stop living on M&S quiche

Someone was going to have to turn her family's fortunes around, and clearly that someone was her.

That's why she was off to see Freddie. Rock stars and rappers would have to wait for now. It was time to go girlfriend on his ass.

An hour later, Bex was in Freddie's favourite Saturday-night haunt, a stunning thatched country gastropub called The Coach and Horses, wearing a slinky deep-blue pantsuit.

She'd bought herself a drink on her dad's bar tab (luckily, his credit was still good there – for now, anyway). She'd joined Freddie's crowd, slipping on to the cosy bench seat beside him. When Rufus and Amir had gone off to play pool, she'd leaned in close to his ear and proposed they go for one of their private rides.

To her surprise, he pulled away. 'Bex, no, this has to stop.'

WTF? Outright rejection. First her parents, now this?? She tried to play it off with a sultry pout. 'Why not?' She wasn't going to deploy the 'G' word now, after such a bad start.

He raised one eyebrow at her, assessing. 'You might not like it. In fact, you definitely won't.'

'What?'

He just shook his head and sipped at his pint.

She nudged his arm playfully. Like it was no big deal. 'You can tell me, we're old friends. This is just fun, *me and you*, you know that.'

He demurred. 'Best not.'

Bex's mind was whirring, in overdrive, although her face didn't show a flicker of it. 'Come on, spill. I know we haven't been hanging out much recently, but I've always got your back.' She kept her voice light, easy. 'Have you been getting with someone?'

'No.' Another sip of his pint.

Thank God. Obviously she'd have had to find who it was, go round to her house and tear the poor unfortunate girl limb from limb.

Freddie cleared his throat. 'But there is someone I like.'

Bex crushed her perfectly manicured nails into her palms. *Which undeserving gold-digger has got her claws into* my *Freddie?*

And then, suddenly, she knew. That new stable hand who thought she was all that but didn't even know how to put on a tail bandage.

Cathy? Cassie? *Carrie.*

She raised an eyebrow, aiming for a blend of friendly, intrigued and supportive. Even though it nearly killed her. 'Aha.'

She wanted to ask him whether this Carrie girl felt the same, whether anything had happened, whether he planned to ask her out, whether he already had. But she didn't trust herself to hold her composure. He'd got with other girls, she knew that. Loads of them. But it had never stopped him seeing her. He always got bored of them after a few nights. But now? He hadn't even *slept* with this girl and he was rejecting her, Bex, over it. 'Exciting,' she forced herself to say. 'I've got my eye on someone, too, actually. But I'm keeping it to myself for now. See what happens.' She shrugged, feigning nonchalance.

Freddie smiled at her and held up his glass. 'New flames for us both then. And here's to old friends.'

She clinked her glass with his and just about choked down her vodka martini. The only new flames would be the ones she'd use to burn Carrie's house to the ground, with her inside.

Bex hung around for a few more drinks so she didn't look sus then ordered an Uber straight to Luella's house. She knew she shouldn't be wasting money on extra taxi rides, but this was an emergency.

She rang the doorbell hard and when Luella answered in a dressing gown and face mask, Bex walked right in, spitting feathers. 'Do you know about this Carrie person, working at the Langdons'? Freddie's got a thing for her, apparently. Which I cannot understand at all because looking at her Insta the girl literally can't put a top and jeans together, never mind coordinating them with her make-up and—'

Luella followed her as she strode to the kitchen. 'Well, hi, Bex, how are you?' she said, a little playfully.

Bex found this completely inappropriate. 'I'm awful. Dreadful, of course,' she wailed. 'Freddie's just *abandoned* me for some slapper who spends her days covered in horse shit and doesn't know her Prada from her Pringle.'

'Her *name* is Carrie. She's nice.'

Bex was incensed. 'No, she's bloody not! If she were, she wouldn't have taken Freddie from me.'

'Freddie wasn't yours. It was just a bit of fun, you always say it yourself, and the last time was, well, months ago.'

Bex sat down heavily on an ancient chair at the end of the long kitchen table. She glanced up automatically to the shelf over the Aga. She always looked up to see the pottery pig with 'Best Friends Forever', which she'd made for Luella back in primary school. The one Luella had made for her was in her kitchen too, but her mum would always hide it in the kitchen drawer when guests came over.

She sighed. 'He *was* mine. He *is* mine. He's always been mine.'

Luella leaned against the fridge but didn't offer her a drink. Or even a kind word, as it turned out. Instead, she stuck the knife in. 'Bex, come on. There was never some kind of long-term pact between you two.'

Bex stood up sharply. 'There *was*. I know it and so does Freddie. Or at least he did until that basic stable bitch showed up.' She grunted in frustration. 'You are *not* to see that girl, Lulu, do you hear me?!'

Luella's response sounded somewhere between shock and laughter. *The cheek!* Bex thought. *Has she completely forgotten what loyalty is?*

'Bex, you can't tell me who to—'

'No, I can't. But I *can* tell you that if you value my friendship, you'll steer clear of that scheming little cow.' She wanted to tell Luella how betrayed she felt by her hanging out with Carrie, and how devastated she was about Freddie's rejection, and the money, and – very worst of all – what her father had said about her beloved ponies.

But she couldn't. She tried, but it all just sat on her chest, squeezing her lungs so tight her breath came out strangled in her throat.

'Bex, what is it?' Luella asked gently. 'You can tell me. Is there something else?'

All Bex could do was shake her head, while fighting back tears. *Don't be a cry-baby*, she told herself.

Luella gave her a smile, so full of love and kindness that the wretched tears almost spilled down her cheeks. 'Look, Carrie really likes Freddie. For himself, not his money. And I think he really likes her too, so—'

That was it. Bex knew her only option was to put her walls up or break into pieces. She barged past Luella and headed for the front door, scared that she'd shatter and fall to the floor in a sobbing heap. 'Yes, well, thank you very much for your support, *best friend*,' she said acidly, and then stormed out, with an impressive door slam. Lulu didn't even bother to go after her – clearly she didn't care about her at all.

Carrie Brent had to go. Out of Langdon's, preferably out of Yetbourne entirely, and back to whatever godawful postcode she'd crawled out of in the first place.

But that was no use to Bex right now. She knew her father wouldn't change his mind about her ponies. She shook her head hard. It was still too painful to even think about. She couldn't. It was too awful. But it was happening. It was really happening. The very worst thing she could imagine.

Bomba. Gordo. Estrella. Blanca.

She could only keep two. She'd have to choose.

Chapter Seven
Carrie

Carrie woke up early, excitement thrumming in her chest as it did each morning now she worked with beautiful horses at the Langdon Estate every day. But today, Saturday, was extra special. Today, she was meeting Kit and Luella for her very first lesson in natural horsemanship.

She had a secret plan – well, maybe it was just a delusional fantasy. It was that, if she could learn how to calm Blaze, maybe Freddie would let her train him.

She got dressed in jeans and a T-shirt and trotted down the stairs to the smells of burned toast and the septic tank, as the wind was blowing the wrong way.

'Morning!' she called to her mum, who hadn't noticed the toast quietly cremating itself. She popped it up, chucked it away and started again. Pity it wasn't that easy with the sewage smell. 'I can't believe we're not on mains drainage here,' she groaned.

'Oh, morning, love.' Mum came out of her reverie. Carrie knew she had a lot on her mind. Since Dad had lost his job, and their house in Streatham had been repossessed, she drifted off a lot. Plus, she was tired, from taking on loads of cleaning work in the village.

'Thank God we have Wi-Fi, or I'd, well . . . just *no*. Absolutely not.'

Mum smiled, which had been her aim. 'Are you catching up on your coursework today?' she asked. 'We can just about afford to get you that maths program now – the school sent an email about it.'

'Sure . . .' Carrie poured herself some orange juice and glugged it down, then buttered the toast, stuck the two pieces together and headed for the door. 'This afternoon. Definitely. And thanks about the program, but I can pay for it. I've got my wages.'

'No way,' came Dad's voice, as he stepped out of the damp downstairs bathroom in a towel, hair wet from the shower. 'If I can't buy my daughter a maths program for her A levels then what has it come to?'

She felt the awkwardness between Mum and Dad then. They hadn't handled recent events very well. They didn't talk enough – instead there were a lot of pointed comments and painful silences.

'Gotta go,' Carrie said, munching her toast. 'I'm going to meet a new friend. Well, two. We're doing horse stuff. Then I'm working. I'll get a sandwich from the staff fridge. Catch you later.'

She threw an arm round Mum as she passed by the back of her chair and pulled a face at Dad. That used to make him laugh, and it raised a smile, at least.

Nothing could rain on her parade that morning, though, and half an hour later she was with Kit, Luella and Charlie in their secret spot, heart pounding with excitement.

'Right, I'll go back to basics for your sake, Carrie,' said Kit, 'and Luella could do with it too,' he added with a wry smile in her direction.

Luella playfully slapped him one. 'Hey, don't be rude! Charlie sprang off her nearside hind into canter like absolute butter yesterday, just from me lifting my energy.'

Kit grinned. 'You must have a great teacher.'

Luella grinned back, wickedly. 'No, I just have a fantastic horse.'

Carrie sighed dramatically, a twinkle in her eye. 'Get a room, you two.'

That sobered them up a bit and they both took a bashful step back from each other. It was cute, she thought. They'd make a great couple. Carrie wondered whether Luella had taken her advice and asked him out yet.

Kit pushed his sandy blond hair away from his eyes and handed Carrie the stick and string, as well as the heavy, long lead rope with the stunning Charlie on the other end of it. The dapple-grey mare was happily munching grass and showed little interest in going round in a circle. 'First things first,' Kit said. 'Rapport. Connection. You're just going to take a walk around the arena together.'

The 'arena' was the level, grassy rectangle that he'd marked out with four yellow flags at the corners. Some cones were set up in a line down the middle of it.

'Sure.' Carrie set off, giving Charlie a tug, so she pulled her head up and came with her.

'Get her off the forehand, stand behind the drive line . . . and stop dragging her!' Kit directed.

She grimaced. *Great start, Carrie. You can't even walk a horse around.*

After a few minutes, Carrie thought they were doing pretty well, walking along together, but Kit called out, 'Use the stick to move her out of your space, she's all over you!' as Charlie started snuffling at Carrie's pockets to see if she had any treats. 'That's it. Protect your space. Project your energy, from your belly button. Send her *out*.'

Carrie focused on everything Kit said and, to her amazement, Charlie stepped away as they went forward, giving her a little more room.

'Good, well done.'

Kit got them going between the cones, and then into moving from a walk to a halt, then a halt to a walk and a walk to a trot, then, most excitingly, a halt to a trot. She could hardly believe it when Charlie burst into motion. Kit and Luella clapped, and Carrie was brimming with pride by the time Kit called a break.

They sat on some jump stands and drank posh hardly fizzy lemonade in glass bottles, with bits in, that Luella had brought with her. Luella and Kit squeezed on to one of the plastic blocks while Carrie took the other. Any excuse to be near each other.

'That was absolutely frickin' awesome!' she cried, glugging from the bottle and screwing up her face at the sharp taste.

'You did amazing,' said Luella.

'We'll do circles next,' said Kit, 'maybe even get her cantering around you.'

Carrie beamed at them, one after the other. 'Thanks for loaning me Charlie,' she said, 'and the teaching.'

'You're welcome,' Luella and Kit both said at the same time.

'So, when do I actually get, you know, *on* the horse?' Carrie asked, desperately hopeful, but trying to sound casual.

'When you have any kind of boundaries whatsoever on the ground,' said Kit wryly.

Carrie shrugged. 'How hard can it be? Sit up there, point forward, go left and right.' She mimed holding the reins.

'I suppose I could take you round the field on one of the kids' ponies at the Langdons',' said Luella. 'On a lead rope, mind you.'

That wasn't exactly Carrie's fantasy – cantering Blaze through an open field with Freddie on Willow beside her was more like it. Even so, her heart leaped with excitement. She was just about to say, 'Cool! When?' when Luella said, 'The problem is . . . Well . . . I wasn't going to tell you this, but Bex banned me from seeing you. And she doesn't even know I'm training with Kit.'

'I'd definitely be blacklisted,' said Kit, laughing easily. But Carrie bristled. *Who does this bloody Bex girl think she is, anyway?*

'She can't tell you who to be friends with,' she said fiercely, watching her first ever ride slip away.

Luella sighed. 'No, she can't. But she's been my best friend for years, and she's going through some kind of tricky patch at the moment, and I want to be there for her.'

'But don't listen to her,' Carrie pressed.

'I'm not. I'm here, aren't I?' cried Luella, indignant. 'Doing all the things Bex would definitely disapprove of.' She smiled at Kit and they linked hands briefly. Clearly neither of them wanted to let go.

Carrie couldn't help but grin. 'Wow, if Bex finds out you two are a *thing*, she'll spontaneously combust!'

Luella flushed and Kit, looking horrifically embarrassed, muttered something about getting the Pringles from the barn.

The second he was far away enough not to hear, Luella gave Carrie a shove and squealed, 'Oh my God! I can't believe you said that! Out loud! In front of Kit! Who has ears!'

Carrie took the last swig of her lemonade. 'I told you, he likes you!'

'He doesn't! He just *ran away*!'

Carrie laughed. 'No, he's awkward because he *likes you*. And before the running away there was the spontaneous hand holding. Have you asked him on a date yet?'

'No!' Luella snapped. 'And I can't believe you said we were *a thing*! We're just friends.'

'You will be a thing soon, after the date you're going to ask him on,' said Carrie breezily. 'And then you'll see *his thing* . . .'

Luella shrieked. 'Carrie! Don't be crude!' She threw her a wry smile. 'Not that I would mind seeing *his thing* . . .'

'Luella! Don't be crude!' Carrie mimicked, and they fell about laughing, making Charlie whinny and shake her head.

'Anyway, let's talk about you and Freddie,' said Luella, switching the spotlight to Carrie. 'Snogged his face off yet?'

Carrie swatted her. 'Ha! You sound so funny, saying "snogged" in your posh accent! But no, I would have told you if I had.' She sighed. 'I don't even know if he actually likes me. I mean, the way people talk about him, I get the impression he's like this with loads of girls.'

'True, he's a player,' said Luella, and Carrie held in the urge to scream, cry, vomit or all of the above. 'But he's always gone back to Bex in between. Nothing has ever got serious, with her or with anyone else.'

'And you're saying I'm just another one of those girls in between bouts of Bex,' said Carrie grumpily.

'Actually, no,' said Luella. 'Bex came over the other night – she was in a terrible state. Really upset. For the first time ever, Freddie rejected her.'

Freddie rejected her! Carrie's heart leaped with joy, which she felt bad about, for a nanosecond. 'You mean, her giant ego took it badly,' she said, guilt-free. *Bex didn't care about Freddie. She only cared about herself.*

'She really likes him, Carrie,' said Luella gently. 'And underneath, deep down, she's not as bad as she seems.'

Carrie raised her eyebrows in disbelief.

'Honestly,' Luella insisted. 'You just have to get to know her. And maybe . . .' She sighed. She looked extremely uncomfortable all of a sudden. 'Maybe take things easy with Freddie? Don't rub it in her face?'

Carrie beamed. 'I'm just excited to hear that you think there's something *to* rub in her face.'

'Yep, Freddie literally *told* her he likes you,' Luella said. 'So, there is *definitely* something to rub in her face. But don't. And maybe wait a bit before . . .'

Carrie did a little happy dance. 'Nuh-uh. She had her chance. Now I get mine. He's single. I'm single. We both like each other. Man, I can't wait until my next shift.'

'You're still employed there and Freddie's not supposed to get involved with the staff. I hate to break it to you, but you are very much staff,' said Luella.

Carrie nudged her and grinned. 'Who cares? Freddie. Likes. Me!'

Freddie likes me, Freddie likes me, Freddie likes me. It was like a chant that had been playing in Carrie's head, and heart, ever since she'd got back on her bike and ridden over to the Langdons'. The rest of the natural horsemanship lesson had gone brilliantly. She hadn't quite got Charlie changing direction on a circle in canter yet, but Kit had promised her that it would come, and their hindquarter yields had been epic.

She'd decided she wouldn't say anything to Freddie about being at the Balfours' – their rivalry was real, and deep, and she was a Langdon girl now. But as she left her bike in the rack and strode down on to the main yard, to her surprise, she found a Balfour right in the middle of it.

Barnaby Balfour, to be precise. She'd seen him around the village, and at some of the polo matches the Langdons had hosted so far. He had dark brown curly hair, deep brown eyes and broad shoulders. If she hadn't been completely into Freddie, and hadn't heard how awful Barnaby was, she might have even thought he was attractive.

She tried to slip into the office unnoticed, sliding the rucksack with the ultrasound machine off her shoulder as she went in.

'Hey, new girl!'

Damn. He'd seen her.

He strode over, in that same purposeful, confident way that Freddie had. 'You're Carrie, right?'

She didn't smile. 'Can I help you? Are you looking for someone?'

'Looking for someone,' he repeated, slow and lazy. 'Well, I was going to stay single, play the field. But,' His eyes raked across her body before settling on her face. 'But I might be.'

Flustered, Carrie took a physical step back. 'I didn't mean that. Obviously.'

He laughed. 'Relax. I'm joking. Don't be so tense.'

She felt intensely uncomfortable. 'I have to get to work.'

'His Lordship Junior about?' He said it with a sneer.

A moment was all Carrie needed to get a handle on things. One more comment or look like that and she'd crush the little worm into the dust, or maybe run him over with Blaze. 'He's out,' she said, arms folded. 'So you can leave.'

Barnaby raised his eyebrows. 'You're a handful.'

'I'm here. What do you want?' came Freddie's deep voice from behind her, edgy and tense.

Barnaby glared at him over her shoulder and bristled. 'The VIP area, for the Tenterden Cup final next weekend. We need more seating, and we aren't happy with the quality of the canapés.'

Freddie shrugged. 'Then you've got no taste. Organic, local produce – and our catering team is award winning.'

Barnaby glared at him. 'It was rubbish. *Local?* The whole *point* of the best is it has to be *flown in*. My father has some very important business associates coming to that match, so make sure there's a marked improvement, got it?' Barnaby squared up to Freddie, right in his face, but Freddie just laughed. Though Carrie noticed his hands ball into fists. 'I'm not going to fight you over canapés,' he said. 'Get off our yard. Now.'

Barnaby nodded towards her. 'Nice bit of skirt. Perks of the job, I suppose. I know I would.'

Carrie was about to thump him herself, but a second later, she shrieked as Freddie grabbed his shirt collar and pushed him back against the wall. 'Don't you dare speak about her like that! Or any girl!'

For a moment, time seemed to stand still. Then Freddie let go, shoving Barnaby out of the office door. For a moment, Barnaby faced him off, eyes blazing, but then, seeing the fury in Freddie's, he thought better of it. He held his hands up. 'Fine. I'm going.' He walked out, submissive, but then turned, winked at Carrie and said, 'See you later, sweetheart.'

He left before Freddie could floor him.

'You OK?' Freddie asked, as they both stood in the office doorway.

'Any more of that and he's heading for a knee in the balls.'

They both tried to step through the door at the same time, bumping up against each other. It felt so awkward, after Barnaby's comments. That was how everyone would see it, if anything *did* happen between them, she realised. Freddie crossing a line and taking advantage, or Carrie sleeping with the boss to get ahead. She might even get fired. It made her shudder inside.

She thought of how excited she'd been to come to work and see him, and felt silly. *Freddie likes me, Freddie likes me.* The chant in her head felt like it was mocking her now. She stepped through the doorway, putting about two metres between them.

'Well, I'd better get on,' he said stiffly.

'Me too.'

'Lots on today.'

'Absolutely.'

Urgh! They felt like strangers. Or robots. Or robot strangers.

The flirting has to stop, Carrie told herself firmly as she grabbed a broom and started sweeping, taking her frustration out on the stray hay flying about the yard. There was too much at stake. It was for the best. Definitely.

Maybe.

Chapter Eight

Luella

Luella finished up another dressage session with Charlie, in her own arena at home. They were doing better, that was for sure. Charlie still kept leaving a leg behind in the square halt at the end of the test and Luella kept getting distracted, thinking about what Carrie had said – *ask him out*. But apart from that, it was looking good.

'Good girl. Good job.' She gave Charlie a big pat on the shoulder and a loose rein to warm down. She was due over at the Balfours to train with Kit, and she planned to walk Charlie over rather than load her into the horsebox, as it wasn't too hot. Her heart caught in her throat as she thought about leaning back into Kit's chest while he showed her how to direct her energy. His warmth, his smell, his hand closed round hers on the stick and string . . .

Ask him out, said Carrie's voice, in her head.

'Shut up,' she said, out loud.

On the ride over, she kept herself busy running through dressage tests and points they could improve on, so that she wouldn't start fixating on Kit's shoulders, his hair, his eyes, his hips, his bum in the blue jeans he always wore. Oh God. There she went again. It was both amazing and awful, having a mind-numbingly intense crush.

For a moment, she let herself imagine asking him out. But what if he said no? Their training would be so awkward. Was it better not to risk it? Or what if Carrie was wrong and he *didn't* like her that way?

Again, she realised how much confidence in herself she'd lost recently. She felt bad for not fully supporting Carrie asking Freddie out. Then she felt bad for not taking Bex's side more. Then she felt bad for being a drama queen and obsessing about this kind of stuff. Then she thought about Kit's shoulders again ... *Urgh, make it stop*, she groaned to herself.

She leaned down and opened the latch of the secret gate, then rode Charlie through into her and Kit's training field. She could see the quad bike by the barn, but as she rode closer she couldn't see Kit anywhere.

She slowed to a walk as she neared the barn and dismounted, ground tying Charlie. She gave her a quiet stroke on the neck rather than a loud pat, though, as she listened, focused. She could hear Kit talking in the barn.

Why am I sneaking around? she wondered. But she didn't shout out to announce herself.

It's not sneaking – I'm just checking he's OK, she answered herself. *And it's not eavesdropping – it's a public place.*

Yeah, right.

Then another voice. Female. She couldn't make out the words, but there was a giggle, and a flirty tone. She felt fiercely possessive and scared of what she'd see. She walked quietly up to the side door of the barn and peered in.

Oh, thank goodness, it was only Felicity. For a moment there, she'd thought he was with a girl. As in, *romantically*. It struck her at that moment that he wouldn't be doing anything wrong if he had been. Her stomach flipped. She and Kit weren't together. They hadn't kissed or talked about seeing each other. He wasn't *hers*.

She had that rush of relief that happens when you think something's gone badly wrong, but it hasn't, and you feel like you've been given a second chance. Then she heard Felicity say, 'I thought we could . . . Kit, would you like to come to the multiplex with me? And then we could go to the Nando's there and . . .'

Luella took a step back and tucked herself behind the barn door. Oh my goodness, Felicity was *asking him out*!

'It's so kind of you to ask, but I don't think—' Kit said, sounding mortified. She'd better go in there and rescue him, the poor guy. But then Luella watched in horror as Felicity lunged forward and kissed him, full on the lips. Kit stood there completely frozen.

Luella's body reacted before her brain then and she strode into the barn. 'Hey, guys, what's up?' she said, as breezily as she could, like she'd just got there.

Kit jumped backwards and Felicity turned bright red, flustered. 'Oh, hi, Lulu! I was just . . . looking for . . . baling twine . . . Well, anyway, I'd better dash.'

With that she fled past Luella and out of the barn. They watched in silence as she ran right up the lane and rounded the corner. Then Luella turned to Kit, put her hand on her hip and raised her eyebrow. 'Well, *that* I was not expecting.'

Kit sat down heavily on a hay bale and sighed. 'Tell me about it. God, how awkward. I hope she doesn't tell anyone. And I hope no one thinks that I . . .' He groaned and put his head in his hands.

Luella sat down beside him. 'What – encouraged her? Kissed her back?'

He nodded, still clutching his head. 'She's only fifteen. And the boss's daughter.'

She put her arm around him, automatically. 'Don't worry. If anyone says anything, I'll be clear with them about what happened. I saw it all. You've done nothing wrong.'

'Thanks, Lu. I don't know what I'd do without you.' He looked up, meeting her eyes with his, and she melted inside. God, she wanted to kiss him so much. She gathered up her courage. She'd got that second chance. *Seize the day.*

She smiled shyly. 'Would you like to go out with *me*? On a date.'

He smiled too. 'Yes, I would love that. Very much.'

Luella felt a rush of elation through her chest. Relief and excitement all at once. *Thank you, Carrie.*

Kit smiled wickedly. 'As long as it's not to Nando's.'

Luella snorted. 'As if! Although . . . their grilled corn is amazing!'

'Come on, let's go train,' said Kit. He entwined his fingers with hers, her breath caught in her throat and for a moment the places where his skin touched hers felt like the only thing in the world. He leaned towards her and she pulled him close . . . and then his phone rang.

They leaped apart, like they'd been caught, then laughed. 'I'd better take it,' Kit said. 'It's the boss.'

For one horrible moment, Luella was filled with a fear that Felicity had run straight home and told Jasper Balfour that Kit had rejected her. Or, worse, that he *hadn't* rejected her.

But no. Kit was nodding, smiling, and saying, 'Yes, absolutely, sir.' Pause. She strained to hear but Kit had the phone pressed tight to his ear. 'It would be a privilege.' Pause. 'Thank you. I won't let you down. You too. Goodbye.'

He hung up and blinked at her in astonishment and then a big, beaming grin spread across his face. 'I'm playing in the Balfour team for the charity polo match,' he said, staring into her eyes in wonder.

She gasped. 'Oh wow, Kit! That's amazing!'

He stood up and paced about, fizzing with energy. 'I couldn't have done it without you, Lu. You encouraged me to ask and I went for it.'

'You're talented,' she said firmly. 'It's great he's giving you a shot.'

'If I do well, I'll be chosen for their Guillards Cup team,' said Kit, looking dazed. 'Lu, I can't believe it! A real chance to make my way to the top! This could be the start of a whole new future for me!'

'It's awesome!' said Luella, standing too. As they went out into the sunshine, she smiled to herself as she thought, *a whole new future for us.*

Then she caught herself. *Steady on!* she thought firmly. *Let's start with a date.*

Chapter Nine

Bex

Bex sat on the fence, watching her ponies graze in the field. She'd turned them out, just the four of them, in the empty top field, so that they could have a good run around and play together for the last time.

They didn't know it was the last time, of course. She watched Estrella assert herself in the herd, moving Gordo out of her way. So Gordo went and moved Blanca, who pulled her ears back and leered at him, but then went and grazed with Bomba, who held the lowest position in the herd, even though she was dynamite on the polo field. It could look bad to people, the way horses moved one another around, or took little pops at each other, but knowing their place in the herd actually made them feel safe.

Bex used to think that that was a lot like life – if everyone just knew their place then things would be much better. But she wasn't at the top of the tree any more. What *was* her place? She didn't know. Everything was crumbling. She did know one thing, though. Whatever her place in life was, she'd have to find it on her own now, because her Langdon plan had failed.

She had to give up two of her beloved ponies.

She'd had a sleepless night when she'd got back from being rejected by Freddie and betrayed by Luella, made the painful decision and then thrown up her breakfast. The phone calls had been made to *good old Jonty* and the day had come. Far too quickly.

Estrella and Blanca were leaving. The lorry would arrive in an hour.

She'd felt too rubbish to put any make-up on. She was wearing a giant pair of sunglasses and planned to spend this final hour watching her darling horses play, sobbing her heart out in privacy.

But—

Oh God.

Who was that vaulting over the gate?

A willowy blonde figure.

Luella.

'Hi, Bex.' She sounded sombre, as she reached her. Damn. Mum must have told her where she was. For a moment, she panicked that she may have told her the full story, too. But no, surely not. Dad had sworn them both to secrecy.

'Why didn't you call me?' Luella asked. 'You know I love Estrella and Blanca!'

Bex just shrugged, holding back the tears, thanking God for the sunglasses. 'Oh, I . . . You know . . .'

'It's amazing that you got that last-minute spot. For both of them, too! Isn't there, like, a two-year waiting list for residential training places at Fuente Polo?'

Mum had delivered their agreed cover story to perfection, then. 'Yeah, but, you know what my dad's like. Anything for me. He pulled some strings.' She couldn't hold the tears in any more and broke down, rocking back and forth, howling.

'Hey!' In a moment, Luella's arms were around her, helping her slide down off the fence before she fell backwards. 'Why are you so upset?' she asked, gently rocking her. 'You've always wanted your horses trained by Carlos Fuente . . .'

'It's just, it's three months! I'm going to miss them so much,' she sobbed. *If only. If only it were just three months.*

'I completely understand,' said Luella then, stroking her hair. 'I'd be the same if Charlie or Captain were going away for that long, even if it was for such an amazing opportunity.'

She hugged Bex and was surprised to find her best friend clinging tight to her and sobbing her heart out. Bex herself was even more surprised. She cried and cried and couldn't stop. She'd been too angry to cry in front of her parents – not that they'd have known what to do with her if she had. There might have been one of those awful *'Be a brave girl, Bex'* peptalks from her dad and her mum would probably have suggested a comforting cup of tea. Or some vodka shots.

Luella was amazing – she'd always been good with emotional stuff. As Bex sobbed and wailed and moaned, she just held her tight. She didn't try to make her stop, or tell her that everything would be fine, or fuss about her face getting puffy. Bex wished that everything could go back to how it had been before Carrie came along, and before she'd found out about her parents' huge mess. She'd been growing apart from Luella, obsessing over her personal brand and her social media profile, but now she desperately wanted them to be close again. Someone to laugh with, hang out with, ride her remaining ponies with.

She stopped crying eventually, blowing her nose on the pristine tissue Luella handed her. 'This is all Carrie's fault.'

Luella stepped backwards and looked at her, troubled. 'What's this got to do with Carrie? Your ponies are going to a top trainer!'

Bex got a hold of herself. God! She'd almost let slip the truth – that they were going to a polo club for their rich clients to try and buy, like haute couture dresses, when they were living beings. *Puke.* She'd probably never see them again.

But she couldn't let Luella know. She couldn't have it getting out. 'Freddie, I mean,' she said hurriedly. 'She's stolen him from me.' If Carrie hadn't come along, Freddie would be bending the rules to help her keep Estrella and Blanca at the Langdon Estate right now – she was sure of it.

Luella sighed. 'I know it's hard,' she said. 'And I've tried to talk to Carrie, ask her to consider your feelings . . .'

Bex stared at her, stung. So now her best friend and that Carrie were having cosy little chats about her? *Urgh!* She couldn't stand it.

'Don't bother,' she said coldly, pulling away. 'Don't talk about me at all.' She wiped her eyes. 'Right, I've got to go and get these guys' stuff together, so . . .'

Luella didn't take the hint. She stayed right where she was.

'So, can you go and let us have our last bit of time together in peace?' Bex snapped.

Luella just sighed and held her hands up. 'Fine. I'm not going to argue with you, Bex. Just know I'm here for you if you need me, OK?'

'I won't.' However hard she tried, Bex couldn't crack through the wall that had sprung up in front of her. And right now, she didn't want to. Carrie had taken Freddie, and now, it seemed, she'd taken Luella too. From this moment on, Bex decided, she was on her own.

Well, maybe not *quite* on her own. Maybe she still had Freddie, sort of. An hour later, she'd got Estrella and Blanca on the lorry and was just running back into the tack room to grab Blanca's fly mask, when he walked in.

'Bex.'

She startled. *Oh no.* She looked horrendous.

'Are you all ready to go?'

She nodded. She was sure she wouldn't be able to speak without crying.

'I'm sorry it's come to this,' said Freddie.

She shrugged. 'It is what it is.' Her voice cracked, but he didn't push it and go on about how devastated she must be, thank goodness. He seemed to understand that she was already at breaking point. She reached for her sunglasses to hide her red, puffy eyes, but then left them on top of her head. The tack room was pretty dark, and Freddie had seen her look worse. When Shelka had finally had to be put down, he'd stayed up all night with her.

'It's just . . . It's so unfair and it's not their fault. They'll think they've been sent away and they won't know why.' That was it, the floodgates opened again.

'Bex . . .'

'What's done is done.' Bex stood, grabbed the fly mask and tried to push past Freddie.

He caught her up in his arms and hugged her close. She stood braced, her arms by her sides. 'It's shit and it's awful,' he said. 'And I won't say you'll feel better soon. Maybe you won't. Maybe you never will.'

She relaxed into his embrace and breathed out. He was letting her have all her pain, and all her grief. He knew her so, so well, and she couldn't hide it from him. It felt good to let the tears fall on to his shirt as she breathed in the familiar, comforting scent of him.

He kissed the top of her head. 'And I promise you, no one will know where Estrella and Blanca have really gone. Or why. Mum,

Dad and Terrence are completely trustworthy, you know they won't breathe a word.'

Bex nodded against his chest. 'I know.'

'And I won't tell anyone either.'

She looked up at him, taking in just how beautiful he was, inside and out. They had such a long history together. Maybe this Carrie thing *was* just a blip. Maybe there *was* some hope of getting him back, one day. 'Not even Carrie?' she asked.

He squeezed her tight. 'Not even Carrie.'

Chapter Ten

Carrie

'Sahara Bright Blaze, I am not going to give up on you,' Carrie said through gritted teeth, as Blaze pulled back at the end of the rope, rearing up in her face. Then he put his head down to munch on the grass as if nothing had happened. This had been so much easier with Charlie. It turned out that if Blaze was asked to do anything he hadn't been expressly trained to do by Keiran, the Langdon head polo pony trainer, then you could forget it.

Carrie took a deep breath and felt her cheeks burn with embarrassment and fury. She should be the one called *Blaze*. Worse, Heather was sitting on the fence nearby, eating a granola bar and watching. Because she'd invited her.

She'd been so confident in her skills after four natural horsemanship sessions with Kit, Luella and Charlie that she'd asked Heather if she could have a try with Blaze. They were all still having problems with him – both on the yard and the polo field. He would suddenly get really angry and try to bite them, ears back and face leering. Or he'd freak out during exercise and bolt off or dance about in the air. If he carried on like this, well, he wouldn't be fit for purpose and Carrie didn't want to think about what might happen to him. The polo world was harsh on the ponies, in the main, and there was no room on a working yard for an unusable one. She pulled herself together and sent her energy down the rope as Kit had shown her. It worked like a charm with Charlie – she felt it and connected, open and ready to play together. Blaze just ignored it and continued to munch the grass.

'I can't just *watch* him do that,' Heather called. 'For one thing, you just totally let him get his own way, and for another, laminitis . . .'

Damn. Too much sweet, lush, early summer grass would actually harm Blaze, *and* she'd shown zero leadership. She had to get a move on. This wasn't going well. Her fantasy that Heather would be amazed and instantly call Keiran to watch, and that she herself would then end up as a junior on the polo training team vanished – *poof* – into the crisp early morning air.

She waved the stick behind Blaze, but she wasn't as confident as she'd been with Charlie. If she did too much, he might freak out, turn and boot her one. 'Blaze, you're showing me up,' she muttered. But she knew it wasn't him, really. It was her. She wasn't stepping up and projecting her energy. She was too scared, to put it bluntly.

'Finish up,' called Heather. 'There's tons to do today and I'll need to find time for a full English down the pub later – this little thing isn't going to get me through on its own.'

Carrie took another deep breath and thought about Kit's mantra, *'Lead from within.'* She forgot about Heather, and being judged, and looking good (or rubbish) and just focused on the connection between her and Blaze. 'Right, mate, get with the programme,' she told him. She let go of the string at the end of the stick and flicked it behind him, like she meant it.

He startled a little and shot forward into a chaotic trot, but she kept her breathing steady, dropped her shoulders and opened her hand – the last thing to do in a situation like this was tense up.

At last, feeling the shift in her energy, Blaze started to move more smoothly, on an even circle, and she asked for a change of pace, to walk, and then up to trot again. He sprang off his inside hind nicely and Carrie ended there. Something else Kit always said was *'End on a good note.'* The whole thing had lasted about four minutes. But inside she felt like she was flying, elated, like she'd won the Guillards Cup singlehandedly and passed all her A levels with flying colours and had the hottest night of her life with Freddie Langdon.

She turned and saw Freddie himself standing there, next to Heather, leaning against the fence with his easy smile. *It's OK*, she assured herself, *he's not a mind reader*. She composed herself as she and Blaze walked to the gate. Freddie opened it for them and Heather leaped down from the fence.

'Impressive,' he said. 'You got him going nicely, without upping the pressure.'

'We can all lunge a horse, no offence,' said Heather. 'I'm not sure what exactly you did differently.'

'Well, from what I've seen, I'm happy for you to keep going with old Blazers here, help him sort his shit out,' Freddie said.

Carrie's heart leaped with joy. 'Oh wow! Thank you so much!' she cried. 'I won't let Blaze down, or you.' A pony to practise with! Heather kindly didn't mention how badly the rest of the session had gone.

'It can't do any harm, anyway,' Freddie added. 'Supervised, of course.'

She promised herself that she'd study up online too and work hard to come on leaps and bounds and amaze Kit and Luella. She wanted to throw herself on Freddie and give him a huge hug but she just about managed to hold it in and say thank you again. They'd both been distant, more professional, since their run-in with Barnaby. *Or maybe he didn't like me that much in the first place*, a harsh voice in her head cut in.

As they neared the yard, he looked suddenly awkward, which never, ever happened. 'Erm, Heather, could you give us a minute, please? I need to talk to Carrie about something. We'll bring Blaze in.'

'Sure.' She tucked the granola bar wrapper into the top of her jodhs, along with her phone, and headed back to the yard.

Carrie's mind was racing, almost as fast as her heart. *A word alone? Why? What could it possibly be about?*

Asking her on a date, maybe? Her heart leaped with excitement, and fear. They couldn't, could they? What about the rules? What about her job? *No one has to find out*, she told herself. *We could find a quiet little place . . .*

When Heather had rounded the corner, Freddie shuffled from foot to foot and cleared his throat. Carrie smiled slowly. Here it was. Their moment. It was happening. 'Freddie Langdon, are you nervous?' she teased, a flirty tone in her voice. An invitation. She just couldn't help herself. 'What's up?'

Then, she had a sudden, illogical fear that she'd misjudged the whole situation and that he looked awkward because he was about to fire her. 'I stayed late and scrubbed out all those feed buckets I missed,' she gabbled. 'I know Terrence was annoyed but Michael put them round the corner and I didn't see them so—'

Freddie relaxed then and his easy smile came back. 'It's nothing to do with feed buckets. You're doing a great job – I think so, and so does Terrence. The grooms like you and even Mum and Dad are impressed, which is saying something.'

Carrie felt relieved and proud, both at once. Maybe Lord and Lady L could like her so much that they'd overlook the employee rule and she and Freddie could date and . . .

'I was thinking about what you said a while ago, before you started insulting my face.' said Freddie playfully. 'I reckon it's time . . .'

She held her breath. Their eyes locked. Was this really it? Would he ask her out? Or just lean straight in for a kiss?

'Let's get you riding,' he said. She rocked back on her heels, in shock, and because, *embarrassingly*, she realised that she'd been leaning in herself.

OK, so, not a kiss but . . . 'Oh, wow, seriously?!' she gasped. It felt like all her horsey wishes had come true at once. An image of herself and Blaze galloping across the countryside flashed across her mind, the two of them jumping gates, crossing streams and galloping across a meadow together. She couldn't help throwing her arms around Freddie's neck. He laughed and pulled her close. 'Thank you!' she cried. 'Thank you so much!'

Then, there was a breath, as their eyes met. Their lips were a whisper away from one another. Carrie was lost in the heady scent of him, his eyes, his lips, his open shirt.

Blaze tugged at the rope in his hand, pulling them out of the moment. 'See you by the mounting block, ready to go, in twenty minutes, then,' Freddie said briskly, striding off with Blaze. 'Beatrice knows the drill. Go and find her, she's up in the hay barn.'

'OK, thanks, I will.' She watched him go, heart pounding, waves of desire coursing up her body. Would they ever get it together and kiss? Or would that be the worst mistake of her life?

Both Beatrice and Heather helped her tack up Bounty, a sweet, experienced, calm yellow-dun mare whom the beginner children learned with in the Saturday morning kids' polo club. They'd had hysterics when she'd mentioned riding Blaze. 'Not yet, missy,' Heather had said kindly. 'Our job is to get you going in the saddle, not land you in A&E!'

Soon she and Freddie were riding out together, through the fields at the far side of the Langdon Estate, which was much bigger than she'd realised. The only thing that wasn't part of the sexy, romantic fantasy she'd been having about this moment was that he had her on a lead rope. Oh, and the fact that the hat which fitted her best from the tack room had a Disney princess on it.

Still, she thought she might actually die of joy, with Bounty walking along beside Willow, and her hips and pelvis rocking to the rhythm of the mare's footsteps. The sound of them clip-clopping along the lane, and the smell of slightly hot horse in the warm June air, and the sunshine and the reins in her hands . . . it was heaven. And finally being properly alone with Freddie. He looked so incredibly hot in his jeans, checked shirt open a few buttons at the neck and deck shoes with polo bandages wrapped around them. Paradise, absolute paradise.

Of course, Bounty chose that moment to do a huge fart. Carrie blushed bright red. 'That was the horse, obviously.'

Freddie laughed. 'Don't blame Bounty.' Usually she would have laughed too, but liking him so much and . . . urgh . . . *fancying* him so much . . . it made her want to look sexy and cool all the time. Which was not happening, thanks to the princess hat and Bounty's bum.

She rode along looking at the beautiful countryside – it was the perfect day for riding out with a fit boy you couldn't stop thinking about. Warm, with a good breeze, so she wouldn't end up looking too grossly bright red and sweaty. But not so windy the horses went wappy and she got bucked off in the mud or something. She stole a glance at Freddie and found him looking her body up and down, intense and focused. She smiled to herself. *Not that unsexy then.* He saw her looking and said quickly, 'You're doing really well. Good . . . leg position. Nice rhythm with your hips.'

She dared herself and raised an eyebrow flirtatiously. 'Oh, you like the way my hips move, do you?'

Freddie looked like he was about to say something flirty back, but then he raked his gaze down her body again and seemed lost for words. 'It's . . . yeah . . . it takes the pressure off the pony's joints . . .' he stuttered, looking flustered, '. . . when you . . . like that . . . it lets them move naturally.'

Confidence boosted, she gave him a sultry look from beneath her eyelashes. 'So, as I've got really great hip action, can we gallop across this field?' Bounty was springy-stepped and alert – definitely up for going faster. *Make my fantasy come true*, she thought.

Freddie smiled back at her, slow and sexy. Then he rode Willow close, right up beside her, so their thighs were touching. He leaned across.

Wow, is he going to kiss me while riding? she wondered, waves of desire pulsing up her body. She leaned towards him. Their faces were so close, their lips almost brushing.

'Patience,' he said. He was teasing her now, she thought – making her wait for that kiss they were, clearly, both so desperate for. *That confidence in him was so, so sexy, and his shoulders, his hips, his thighs – oh my God . . .*

He urged Willow on a little and his thigh moved off hers, then he reached out and unclipped the lead rope. 'Trot will do, for now.'

Carrie blushed. 'Oh, you meant no galloping yet.' It was out of her mouth before she could stop it.

He grinned, enjoying the game. 'What did you think I meant?'

'Never mind!'

Trotting, off the lead rope, across a sunlit field with Freddie Langdon was almost as good as kissing him, though. She leaned forward to stroke Bounty's neck, heart just about bursting with happiness.

'Shorten your rein a little but don't grip too much and squeeze her on if she loses pace, but don't kick,' said Freddie.

'Are you secretly a bit of a horse hippy?' she teased.

'Less chat, more focus,' said Freddie – hot, in control – and she thought she'd die of wanting him. She did as he'd said and Bounty moved easily into trot. She bobbled about a bit at first, but, watching Freddie, she soon got the hang of how to let her hips be jogged forward with the rhythm.

'Very nice,' he said, Willow matching her stride.

'Let's gallop,' she said. 'We could race to the tree. I'd beat you.'

He raised an eyebrow at her, amused. 'No way.'

'Oh, come on. Look, I'm doing so well. Canter, at least . . .'

Freddie gave her a stern look. 'Carrie, no way.'

She sighed and pouted, letting her shoulders slump.

He grinned. 'I mean, no way will you beat me.' And with that he and Willow took off, through a few strides of canter then galloping across the field. Bounty took off too, and Carrie gasped, hanging on to the front of the saddle, beaming, feeling like her heart would burst with thrill and joy. Freddie Langdon may have been from a different world, but she felt like they were two of a kind.

Chapter Eleven

Luella

Luella wanted Kit's jaw to drop when he saw her. That's why she'd worn the silver slip dress with strappy heels, and matching beautiful underwear. Not because she was going to do anything on a first date, but just to feel confident and sexy.

Feeling good was also the reason she'd borrowed her mum's Lamborghini and booked her dad's favourite table at Source, their nearest country town's only Michelin-starred restaurant. She wanted to come alive again, especially after feeling so rubbish recently. Kit was definitely helping, as was her friendship with Carrie.

She walked in and saw Kit sitting at their table, sexy and tanned in an open-necked pale blue shirt. Yes, his jaw did drop. Satisfyingly.

He stood, as the maître d' welcomed her and pulled out her chair. 'You scrub up well, lass.' It was cute. He was actually blushing.

'Thanks. I tried to get most of the horse poo off me, anyway.' She settled into her seat. 'What do you fancy?' The question made Kit blush again. 'From the menu,' she added, her own cheeks turning pink too.

He shrugged. 'The prawn salad and then the beef, I think, although I don't know what half the stuff that comes with them is.'

Luella smiled warmly, wanting to help him relax. 'Me neither. But that sounds good, I'll have the same.'

The maître d' came and suggested something from the wine list to go with the starter and then something else to go with the main. 'Excellent choices,' said Luella, and he nodded and swished the drinks menus away. She noticed that Kit looked a little uncomfortable, but she didn't think anything of it. It was pretty warm in there, or maybe it was *her* looking so good that was flustering him.

They chatted a little about Charlie and life as a stable hand at the Balfours and then the starters arrived. As Luella expertly shelled her prawns, pretending not to notice Kit struggling, she said, 'You know, you could use the Balfour charity match opportunity to go pro as a player, and move up from being a stable hand.'

There was an awkward silence, then Kit said, 'Yeah.'

'I'm sorry, have I offended you?' she asked, her heart pounding, suddenly anxious.

'No, not at all. It's just . . . these bloody prawns.' He pulled the head off one forcefully and she thanked God it didn't fly across the room.

'Not that what you do now isn't *brilliant*,' she said. 'But, as you say, there isn't a lot of opportunity to progress.' More awkward silence. Luella had the horrible realisation that Kit's father Daniel had been a stable hand all his life too. *Urgh.* 'I mean, you have a lot of talent training horses, that's what I'm saying,' she clarified. 'And you ride so well. I know you filled in exercising ponies with the grooms last year when Tom broke his ankle.'

'I'm fine, really. It's just the prawns.' He wiped his fingers on his napkin and Luella automatically wiggled hers in the small bowl of lemon water the waiter had put on the table in front of each of them. He didn't seem to pick up on it. He sighed and finally met her gaze. 'Sorry if I'm a bit tense. Places like this aren't really my thing, and the prices . . .'

Luella felt horrified. 'Oh, no – I asked you out, so of course I'll pay. I never would have suggested it if . . .'

His face darkened. 'What, because I don't earn much?'

Her anxiety spiked. 'No, it would be the same with anyone, honestly. I invited you, so I'll pay.'

'That's not OK with me,' he said stiffly. 'We'll split it.' He suddenly seemed much further away from her than just across the table. More like miles. And closed off, too. There was tense silence until the waiter came to take away their starter plates. Luella smiled brightly. 'That was delicious, thank you. Could we cancel the wine with the beef, though. It's hot this evening. I'd prefer just water.'

'Certainly, madame.'

When she looked up from adjusting her napkin, Kit was glaring at her. 'Have wine.'

'I'm fine.'

'You're getting an Uber home anyway, right?'

'I brought my car. I was going to leave it, but it's fine. This way, I can drive home.'

'Have what you want. Don't cancel it on my account.'

'I'm not. I just don't want it.' *Lie.* She just didn't want him feeling that he had to pay for half of it. And he knew it.

Kit sighed and leaned back in his chair. 'Well, this is going well.'

'Only because you're not making an effort!' she snapped, surprising herself.

Then it got even worse – Alicia, a friend of Bex's from tennis club, walked in and Luella instantly stiffened and pulled a face, then quickly hid her dismay. She'd been fine because she knew Bex was out in London for the night. But she hadn't thought about any of Bex's other friends seeing them.

Then she berated herself – why did she care? Was she really as spineless as that? Surely if she liked Kit she should just . . . She gazed across at him and was shocked to see how angry he looked. 'Embarrassed to be seen with me?' he asked, straight out, direct. 'I know Alicia's friends with Bex.'

'Of course not,' she insisted. 'She and I just don't get on well, that's all.' *Lie again.* Made worse by Alicia spotting them and giving her a friendly wave and smile, which she was too well-mannered not to return.

Kit raised his eyebrows at that but didn't comment. Then, 'And as for turning pro, I wish you wouldn't mention it so much,' he said, more to the selection of sourdough breads in the basket than to Luella. 'I feel enough pressure to prove myself at this charity match already, and . . .'

'What?' She put her hand on his but he pulled it away.

'I get the feeling that you're more interested in who I *could be* than in who I actually *am*.'

Ouch. That was so unfair. And untrue.

She was about to tell him so when the main course arrived but he ducked his head to focus on the plate in front of him and avoid her gaze. She stared at him across the table and felt like he might as well be in another galaxy.

Luella was still feeling bad about the awful date the next morning. She and Kit had just about made it through the beef without falling out completely and skipped dessert on the excuse of needing to get home. *Early starts and all that.* She'd paid the whole bill when he'd popped to the gents, too – something else he could add to his list of Things Luella Did Wrong.

She texted Carrie about the date from hell (using crossed-out eyes emojis for the first time ever) while she had a whole tub of Häagen-Dazs standing by the kitchen counter, followed by two coffees. She got her head down and took her frustration out on her maths, chemistry and physics coursework, then training Charlie, which kept Kit Pearce nicely out of her mind.

But, annoyingly, at about seven p.m. she started missing him. She opened Signal and stared at their chat. They hadn't messaged at all – and they usually pinged photos and things back and forth at least two or three times a day. Almost as if he was psychic, she saw three little dots appear. Her heart leaped and then came crashing down. For the first time since the night before, she let herself be completely and utterly disappointed with how the date had gone, and the distance between them. *If he's messaging to have a go at me then he can just—*

> Come to our place, as soon as you can. Please, Lu.

No, no bloody way, she thought. *Not for more broody, mardy, sulky treatment. No thank you.*

It was half seven, and there were still a good couple of hours' light in the summer sky. The horsey chores were all done for the day and Charlie and Captain were tucked up in their stables, so she'd cycled over. Only to tell him how out of order he'd been, of course.

Kit wasn't in their usual place by the jump stands and at first she was confused. Then she heard music coming from the old barn and went to investigate.

She gasped in surprise. There were fake candles flickering on the hay bales and a checked tablecloth on an upturned cable drum between two hay bales. Hearing her come in, he turned and smiled. She could almost forget everything that had happened the night before when he smiled at her like that. 'Madame. Welcome to Chez Kit. Please, do sit down.' He flounced over to her comically and steered her towards one of the hay bales.

She frowned. 'Kit, what are you doing?'

Now he was rummaging in a rucksack and pulled out two cans of Fanta. She instantly forgot her annoyance as she laughed out loud. He put one on the cable drum table (she now noticed that the tablecloth was, in fact, a checked shirt). He held the other up to her, laying it along his arm like a wine bottle. 'May I recommend the Fanta a L'Orange,' he said. 'This is the perfect complement to our starter, Le Fromage et Onion delicately sliced Pommes de Terre.'

She smiled wryly at him. 'Cheese and onion crisps?'

'Some common folk do know them as that, yes,' he said, with a grin, pulling two packets from the rucksack and placing them carefully on the table. 'Oh, and they come with a side of . . . Skips.' He put them on the table too, with a wink. 'You know how much I love prawns. I just don't love having a full-on wrestling match with them.'

She laughed. 'OK, OK! I'm sorry about last night!'

He held her gaze and smiled. Luella's stomach flipped with desire. 'I'm sorry, too,' he said. 'I was out of my comfort zone and I acted like a twat. Especially about that Alicia girl knowing Bex, and accusing you of being embarrassed to be seen with me.'

Luella blushed deeply. She didn't want the distance to open up between them again. She wanted to tell him the truth. 'That face I pulled *was* about Alicia knowing Bex,' she said. 'I was an idiot. I'm sorry I care what Bex would think and I'm sorry I lied about it.'

She thought he might take that badly again, but he was his usual easy-going self. 'I get that it must be hard for you,' he said. 'You two have been friends for years. And I'm a big old pleb, and a Balfour pleb at that.'

She couldn't help smiling at that. 'I'll tell her, in time, about us.' Then she was horrified. *Was there an 'us'? Was she jumping the gun? Sounding desperate? Urgh.*

Kit just smiled, though, then sat down opposite her. They tore into the crisps and opened the Fanta. 'Dare I ask what the main course is?' she joked.

His vibrant blue eyes twinkled. 'Two pasties, the last ones in the shop.'

She arched an eyebrow. 'That's reassuring.'

'Steak and onion, or curried veg.'

'Sounds divine.'

He took her hand across the table and looked deep into her eyes. 'Seeing as you're the most beautiful girl in the world, I'll let you have first choice.' He began to lean towards her, and she tilted her chin and closed her eyes.

Instead of a sublime first kiss, there was the clang of hay rakes falling to the floor. Luella's eyes shot open, and she and Kit stared at each other in surprise.

It was Felicity. 'What's going on in here?' she said as she clocked the candles and the checked tablecloth. Even the Fanta seemed romantic in the flickering candlelight. She looked completely mortified.

Kit sighed and gave Luella an apologetic look. 'Does your mother know you're out this late?' he asked Felicity, looking extremely uncomfortable. 'You know you're meant to be in by eight.'

'I don't care.' Felicity batted her eyelashes at him. *Seriously, with me sitting right here?* thought Luella. *OK, the crush was cute and everything, but enough was enough.*

'Come on, kid, we'll walk you home.' He glanced at Luella again. 'If that's OK, Lu?'

Luella stood and stretched. *No first kiss tonight then. And not even a suspect pasty.* 'Sure,' she said.

Halfway up the lane, Luella gave Kit a 'walk ahead' look, and he was more than happy to go, saying he needed to call Eric and check on hay delivery times for the morning.

'Isn't Kit handsome?' said Felicity, when he was out of earshot, like Luella was an older sister she was confiding in. 'I think he's dreamy.'

Luella smiled. 'I know you do,' she said kindly. 'But, look, he's too old for you, and as you may have noticed in the barn, he and I have something going on.'

Felicity looked crestfallen. 'Oh. I wondered, and I mean, I'm happy for you, but . . . he's always so nice to me and . . .'

Luella put her arm around Felicity's shoulders and pulled her close. It couldn't hurt to bend the truth, let her down a bit more gently. 'That's because he thinks really highly of you,' she said. 'He sees you as a little sister.'

Felicity's lip wobbled. 'I guess that's something,' she said. Then she glanced up at Luella. 'Oh, I'm sorry, I hope you're not mad with me. For liking him. I didn't know.'

'Not at all,' Luella reassured her, with a smile. 'We all get crushes when we're young. They don't mean anything. You'll get over it quickly enough. And in a couple of years, you'll meet someone as wonderful as my Kit, I'm sure you will.'

Felicity managed a small smile back. 'I hope so.'

They carried on in silence and caught up with Kit. She linked fingers with him as they walked along. *My Kit*, she'd said. Subtle, but a clear signal. Kissing him would have to wait, but Kit was *hers*, and that was that.

Chapter Twelve

Bex

'Daddy's just signed a huge deal in Saudi, it's a renewal of the contract his company have had out there for the last five years. Only this time it's bigger and better.' *Being able to lie through my teeth*, thought Bex, *without a flicker, while drinking this ghastly coffee and having to look at this hideous carpet, is a definite skill.*

She saw a look pass between Jasper and Delia – sheer delight, as well as the sharp-eyed, quiet smile of their business manager, Eric. Obviously seeing an opportunity in there somewhere for the Balfour Estate. Just as Bex had intended.

Coffee with Mr and Mrs Balfour was going excellently so far – well, apart from the actual coffee, which looked and tasted like mud. Jasper and Delia, and Eric, had no idea that her father's contract – overseeing the manufacture and export of steel, aluminium and silica for the building industry – hadn't been renewed. They could probably have done some digging and looked it up on a website somewhere, but she doubted they'd bother. And she'd think of a way to explain herself if they did.

The meeting was to discuss her moving stables. Well, the Balfours didn't know that yet – so far they thought it was a social call. Keeping Bomba and Gordo at the Langdons' was no longer an option. Things were so awkward with Freddie now since that Carrie girl had got involved in *their* love life and ruined everything. Plus, even Bex could see that she'd blown up at the grooms one too many times, despite repeated warnings. And then there was the looming question of money. Luella had settled the April and May invoices, yes, but June's was now overdue by a week, and it wouldn't be long before the shit hit the fan, big time. The Langdons had seen a red flag, and they'd certainly follow up any unpaid bills quickly from now on. There would be no sweet-talking or delaying her way out of it.

The Balfours on the other hand . . . She'd just filled them in on how she didn't feel the Langdon Estate was the right place for her horses. She was staying within the lines, polite at all times. But the subtext was clear – Langdon's wasn't up to scratch, not for the new, young face of British polo. 'It's only Bomba and Gordo at the moment,' she said. 'Estrella and Blanca are away for three months, for top-level training. Bad timing, I know, during the season, but I couldn't pass up the opportunity. There's a two-year waiting list. And you know how it is – local trainers, even the best, can only get you so far. It's an investment in next season.'

Please don't ask me which trainer they've gone to, Bex silently begged. Her voice had strangled in her throat a little when she'd said their names, and she'd had to cough to cover it up. The pain of losing two of her beloved ponies crackled agonisingly inside her. She couldn't lose the other two as well. It was vital she secured their future, and if that meant sucking up to the vile Balfours, then so be it.

'Well, that simply will not do at all. You must come *here*,' said Delia.

Bex felt a huge wave of relief flood over her. *Thank goodness*. 'Oh,' she said, as if in surprise. 'Well, I hadn't thought . . . I was looking at Kings . . .' (Cue name-drop of extremely expensive polo club) 'But it is quite a drive . . .'

'Well, of course you must come here, darling!' said Jasper. 'Kings is bloody miles away! And you'll fit in better with us than the Langdons, my dear. We're a better class of class.'

Bex managed to smile without wrinkling up her nose. The fact that they had *mentioned* class at all said everything. *But needs must*. She felt a mix of thrill and fear as she played her riskiest card. 'Thank you so much for the offer. I'll certainly consider it,' she said. 'And, as I'm a new client, I fully expect to pay three months in advance, of course . . .'

Jasper looked keen. *Damn*. 'Well, that would be—'

Bex laughed sharply. 'I mean, the dear old-fashioned Langdons find talk of money vulgar and everything there is very *as and when*. But of course I can understand that you'll need payment upfront. You're businesspeople, and as such you have to watch the budget.'

Delia looked as alarmed as if a mouse had just shot up her dress and Jasper, always slow, caught on and blustered, 'No need to pay anything upfront, dear girl. How sweet of you to offer. Very *modern*. But no, no, no, you're a friend, it's not about the money.' He stressed the last word with a sneer for extra effect. Bex was the only one who noticed Eric quietly rolling his eyes.

'You must have the best of everything, we'll see to it,' Delia said then, signalling to their maid to pour Bex some more of the disgusting coffee.

Inside, Bex celebrated. She'd secured her darling Bomba and Gordo a good home for two or three months, at least. Things were going so well that she pushed on to secure part two of her plan: Operation Balfour Polo Team. She acted like she'd just had some kind of epiphany and made a decision on the spot. 'You know what? I'd usually take time to think over a huge decision like this. Kings is very prestigious, after all. But I've got a good feeling about bringing my horses here. And I always follow my gut. So, I'd be delighted to accept,' she said.

'Marvellous,' said Delia, and Jasper beamed to see his wife looking so happy.

'I do love Freddie and the whole setup at the Langdons' is very sweet, but they're just not bringing out Gordo and Bomba's full potential. And one must always think of the horses first, mustn't one?'

'Absolutely,' said Jasper. 'The horses and the games, and sponsorship, and winning the Guillards Cup.'

Bex shot him her killer smile and then beamed it at Delia too. 'Well, of course, when I say the horses, that naturally includes bringing home the Guillards Cup to where it *rightfully belongs*.'

'Damn right it belongs here,' said Jasper broodily.

'As we all know, you'll be playing the Langdon team in the opening game of the Guillards Cup this year,' said Bex smoothly.

'That's old Lord L's smart move,' scoffed Jasper, 'to get us out in the quarter finals and not have to face us later in the tournament. But it's going to backfire spectacularly when we win and his team is out of their own tournament in the first game. Shame. Embarrassment. And a long grind sitting on the sidelines, all the way to the final, where he can hand us the trophy, the old git.'

'Jasper!' cried Delia. 'I apologise, Bex,' she tittered. 'My husband's blood does get up rather at the mention of the Guillards Cup. The referee wasn't fair last year and it cost us the win.'

'Oh, I know,' said Bex. She beamed at Jasper. 'And I agree with you. *Everyone does.* Lord L's plan is your opportunity – a great chance to show them all who's really in charge round here, settle old scores. Maybe bring in some new blood.' *Plant the seed, watch it grow.*

Delia glowed and Jasper looked like he'd died and gone to heaven. 'Couldn't agree more, my dear,' he said warmly. *God, they were so easy.* 'That's the last time I give my son the patron's place on the team, I can tell you.'

Delia looked sour then. 'Yes, Barnaby's a darling, but he obviously thinks we should just *hand* it to him. He'll probably have a tantrum when he finds out we won't.'

Jasper sniffed. 'Too right, we won't. Boy needs to grow up – shame they've banned caning from schools now. Soft-touch Britain – the place is going to the dogs.'

Wow, thought Bex. *My dad might be a coward, but at least he isn't a total psycho like Barnaby's.*

Eric stepped in at this point, probably to stop Jasper saying anything that could actually be brought against him in a court of law. 'And as for the pros, we have a new chap arriving on Wednesday to stay as a house guest and bring a lot of fresh ideas to our training team. Alfonso, he's called. He'll be helping us to victory against the Langdons this year, no doubt.'

Bex hid a sly smile and nodded along as Eric got far too involved in explaining training methods. So Barnaby wasn't in favour, a hot new polo player was on his way and the patron's place on the Balfour team was up for grabs. Interesting.

Eric finally paused for breath and she went for it, smiling at Jasper and then Delia. 'About the patron's place . . . If Barnaby won't be taking it this year, then I'd love to volunteer. It would be an honour to represent the Balfour Estate.'

'Excellent idea,' said Jasper, which earned him a sharp look from Delia, and a whispered, 'Don't forget . . .'

He frowned. 'Oh, yes. Christopher Pearce is having a crack at it too, so you'll have some friendly competition. He said Luella encouraged him to ask us – she's a lovely girl. Your friend, isn't she?'

'Yuh,' Bex croaked. *Not any more*, she thought savagely. She hadn't even known that Luella had anything to do with Kit Pearce. *What the hell was going on?*

'I've got a marvellous idea! You can both play in the charity game this weekend and we'll see what we think!' cried Delia, excitedly.

Bex kept smiling and nodding along, but inside she almost blew a gasket, whatever one of those was. *Kit? Kit? That scruffy stable boy?*

Jasper threw back the vile coffee. 'Wretched charity thing is a waste of time in my opinion, but the locals seem to like it and it's good to keep in with them.'

She barely heard him; she was still reeling. How could they, the new-money, brash, vile idiots? How could they be so trashy – a stable hand getting the patron's place?! She felt so sick, she couldn't keep control of her facial expressions and had to excuse herself to go to the loo.

After giving herself a stern look in the mirror and thinking of Gordo and Bomba, she pulled herself together and came out of the bathroom into the deserted upstairs hallway.

Not deserted as it turned out. Barnaby was waiting for her and caught hold of her wrist roughly. 'Hey!' She tried to twist out of his grip but he held on tighter and dug his nails in. He put his vile face close to hers, and she could smell stale garlic on his breath. *Rank.* 'I know what you're doing and it won't work,' he snarled. 'I'm having father's place on the team for the Guillards Cup – in *all* the games.'

Bex glared at him and yanked her wrist free. 'I don't know what you're talking about.'

'Don't lie. I heard you downstairs, I was on the patio outside.'

Bex laughed, but even to her it sounded too loud, too forced, too hollow. He smiled. He was rattling her and, annoyingly, he knew it. 'They invited me, what can I do?'

'You set it up and they walked right in.' He snorted. 'You may have fooled my parents into thinking you're doing them a huge favour by being here, but you don't fool me, Bex. I see right through you. Why are you really here? Has Freddie finally kicked you to the kerb?' He peered closely at her. 'Or is this about money, I wonder?'

She kept her face carefully impassive. Damn, he was good. She'd have to be careful – Bomba and Gordo were depending on her. She knew Barnaby hated her, but she hadn't realised quite how much. 'Whatever.' She sighed impatiently and tried to walk past him, but he blocked the way.

'Don't get too cosy here, with your feet under our table. I'm watching you.'

She laughed, hard and sharp. 'Wow, did you really just say that?' She pointed to her eyes and then to his. 'Do you want to do the little sign as well?'

He glowered at her and walked away. Once he'd rounded the corner she took a deep breath, shaken. *Damn, that hurt.* She rubbed her sore wrist and blinked back the few betraying tears that had sprung into her eyes. Then she straightened her dress, put her shoulders back and swished off downstairs.

She said her goodbyes soon after, struggling to keep her social mask up after her run-in with Barnaby. By the time she'd made her way back across from the house to her car, though, and down the long Balfour Estate driveway, she was pretty much over it. And as she sped down the back lanes, she was feeling on a high again. She could handle Barnaby and she'd take Kit down, easily, in the charity game. There was nothing like a little competition to bring out her best and give her an edge. Same team or not, she'd make sure he didn't even *touch* the ball, and he wouldn't know what had hit him.

And then, she rounded a corner and almost *did* hit him. She slammed on the brake and Charlie reared up and skittered backwards, with Lulu on board. That Carrie girl was there too, sitting on a bicycle like a ten-year-old. Kit looked angry, so Bex quickly shoved down the concern she'd felt for Luella. Her father had taught her young that attack was the best form of defence.

Kit had taken hold of Charlie's rein and was soothing her while Luella gathered herself. Carrie's face was a picture of fury, her gaze laser-focused on Bex. Bex struck first. She got out the car and marched over to the group. 'Could you *not* stand talking in the middle of the road?!' she yelled, unleashing her frustration on them.

'Could *you* not bomb down here like it's the M3?' Kit countered.

Bex ignored this and looked up at Luella. 'So this is what you've been up to?! Hanging out with a stable hand and this little chav, when I expressly asked you not to!'

'Whoa! Watch your mouth!' warned Carrie.

Bex noticed that Luella's hands were shaking. For a moment she had another flicker of regret that she'd come round the corner so fast and scared her, but she shoved it away. She couldn't show any weakness in front of smug Carrie, who thought she was girlfriend material for Freddie. *Wrong.* And smugger Kit, who thought he was polo-player material for the Balfours. *Wrong again*.

'We're training Charlie, natural horsemanship,' said Luella, a tremor in her voice. 'To help with the Nationals. It's working, Bex. She's doing great.'

'And Carrie's what, just hanging out, stealing my best friend as well as my boyfriend now, is she?' she snapped. 'Bitch!'

Carrie let out a sharp laugh. 'Come and say that to my face.'

Kit shook his head, as if he couldn't believe what was unfolding in front of him. Bex turned on her heel to face Carrie, who dropped the bike and strode right up to her, fearless. For a moment, Bex thought, *Shit, she's going to punch me.* She couldn't help bracing herself, just a bit. *Not the face.* She saw Kit notice and look even smugger.

Carrie laughed again. 'You're not worth it.'

Bex stormed back to her car, absolutely livid at such a betrayal from Luella. Her so-called best friend. *Ex-best friend.*

'Be careful, Lulu,' she said coldly. 'Common rubs off.' Then she got in, slammed her door, started her engine and roared past them. Charlie startled again but she didn't care. She was Team Balfour now, and the lot of them could go to hell.

Chapter Thirteen

Carrie

The dress was Carrie's mum's, and not designer, of course, but it seemed like the perfect thing for hobnobbing with the spectators and Team Langdon at the charity match.

She'd taken the early shift at the yard, at even stupider o'clock in the morning than usual as it was a match day, and a high-profile event at that. She'd offered to stay on and work the afternoon but Terrence had told her to go and enjoy the game – she'd be on duty again bright and early in the morning, after all. So, she'd cycled home, had a quick shower, borrowed the dress, and here she was, getting in free as staff this time, a green pass on a lanyard round her neck. It felt incredible, like she was really *in*, really part of the polo scene. And, of course, in suitable wedges.

She ended up under the Langdon canopy, called over by Lady L, on the opposite side of the pitch from the Balfour one. She could hardly believe it – she definitely hadn't been expecting that. She helped herself to sparkling elderflower and filled up on the delicious food (Barnaby was so wrong about the catering). Freddie's mum was lovely – down to earth and no nonsense, and she took Carrie under her wing, introducing her to everyone as 'our marvellous new stable hand'. Even Lord L said that she scrubbed up well and they had a chat about yard life. The whole place was buzzing with everyone from the village and surrounding towns – the charity game was a local tradition and even people who knew nothing about polo loved to come. It was a chance for the Langdons to engage with the local community, and Freddie's parents soon went off to mingle with the crowd.

Carrie sipped her drink and watched Freddie talking to the grooms at the Langdon pony lines down at the far end of the pitch. He was playing, of course, and so was Sims, who was the best young player in Yetbourne and easily good enough to go pro. According to the programme, Bex was the number three. Carrie tried not to think about how stunning she was going to look in her Langdon team colours – vibrant blue with deep-pink numbers – and her tight, white jeans and sexy calf-high polo boots.

'Oh, I wish Freddie Langdon was my boyfriend, he's so dreamy,' came a voice from behind her.

She whirled around, hissing, 'Oh my God, Luella, shut up!'

They hugged warmly. 'How did *you* get alcohol?' Carrie protested. 'They won't serve me now they know me.'

Luella lowered her glass out of sight behind Carrie as she waved to Lady L. 'Contacts, darling.' She smiled cheekily and clinked glasses with Carrie. 'Life's pretty sweet right now, huh? Doesn't Freddie look sexy in his polo shirt?'

'Shhh!' Carrie blushed and changed the subject rapidly. 'How's Kit feeling about the match?'

'Nervous, but ready,' Luella reported. Carrie searched the packed field and spotted him over by the Balfour pony lines. She made to wave, but Luella pulled her hand down. 'Don't! We're Team Langdon!'

'Mind my drink!' Carrie gave her a sideways look. 'Wow, this rivalry thing is serious! Your boyfriend is Team Balfour. You're like Romeo and Juliet!'

Luella smacked her arm playfully and said, 'He's *not* my boyfriend! We haven't even kissed.'

Carrie wrinkled up her face. 'You will. You would have kissed in the barn if you hadn't been interrupted and, as we both know, he thinks you are absolutely bloody gorgeous. Which you are.'

Luella smiled at that. 'Anyway, this is the first step in his exit plan from the Balfour clutches. If he gets chosen for the Guillards Cup team after today he could turn pro.'

Just then, there was a kerfuffle opposite, in the Balfour marquee. Delia and Jasper Balfour were there, among their guests, with Eric and a grey-haired man in a smart suit. Delia was loudly complaining that the champagne wasn't chilled enough, and a red-faced waitress was hurrying off to fetch a bottle fresh from the ice bucket on the bar. Barnaby was slinking around under a black cloud looking very sore – presumably about not playing for Team Balfour.

'Who's that with them?' Carrie asked.

'Some business bigwig, I don't know his name,' said Luella, reaching for a canapé on a nearby tray.

'Ronan Blake? He's a property developer,' Carrie said. 'Freddie told me about him. There's a big project on the table for one of the estates, a conference centre – it's a fifty-million-pound development.'

Luella raised her eyebrows. 'So, the Balfours and the Langdons are going head-to-head in business as well as polo? That could mean fireworks. Let's just hope they don't take it out on one another on the pitch. My Kit is going to be out there.'

Carrie raised an eyebrow and grinned. '*Your* Kit? Noted.'

Carrie had been keeping an eye out for Bex around the pony lines, hoping she didn't look too devastatingly attractive. But she couldn't see her anywhere. As the Langdon team rode out on to the field to warm up, a close friend of Lord L, Henry Selwyn Jones, was wearing the number three shirt, and a change of player was announced by the commentators. 'Young Rebecca Chapman-Foster has wrenched her shoulder, apparently,' said a horsey lady next to Carrie, 'so Henry is stepping in. He'll be slower than the youngsters, but he's got a lot of experience. They should still give the Balfours a good game.'

Plus, Henry Selwyn Jones won't be out there looking hot in front of Freddie, Carrie thought. She was sorry for Bex, though. A wrenched shoulder, today of all days. She didn't like the girl, and she'd never trust her around Freddie, but she didn't wish anything bad on her.

A few minutes later, there were gasps, nudges and a ripple of chatter ran through the crowd as Bex made a big entrance on to the pitch on Gordo . . . in the Balfour team number three shirt. 'Oh my God, look!' gasped Luella.

'Well, it seems there's a late change in Balfour, too,' said one of the commentators. 'Rebecca Chapman-Foster appears to have switched teams!'

'What a shock!' said the other. 'So, she isn't injured after all. Well, this move will only add fuel to the fire of this age-old rivalry between the two teams. There's no love lost there, as we all know, and now it looks like the Balfours have poached one of the sports' most promising young players!'

'What the hell is she playing at?' Luella muttered. 'This is so unlike her!'

'When are you going to see that this is *totally* like her!' hissed Carrie. 'And poor Kit! This was supposed to be *his* big moment!'

Luella bit her lip and nodded. Lord L, now back in the marquee with them, was clearly furious, but he managed it well, and so did Lady L and Terrence. Lord L leaned in beside Carrie and said, 'Well, I assume we can take this as the young lady's notice.'

She smiled grimly. 'I guess so.'

With that, play started. Carrie had googled the shit out of polo since she'd been working at the Langdon Estate and she could follow the game pretty well. They shared Luella's champagne and cheered loudly for Freddie, Sims and Kit.

They all played well, and Kit kept calm and had a great connection with his first bold Balfour polo pony, Libre, as Carrie had expected. Luella, standing on the other side of her, had to close her eyes when it got too intense.

Bex played well too and Luella clapped for her occasionally, which Carrie thought just showed what a kind heart she had, and how Bex didn't deserve a friend like that.

There was some extra excitement when Sims smashed his mallet and Beatrice had to ride on at top speed and give him a new one, doing the exchange at the sideline. Carrie's heart pounded in her chest throughout the whole thing – partly because it was so bloody exciting, and partly because Freddie looked absolutely, breathtakingly freaking gorgeous out there.

Kit and Bex both scored a goal each in the third chukka, but Kit was clearly far more of a team player – setting up hits for his teammates where that was the best thing to do, whereas Bex often slammed past him, keeping possession of the ball, chasing glory for herself.

Freddie took Kit on in a fierce ride-off a few times, and Carrie and Luella both peeked out from behind their hands, too scared to watch. Kit was as forceful with Freddie, and Sims too, staying just the right side of a hooking foul to take the ball from him. That got him another goal and put the Balfours one up right at the end of the sixth chukka. Carrie felt thrilled for him, gutted for Freddie, happy for Luella and angry that the Balfours were suddenly acting like Kit was their prodigy, instead of someone they'd treated like a servant his whole life.

There was another short break before the final chukka. Then Freddie and his team would have to really pull it out of the bag to win, especially with Bex heading for goal every chance she got, safe or not, and with Kit on such fantastic form.

Carrie noticed Lord L looking stressed, glancing at his watch, and some discreet talk with Lady L, who caught her eye and called her over. 'Carrie, dear . . . Lord L's medication. He's left it in the office – third drawer down in the main desk. I know the timing isn't ideal, but could you possibly go and fetch it for us? The key's in the lock box.'

'Of course,' she said.

Thank goodness she had the wedges on this time, but it still took a good few minutes to make it to the yard. She heard the commentators start up again as play commenced, but tuned them out, turning the game so far over in her head.

Luckily the pill box was right there as she'd been told, with the days of the week marked. She grabbed it and rushed back, but she began to feel uneasy. Something didn't feel quite right. As she reached the pitch, the crowd was quiet, the commentators subdued. Beatrice was rushing towards Willow, who was rearing and bucking, and going crazy . . . riderless.

Her stomach turned over and her heart was in her mouth. There was a player on the ground, face down. *Freddie*. As she raced to him, stumbling in the wedges, the commentary drifted over her.

'The paramedics hurry on to the field, but he isn't getting up, John.'

'No, he's not. I'll be honest, it's not looking good.'

What the hell happened? What if he's seriously injured? What if he's dead?

God, at that moment she wished she'd kissed him, all those times. Sod the stupid yard rules. Her heart lurched, with love, and terror. 'Freddie!' she screamed, as she neared him, feeling sick to see his leg at such an unnatural angle.

'Carrie!'

She looked up sharply. *What?!* Freddie was running on to the pitch towards her. *But how?!* She was flooded with relief, but then, who . . .

She and Freddie reached the figure as an ambulance drove across the grass towards them.

Hugo.

Freddie threw himself to his knees beside his friend, checked his airway and breathing, then felt for a pulse. 'Mate! Wake up, mate! Hugo!'

'Carrie!' shrieked Beatrice, and Carrie looked up sharply to see Willow pull away from her, rearing up and turning, snapping the rein.

'I've got this, you go,' said Freddie. Willow was bolting towards her, straight at the crowd of families watching, who tried to scatter in a panic, grabbing toddlers and stumbling through picnics. Carrie stood in the way, arms raised, making herself look as big as possible. Bex, the closest player, was off Bomba and pelting towards them too, circling her arms in the air, yelling, trying to head Willow off. Carrie did the same, and time slowed down as she waited to be trampled under her thundering hooves.

But Willow came to a sudden halt and danced on the spot before them, eyes wild, sweating, foaming at the mouth. For a moment, she and Bex shared a genuine, deep look of relief.

'Good work,' said Carrie.

'You too.'

The paramedics were with Hugo by then and Freddie was suddenly beside them, taking Willow's rein. It was only then that Carrie registered the bloody, gaping wound across his forehead.

'Your head!'

'It's nothing.'

In seconds, the vet was with them, holding her medical bag and a lead rope.

'What the hell happened to her?' Freddie gasped. 'She just went crazy!'

'Looks to me like drugging,' said the vet. 'Let's get her off the pitch.' She raked a glance over the three of them. 'Only two,' she said firmly.

Bex and Carrie both looked at Freddie. He didn't hesitate. 'Carrie.'

Chapter Fourteen

Luella

'She just lost the plot, there was nothing I could do.'

'You did really well to stay on for as long as you did.'

Luella sat on the chair beside Hugo's hospital bed, with Carrie beside her. Two days after the accident he was still there. He had bruises, fractured ribs and his right leg was broken in several places, as well as concussion.

'He's got to have an op, at least one, and then he'll have pins sticking out of his leg attached to one of those Bionic Man cast things. Gruesome,' said Sims, who sat alongside them, stuffing grapes.

Carrie and Luella exchanged a glance. That was bad. They both knew it would take him months to recover. 'God, Hugo, I'm so sorry,' said Luella.

'That's awful,' echoed Carrie.

'Yeah.' Hugo's attention was on Sims. 'Hey, Loops brought those for *me!*' he protested.

Sims broke off a small, measly bunch and handed it to him with a wicked smile. Luella wondered when the boys were going to grow up and handle tough emotions head on. She was glad she'd come, though. She'd woken up that morning and just thought, sod it. Never mind that they weren't that close now. She still cared.

The game had got going again, which, she knew, Carrie had found astonishing. Sims had subbed in for Hugo, the Balfours had won by two goals and Willow had been looked over by the vet. 'Jennifer found elevated magnesium levels in Willow's blood,' Carrie told the boys.

Hugo nodded. 'I heard. Lord L was in here earlier, and Freddie, plus half the staff and my entire family. I can't get any bloody peace.' He laughed.

'Elevated levels aren't always easy to spot but in this case we were lucky and it did show up,' said Luella, sticking to the topic. 'It proves that somebody did something to Willow.'

Hugo shrugged and winced in pain, then tried to mask it with a grin. 'There's magnesium in the feed room cupboard along with everything else.'

'In the right measure it's completely fine,' added Sims, through a mouthful of Hugo's grapes.

'But who would have given it to Willow, when it wasn't on her feed chart? And that much too?' asked Luella.

'One of the grooms, probably,' said Sims, now swigging Hugo's Lucozade. 'Or the stable hands. By accident, I'm sure. Lord L trusts all his staff and so do I.'

'Me too,' said Hugo. 'But the person could be too scared to own up.'

'Well, it's serious. You've been badly injured and it could have been even worse,' said Carrie gravely. 'And what if someone did it on purpose? They could try again.'

Hugo sighed, clearly resigning himself to the fact that he wasn't going to get out of the conversation. 'Well, then it could have been almost anyone, I suppose. The security on the yard is tight, but if someone was determined, they could have got into the feed room. There are no cameras in there – well, there weren't. There will be now, of course.'

'But who would do that?' said Luella. 'Willow could have been seriously injured too. There was a chance she could have had a heart attack. Thank goodness she was OK.'

They all fell silent. Then, after a moment, Carrie said what they were all thinking. 'You swapped in at the last minute. What if it *was* deliberate, and the real target was Freddie?'

Luella flicked her gaze to her, a secret look of support. She knew that while Carrie felt awful about Hugo, she was also relieved it hadn't been Freddie. Freddie had swapped out to have a bad cut on his face treated – the medics had insisted. *Minor facial laceration*, he'd called it. It hadn't looked very minor, in Luella's opinion.

'The question is *why*, really,' said Sims. 'When you understand the *why*, you'll find the *who*. Then, if it wasn't an accident, the police would be interested, I'm sure. But it probably was.'

'I'm not bothered about police. I just want to recover and get back on with things,' said Hugo. 'It's a dangerous game – I take big risks every time I play, so I'm not going to get obsessed about this.'

That was classic polo-player bravado. He looked exhausted, though, and vulnerable. Luella's heart went out to him, and she wanted to give him a big hug – which, of course, would have hurt like hell.

For the first time in a long time, though, they were talking. She gathered her courage and bit the bullet, bringing up something she'd wondered about for a long time. 'So, are you two ever going to tell anyone what you fell out about?'

Sims looked startled, and a glance passed between the two boys – Sims looked like he wanted to say something, but Hugo's glare and slight, painful, headshake was a firm *no*.

'You didn't have a problem with Hugo coming out, did you, Sims?' Luella pressed.

Sims was offended. 'Of course not!'

'Just asking!' She turned to Hugo. 'So, have you dated anyone since?'

'No time for that – I'm all about the polo,' said Hugo. 'Well, I was. I won't be playing any more this season, that's for sure.'

'I'm so sorry, Hugo,' said Luella. He was all out of jokes by that point, and clearly in pain. They all sat in silence for a while and things felt awkward and weird. She didn't push the subject of why the boys had fallen out.

'How's Bex?' asked Sims in an artful subject swerve. He smirked to himself. 'Switching teams last minute is low, even for her. And I'm sure she didn't *mean* to hit Freddie in the face with her mallet.'

Luella couldn't smile at that, and Carrie had scowled at the mere mention of Bex's name. 'I wouldn't know. We're not speaking. She's angry with me because she thinks I shouldn't hang out with Carrie, or train with Kit. She sees it as this terrible betrayal.'

'Sorry to hear that,' said Hugo.

'Me too,' said Sims. 'But I'm not surprised. She's possessive and attention-seeking. Nice girl and everything, but hard work as a friend.'

Luella sighed. 'Not much chance of the old gang getting back together, then.'

'Zero,' said Sims. Luella tried not to show how much that stung. Was Bex the reason they hadn't all come back together after the boys' fall-out? 'But I've got to hand it to her, she played well, and so did Kit,' Sims continued.

'He did, *really* well,' said Carrie, fiercely. 'Much better than Bex. It's a no-brainer for the Balfours.'

'Yes, hopefully they'll choose him for their team spot,' Luella said carefully, not wanting to give away her feelings for him – the boys would rib her and never shut up.

She texted Kit about once an hour, but they were still waiting to hear whether he'd been successful or not. Hugo had been taking a sip of water, and now he coughed and cried out in agony, clutching his ribs. 'Jesus! Fuck!'

Luella was on her feet. 'You OK?'

He was clearly distressed. 'Yep, but will you help me sit up a bit more?'

Sims and Carrie sprang up too, and together they all gently moved him forward, sat him up and rearranged the pillows.

Then Sims sat down next to him on the bed. 'This is shit, but you'll come through it, mate,' he said. Carrie gave Luella an encouraging smile and inclined her head slightly, meaning *'You, too.'* In a sudden bold move, Luella sat down on his other side. 'Room for a little one?'

Sims and Hugo smiled at her. 'Always,' they said, at once. Hugo looked much more comfortable in the new position. The old gang may not have been reunited, but she felt like she had the two boys back, and that was a start. Soon, visiting time was over and Luella and Carrie said their goodbyes. Sims stayed, to chance it until he actually got chucked out by the nurses.

'If this wasn't an accident, who would do something so heartless as to poison a horse?' asked Carrie, as they walked down the wide, empty hospital corridor.

Luella shrugged. 'I don't know. It's awful. And like Sims said, *why*? It wouldn't really affect the game – a new horse and rider would just sub in. And there was too much of a chance the magnesium would be detected for it to be anything to do with devaluing Willow – you know, making out that she's suddenly unrideable or something.'

'One of the Balfours could be behind it, to get the Langdons on the back foot before the Guillards Cup,' Carrie reasoned. 'Putting Lord L's son in hospital, if that was the plan, would definitely have disturbed things in the Langdon camp. I know the Balfours are riled about the head-to-head quarter final, but would one of them really cook up something like that?'

Luella grimaced. 'Well, they are truly terrible people. I wouldn't put it past one of them. Not Felicity, of course – she's just a kid, and she's not in on any of their business plans or schemes. But Jasper, Delia or Barnaby, absolutely. And Eric, their business manager – he's in on everything.'

'Hmm,' said Carrie. 'Or maybe they all planned it together.' She shook her head, as if to shake the thoughts away. 'Let's look at what's likely, though. It probably was just an accident – one of the grooms. Maybe whoever did it is too scared to come forward now, in case they lose their job.

Luella sighed. 'You're right. That's the most plausible explanation.'

Carrie had drifted into thought again, and then, suddenly, she looked fierce. 'Or . . . Do you think Bex could have hurt Freddie on purpose to get him out of the game, because she poisoned Willow but wanted to target Hugo?'

Luella gasped in shock. 'Of course not! Granted, she's not the most sensitive person in the world, but she's not a horse poisoner! Accidents happen all the time. It's a tough game. Yes, Hugo was waiting in case he was needed, and it was a sure thing he'd be the one to take Freddie's chukka. But Bex giving Freddie enough of a head injury to stop him playing? No one could judge that!'

'Sorry,' Carrie said, immediately. 'Of course she wouldn't. I'm just stressing out. I'm worried about Freddie. The magnesium must have been given long before the swap, so it's pretty clear that Freddie or Willow were the targets. Do you think he could still be in danger?'

Luella squeezed Carrie's shoulders. She couldn't tell her not to worry. 'You really like him, don't you?'

Carrie leaned into her. 'Yeah. I really do.'

They walked out into the sunshine. 'Hallelujah, signal,' said Luella. Checking her phone, she was surprised to see a ton of missed calls from Kit, but he'd left no messages. Nothing from Bex – big surprise. She was still giving her the silent treatment.

Carrie caught her mood. 'What's up?'

'Loads of missed calls from Kit.' She was already calling him back. 'But no answer.' She didn't have a good feeling. She hung up and immediately called again.

'He might be up at the hay barn, you know signal's dodgy there.'

Luella bit her lip. 'Maybe.'

She tried three more times as she drove Carrie home, with no luck, so she went straight to the Balfours' yard. There was Kit, sitting on the mounting block, mending hay nets.

He turned. His face . . . He looked haggard, stressed. 'Lu? Thank God!'

Her adrenaline was up right away. 'Are you OK? The horses? What's happened?'

'It's OK, everyone's OK . . . but . . .' He looked around him and pulled her down the row of stables and into an empty one. He checked again that no one was around to overhear them. 'You know about Willow and the magnesium, right?'

'Uh-huh.'

'I was in the Langdon feed room that day, returning the iodine we'd borrowed. One of our junior part-time staff, Ginny, asked me to do it, but, of course, she wouldn't have thought of the potential issues. I should have thought it through myself. I was there after the morning feeds had been made up, but before they were taken out to the stables. And now, there are these rumours going round that I could have done it.' He shook his head, clearly still in shock. 'That I could have poisoned Willow.'

'No,' Luella whispered, in disbelief. She felt sick to her stomach. 'How could anyone think that?'

'I work for the Balfours, and maybe *they* would do something like this. I was so stupid, just to walk in there. I should have thought. It looks bad, Lu.'

Luella tried to take his hand but he pulled away and crossed his arms. She tried not to take it personally, but it hurt. 'There's no way you could have known. Do the Balfours know about the rumour?'

'Yes.' He leaned out of the top of the stable door and checked that the yard was empty again. 'I was called in to see Jasper and Delia, and Eric was there too and, of course, I denied it. But it's bringing bad press to their door and quite honestly I'm surprised I haven't been sacked.'

Luella's head spun. 'Oh my God.'

He paused, sighed deeply. 'Obviously I'm out of the running for the Balfour team place.'

Luella breathed in sharply. 'Kit! No! That's not fair! They can't—'

'They can,' he said angrily. 'They can do anything they damn well like. And I'm not allowed to talk to clients or suppliers.' He kicked at a stone on the ground. 'No smoke without fire and all that, and he has to think of the estate's reputation, that's what bloody Jasper said to me.'

'Kit, I'm so, so sorry,' Luella gasped, then realised she'd forgotten to breathe and drew in a huge lungful of air. 'I wish there was something I could do.'

'Thanks.' He looked tearful – devastated. She felt the same way. 'See you soon, OK?' he said. 'Sorry, I can't face our training session with Charlie today. I'm just going to go home and be with my folks after my shift. This has really affected them. It could cost us our cottage, their jobs, our whole life here.'

Luella felt chilled to the bone. She wanted to stay, to comfort him, but she could tell he needed to be alone right then. 'Call me, OK?' She hugged his shoulders, but he just braced and looked at the ground. She left, feeling sick to her stomach.

When Luella arrived at the Langdons', Carrie was too busy to take a break, so she'd grabbed a poo scooper and was now giving her a hand to skip out the stables while the grooms took some of the ponies out for exercise.

Carrie had been absolutely furious when she'd heard about the rumours and the Balfours' reaction. 'You can't just fire people, and the family have worked there and lived in the cottage for, like, ten generations, didn't you say? And it's hard to evict people for no reason – thank goodness. Unless the Balfours want an employment tribunal on their hands as well they *have* to stay on the right side of the law.'

'Well, maybe that's something, but I don't trust them,' said Luella, feeling desperate for Kit. 'Willow could have been seriously hurt, and Hugo could have been injured for life. Six months of an external fixator on his leg and physio is bad enough. This is awful – if people think Kit was responsible for Hugo's injuries and hurting a horse, he may never find work again.'

Carrie leaned on her fork and sighed. 'I feel sick. Kit's out of the running for the place on the patron's team, and possibly out of Yetbourne – and out of your life too.'

Luella felt utterly bleak. It hurt to hear Carrie's bluntness, but she was right. Worst-case scenario, that's what all this could come to – Kit's family being forced to leave the area. She couldn't bear to think of Kit miles away, hurt and broken. Of Kit not being able to work with horses any more – word got round in horsey circles. She sat down, right there in the wood shavings, feeling hopeless.

'Let's have a look around the feed room,' said Carrie. She glanced up at the huge clock on the archway. 'Everyone else is on their break now, round the coffee pot in the office, so it's a good time. Obviously Kit didn't poison Willow, but someone did, whether by accident or not.'

Luella stood. 'Well, it's better than doing nothing.'

In the feed room there were no obvious clues. They opened the supplements cupboard and had a good look. 'Aha,' said Carrie, reaching to the back. 'Here's the tub of magnesium.' She shook it. 'About half full, I'd say.'

'It doesn't tell us anything, apart from that it was easily accessible,' said Luella.

Carrie peered at the tub, and then at the others. She ran her hand over the top of them. There was a thin layer of dust on them and some of them were sticky in patches. The magnesium tub was clean and dust free. 'Apart from the fact it's suspiciously clean?'

Luella gasped. 'You're right. That suggests someone did take magnesium from that tub to give to Willow, and then wiped it clean to get rid of any fingerprints afterwards.'

'While not thinking that a clean tub would look suspicious,' said Carrie. 'So, they were clever – but not that clever.'

Luella laughed darkly. 'That narrows it down to pretty much everyone we know.'

Carrie took a photo of the tub. 'Let's not disturb anything,' she said. 'We don't want anyone to know we're on to them.'

Next they looked everywhere else in the feed room – the other cupboards, the wall shelves, round the feed sacks and buckets – but they couldn't see anything strange or out of place. They searched every inch of the floor too. Nothing.

'Come on, let's get some coffee,' said Carrie. But just as they were about to head out, Luella spotted something almost tucked away down by the edge of a hay bale and bent to pick it up. She held it up in the dim light.

'An apple core,' said Carrie. 'Not eaten around, though, but smooth. Pulled out with a corer.'

'Yeah. And not the ends, just the middle,' said Luella, 'and it's been discarded, quite obviously.' She gasped suddenly. 'Oh!'

Carrie understood what she was thinking. They cored apples to hide supplements or medication in sometimes, to stop the horses from spitting things out. 'Someone could have filled an apple with magnesium and then stopped the ends back up,' she said.

Luella nodded. 'That would make sense. It fits with the wiped jar.'

'And it suggests someone did it on purpose – a very deliberate action like that,' Carrie reasoned. 'It's not like just chucking a scoop of the wrong thing into a feed by accident. So we *have* learned something.'

Luella sighed heavily. 'It doesn't really help Kit, though. It doesn't give us any clues as to who did it.' She clearly looked as despairing as she felt because Carrie wrapped her up in her arms and gave her a big hug. 'Hey, it'll be OK,' she reassured her. 'This stupid rumour will die down. Kit will be all right – the Balfours will be apologising to him soon enough for taking silly gossip seriously.'

Luella allowed herself to be hugged, but she wasn't convinced that everything would work out. She had an awful feeling in the pit of her stomach that just wouldn't go away. What if Kit lost everything? And what if he had to leave Yetbourne? Leave *her*?

Chapter Fifteen

Bex

'Oi, I want a word with you.'
Bex had come round the corner of the little footpath that led from the car park and found Barnaby Balfour waiting for her. She sighed and looked down her nose at him. 'Don't try to act gangster – you can't pull it off.'

'My place in the Guillards Cup team. You stole it.'

She laughed, but it sounded hollow. Her heart was beating fast. She secretly suspected he was a bit of a psycho, like the rest of his family, and he was angry. Furious, in fact. And they were alone. 'Look, I'm sorry you got the wrong idea. You seem to think the place was yours all along, and that your parents were just trying to teach you some kind of lesson by getting me and Kit involved. But it wasn't like that. The spot was never *yours*. It was up for grabs. It could have been filled by a pro, but your parents gave me and Kit a chance. I think it was very good of them to encourage young talent.'

She held her breath. He looked so angry, she worried that she'd gone too far. Perhaps she should make a run for it.

'Kit was the better player on the day,' Barnaby said. 'You only got the place because the poisoning rumours put him out of the running.'

She knew she shouldn't rise to the bait, but she couldn't help herself. 'That's not true! Yeah, he scored one more goal than I did, but I did more for the team.'

Barnaby snorted with amusement. 'You're so deluded. You couldn't be a team player if you tried. You're only out for yourself. I'm sure you weren't upset when those rumours came out about Kit. You probably spread them.' He glared at her, contemptuous. 'In fact, you probably started them.'

Her eyes flashed. 'I did not!' And she really hadn't. 'Why would I? I have enough talent to have been chosen on my own merit. I'd want everyone to know that, not think I got the team place by default.'

'I'm watching you, Bex,' said Barnaby threateningly, getting up in her face. 'I've seen how you are with my family. But I know you're up to something. And I am going to find out what. And when I do, I'll take you down.'

Bex rolled her eyes. 'Relax, Tony Soprano.' But she felt a chill. An image of her with Mum and Dad yelling about finances in the kitchen flashed through her mind. She shoved it away, as if he might somehow pick up on it. Everything had to seem fine. More than fine. *For Bomba and Gordo.* 'Look, I'm sorry you feel the way you do,' she said smoothly, getting a hold of herself. 'And I hope we can move past this little matter because I'm at your yard to stay, so you'll be seeing a lot more of me.' With that, she pushed past him and strode away, head up, ponytail swinging. She was holding her breath, and her legs were shaking a little, but she kept walking, and she didn't look back.

Twenty minutes later, after decompressing in the ladies' loo and touching up her make up, Bex was sipping champagne outside the front of Brown's. She was with her new bosom buddies Venetia and Aurelia. She hadn't answered any of Luella's calls since the showdown in the lane when she'd found her supposed *best friend* fraternising with the girl who'd stolen Freddie from her and the boy who'd tried to steal her Team Balfour place for the Guillards Cup.

She silenced a quiet voice inside her saying, *Luella didn't even know you were in the running for a place.* She wasn't in the mood for being logical, or reasonable. And anyway, there were other reasons Lulu shouldn't see Kit. For one, he was beneath her, and two, that natural horsemanship stuff he did was hocus pocus.

Bex had chosen a very prominent table on purpose, to see and be seen from all angles of the pretty village market square. *The most important thing when everything is falling apart*, she thought to herself, *is to look like things are better than ever.* That was what the beautiful Saint Laurent pantsuit was about, and the Gucci shades. The champagne.

And the poise, the posture, the composure.

As Venetia droned on about pedigree kittens, Bex wished for a fleeting moment that she had Luella back, but she squashed the feeling down as quickly as it came up. The two girls from her tennis club might be mind-numbingly boring, yes, but they looked great, had their fingers on the fashion pulse and photographed well for Instagram, TikTok and so on. Obviously, TikTok was dire, but you had to be on there if you were anyone. And Bex knew she was far more than just anyone – she was *someone*. Bex Chapman-Foster, It-girl on the London scene, Boudoir perfume ambassador and soon to be the fresh, young face of British polo.

No one needed to know that her family were on their knees, or that she'd already managed to dodge a meeting with Eric about Bomba and Gordo's supplements charges that morning. The Balfours had been relaxed about payment since their chat but their business manager most certainly wasn't. Annoyingly her charm seemed to slide right off him.

'More Bolly?' she asked the girls. 'We shouldn't, but I do so *love* spending time with you two.' This time, Venetia leaped up to go to the bar and order – and pay, of course. The best thing about Aurelia and Venetia, apart from their generous credit limits, was that they worshipped Bex. She smiled sweetly at Aurelia. 'Why don't you go and get us some olives, and maybe a charcuterie board?' she said. 'Then we can stay even longer and spill all the girly goss.'

For a moment, Aurelia looked disappointed. But she went, giving Bex some lovely peace and quiet to put into action her plan to accidentally on purpose run into the Argentine pro, Alfonso. She'd happened to overhear Eric saying that he was popping into the village to register with the private GP. Which happened to be right opposite Brown's . . .

'Alfonso!' she called, waving. He looked confused but came over. 'I'm Bex Chapman-Foster,' she said, shaking his hand. 'I'm on the Balfour polo team. And I know who you are, of course.'

Flattery would get her far. 'Ah, yes. Wonderful to see you.'

That accent. The catch of his expensive aftershave in her throat. She put on her sexiest smile and turned in her chair. 'What a coincidence.' She invited him to join her.

The girls reappeared then, followed by a waiter bearing more champagne. Bex almost sent him back in for an extra glass but Alfonso declined and asked for a lime and soda. Clearly, he took being a pro in training seriously. 'Keeping in good shape for the season?' she asked, a little flirtatiously.

He nodded slightly, amused. 'Of course.'

'Ooooh, are you a polo player?' Venetia crooned. Bex resisted the urge to roll her eyes and made the introductions. The girls were here to make her look good, but if they acted like infants, she'd have to replace them.

'Yes, it is my sport, my passion, my . . .' he reached for the word '. . . vocation.'

'Mine's tennis,' said Aurelia. And, annoyingly, they launched into a conversation about that, as Alfonso was apparently a fabulous tennis player too. 'It was a hard decision to choose between going pro at polo or tennis, but polo was the winner in the end,' he finished. 'My heart will always be with the horses.'

'Mine's with the kittens,' said Venetia. Bex felt like choking her with a long piece of pastrami off the charcuterie board that had just arrived. They were supposed to be sitting here looking fabulous and hanging on her every word, not going on about their own boring interests.

'So, tell us about how you got started in polo,' she said. She knew her stuff. If there was one thing a pro like Alfonso would love more than listening to her, it was talking about himself. She wasn't wrong – and soon he was regaling them with tales of his bravado, and of home-bred horses with incredible pedigrees becoming champions under his family's training regime. And, of course, snatching victory from the opposition in the final chukka time after time after time. Bex glanced at the time on her phone screen, stifled a yawn and pasted on a smile.

'I've been struggling with Gordo's flexibility,' she said, when he finally fell silent. 'I'd love your thoughts on it. Obviously Daniel Hackett is a fabulous trainer, and the standard at Balfours' is extremely high. But clearly you have some really leading-edge insights, to have done so well.'

Alfonso nodded formally. 'Of course. Nothing would give me greater pleasure. We can have a look tomorrow. It's probably best to book the training ground out and we'll have a private session, so that we are not distracted.'

Bex planned on them being *very distracted indeed*. She smiled demurely. 'Thank you so much, that would be wonderful.' She wiggled her fingers, for him to hand over his phone. 'I'll give you my *personal* number,' she said, as if she had *people*.

Aurelia gave Venetia a sappy look, like they were watching a corny romcom unfold right in front of them, which Bex ignored and, luckily, Alfonso didn't see.

Keep them keen and always be the first to leave. She stood. 'Well, I have to make tracks, darlings!' She air-kissed them all. 'Alfonso, it's been lovely to meet you. Girls, always a pleasure.' She wasn't at all worried about leaving him with them – It was more like leaving him babysitting than handing him to the competition.

'I'll see you tomorrow,' he called out, as she sashayed off down the street. She didn't reply or look back. Inside, beneath her poise, she was celebrating wildly. Everything was unfolding according to plan. She, and her family, would be back on top in no time.

Chapter Sixteen

Carrie

A loud, distressed whinny pierced the air, along with a clattering of hooves. Carrie looked up sharply from sweeping the yard. She'd been lost in thought, the only one around on the Monday morning earlier-than-early shift again. It took her a moment to process, but when she then heard a scrape of hooves and a loud bang, she ran towards it.

There was a horse lorry parked in the yard, just in front of the archway. *Oh my God, what if someone is stealing horses?* Her phone was in her jacket on the mounting block, and all she had was a broom. That wasn't much use. Still, she ran at full pelt, yelling, 'Hey! Stop! I've called the police!'

She streaked round to the back of the trailer and there was Bex, shouting at Bomba. 'Just move! Dammit, don't play me up!'

Gordo, tied up to the side of the lorry, pulled back sharply at her raised voice and tried to rear, swaying the whole thing.

'Don't yell at her,' said Carrie, forcing herself to calm down. Not for Bex's sake, but for the horses'.

Bex looked up and fury distorted her beautiful face. 'You again! Don't tell me how to handle *my* ponies.'

Carrie just glared at her. 'You're scaring her. And Gordo. You're so stressed out, and shouting – of course she's not going to think it's safe to get in the lorry. She's a prey animal, for God's sake.'

Bex gave her a contemptuous look, but she didn't pull on Bomba's rope again.

'Can't the driver help?'

'You'd think so,' Bex snapped. 'But he says it's not his job.'

Typical Balfour attitude, thought Carrie. She took a deep breath and reminded herself of the look on Bex's face when Freddie had chosen Carrie over her. Yes, it was to help with Willow, but that moment had been so much bigger. Freddie had chosen Carrie, full stop. Even though they couldn't be together.

That's why she'd gone to Bex's house last night. Yes, she liked Freddie and he liked her, and yes, Bex was awful. But she didn't want to be the cause of another girl's misery. So, she'd gone over to Bex's to talk to her face to face. Sort out some kind of truce and get everything out in the open.

But she hadn't even rung the doorbell, in the end. She'd heard Bex arguing with her parents through the open kitchen window and, well, she hadn't been able to help overhearing about their money troubles. She didn't have any horses of her own, but she couldn't imagine the pain of having to give away not just one, but two. And Estrella and Blanca had always been such sweethearts. The whole thing with Freddie had just seemed like silly, overblown drama after that, and she'd crept away, leaving Bex and her family to their privacy. Now, she tried to remind herself of the awful situation that this mean, snobby, vicious girl was in, and to cut her some slack. She sighed. 'Let me give you a hand.'

Bex pulled a face and her eyes filled with tears, which Carrie pretended not to notice. 'No, thank you. You can get back to scrubbing feed buckets or shovelling shit. I don't need your help.'

Carrie forced herself to stay calm and took a deep breath. 'It's not for you, it's for them,' she said. She'd been using Kit's techniques to load the Langdon ponies when they went to their specialist trainers or for hydrotherapy or, occasionally, on fun days out at the beach with the grooms.

'I said no, so off you go,' said Bex, waving her away.

'I'll just wait here for a moment, thanks,' said Carrie, leaning on her broom.

Bex huffed with irritation and tried to pull Bomba into the trailer again. She reared up sharply with a loud whinny and pulled back hard on the rope, wrenching Bex's shoulder and pulling her over on the ramp. 'Ow! You little witch!' Bex yelled.

Now she really will have a bad shoulder, Carrie thought, but she managed not to say anything. She'd had enough. She strode up to Bex and held out her hand for the rope. 'Give it to me or I'm calling Terrence,' she said firmly. 'Or Lord L.'

That did it. Bex slammed the rope into her hand and slunk off to stand next to Gordo, who turned his rear to her, the horse equivalent of telling her to F off.

Carrie stopped paying attention to Bex and focused on Bomba. She stood on the ramp, the rope slack between them, and felt for a connection with her.

'We're going to the Balfours',' Bex said suddenly. 'I've had an offer to play for their team in the Guillards Cup, now that Kit's had to bow out. Although, I'm sure I would have been chosen anyway.'

Carrie took another deep breath and focused on keeping calm and relaxed for Bomba. She knew Bex was trying to rile her. She couldn't give her the satisfaction.

'As you know, Estrella and Blanca are away for a few months with a top trainer. Once they're back, and with these two getting the very best at the Balfours', I'll be all set for an amazing season next year, especially after we win the Guillards Cup.'

Well, hearing that, Carrie couldn't hold her tongue any more. 'Don't lie, Bex. I know about your situation and your other two ponies.'

Bex glared at her. 'Freddie told you?' Tears sprang into her eyes again. 'He promised he wouldn't.'

'No one told me,' Carrie insisted. 'I overheard you fighting with your parents last night. I was coming to have a chat with you. About Freddie. I thought we should clear the air after . . .'

'After he chose you and not me,' Bex snapped.

'I would never want to hurt anyone,' Carrie said gently. 'And he and I are not together, for the record. But you weren't with him either, so if I *was* with him, I wouldn't be doing anything wrong by you. And . . .' She paused. Bex was still staring at her. Should she risk being really honest? Vulnerable. She went for it, hoping that, somehow, she and Bex could sort things out and get along, for Luella's sake, if nothing else. 'I'll be honest with you – I genuinely like him.'

Bex said nothing. She just scuffed at the ground with her yard boot.

Carrie sighed. 'Look, Bex. I know it hasn't been easy for you, me coming to Yetbourne. And I know you have a lot to handle right now. I could help – I do understand. My family lost money too, that's why we moved here. We've had to massively change our lives. It's really hard. I get it.'

Bex finally looked at her, tears in her eyes. 'I don't want your help,' she said. 'And you have no idea what I'm going through. But . . .' She sighed. 'Look, please, I'm begging you. Don't tell anyone what you know. I'll be finished in Yetbourne and on the polo scene, and so will my whole family. Please.'

Carrie groaned. 'Just tell Luella, Bex. She's not a snob. She'll support you, you know she will.'

Bex shook her head hard. 'No. No one can know. It'll spread like wildfire. Please, Carrie. Promise me. Don't tell anyone, and especially not Lulu.'

Carrie struggled – it would be a secret, and possibly a wedge, between her and her lovely new friend. But, at that moment, she felt for Bex and she did understand, whatever Bex thought. 'OK,' she said. 'I won't.' And then she calmly loaded Bomba and Gordo into the trailer.

It was only once she'd helped Bex put the ramp up and close the doors, then watched the lorry drive off towards the lane, that her legs started shaking and her heart hammering. Whether it was because she'd just braved it out and loaded two unsettled horses on her own, or whether it was the run-in with Bex, she didn't know. But she'd need a strong coffee before getting back to work, that was for sure.

She hadn't expected anyone else to be in the office, but there was Freddie, by the coffee pot. Her heart pounded even faster when she saw him. He looked up – there were Steri-Strips over the wound above his right eye.

'Ouch, that looks bad.'

He shrugged. 'It's nothing. Coffee?'

'Yes, please. I need it.' He gave her a questioning look. She smiled wryly. 'I've been seeing Bex off the premises.'

His fist tightened round the coffee jug handle and his jaw set. 'Why she had to pull that stunt, defecting to the Balfours' team so publicly, I don't know. It's completely disrespectful, really bad form. I thought we were friends. Mum was so upset. And Dad would never show it, but he was really hurt, too. Our families go back a long way.'

'It was an awful thing to do,' said Carrie. 'But maybe she just didn't know how to tell you all she was leaving.'

They looked at each other and then burst out laughing, breaking the serious atmosphere. 'Since when have you had any sympathy for Bex?' Freddie asked. 'I thought it was pistols at dawn between you two.'

Carrie wouldn't have said anything – she'd promised – but her face spoke for her.

'You *know*, don't you?' Freddie asked.

She nodded slightly. 'I overheard. Who else does?'

'Mum, Dad and Terrence,' said Freddie, pouring coffee into two chipped, ancient mugs. 'No one else. It mustn't get out, Carrie. Whatever Bex is like. That would be a disaster for her.'

Carrie gazed into his eyes. 'I know,' she said. 'Don't worry, I won't even tell Luella. I get it – this is huge for Bex, and she's lost her other two horses. It must be awful.'

'It was. She was gutted. She pulls stunts like that charity match thing because she's scared. You know, trying a bit too hard to look like she doesn't care. All bravado. And maybe you're right. Maybe she didn't know how to tell us she was going to the Balfours'.'

Freddie came close, to hand her a mug of coffee. Their fingers brushed as he passed it to her. Her voice caught in her throat as she thanked him. She put the mug down on the bench and stepped up close, thrilled by the feel of his jeans brushing against her shorts. He didn't step back. She reached up and smoothed the hair from his forehead, tilting her chin up. She breathed in the delicious scent of him, as he gazed down at her. 'Carrie, the rules . . .'

Her stomach flipped over. He'd thought she'd been about to kiss him. And he hadn't backed off. And maybe she would have done, if he hadn't just said what he'd said. She ran her hand across his eyebrow, just below the nasty cut, as she'd planned to. 'This must have hurt.'

He leaned his forehead carefully on to hers and closed his eyes. She closed hers too. For a moment, they breathed together. Time seemed to stand still. 'Sometimes it's worth the risk.'

Chapter Seventeen

Luella

The next morning, Luella was leaning against the tack room door of Charlie and Captain's little stable block, waiting for Kit to show up. She was worried about him, and his whole family.

He rounded the corner with his horseman's stick and string in his hand but without the usual spring in his step. She forced herself to smile. Carrie was so good at keeping up a positive vibe, whereas she tended to get sucked into gloomy moods – *not this time, though*. She needed to stay upbeat. For Kit. 'Hey, you!'

'Hey, you.' He sounded downbeat. She wasn't surprised. She decided not to mention the poisoning rumours unless he did.

They hugged, and she stayed for a few moments longer in his arms. After their awful date, and then the cute, disaster-repairing pasty supper in the barn, they hadn't gone out again. And they hadn't kissed or held hands or anything either. But it was still there, the thing between them, stronger than ever.

She beamed at him. 'I'm so excited for you to see what Charlie and I can do. What we've learned with you has really improved things. The flying changes are more balanced for a start and her canter in the half-pass is more engaged and has more cadence. She's really lifting through the ribcage since we've been getting her to work from the hind more on the ground, rather than leaning on the forehand.'

Kit smiled briefly. 'That's a lifetime of being pulled around in head collars for you.'

Luella took the brief smile – she could work with that. She nudged him playfully. 'I know, I know. I've changed my ways!'

He made a fuss of Charlie and they walked over to the dressage arena. Then he gave Luella a leg up, even though the mounting block was right there. She acted like she'd temporarily forgotten it existed, so she'd get the chance to feel his hands on her shin and thigh. Like the hug, that touch lingered a little longer.

The dressage test went well. She was sure she and Charlie would do better than a 5.5 on the half-pass now and they'd pick up extra marks for their shoulder-ins because there was more engagement behind. She ran through a few suppleness exercises and then did the test again and was pleased with Charlie's performance, finishing there to end on a good note.

She swung down and made a fuss of Charlie, then changed her bridle for a head collar and fed her a carrot as a reward. She took off her saddle and pad too and hauled them over the fence, then gave her a brush down on the sweaty patch underneath. Kit made a fuss of Charlie and then they settled in next to each other on the fence. Luella glugged water while Charlie grazed by the bushes at the side of the arena.

'Nice sweat patches.'

She blushed and flapped her arms in the air. 'Urgh! I was hoping you wouldn't notice those. Or that you'd be a gentleman and not mention them.'

He raised a flirtatious eyebrow at her. 'I'm no gentleman.'

She leaned into him. 'Yes, you are. Treating me to that lovely à la carte crisp and pasty dinner, for example. Which we didn't even get to finish.'

OK, she admitted it. She was fishing for another date. She wanted things to move forward, and to date him, and kiss him, and spend as much time with him as possible, especially as he might have to— *No, don't think about it.*

He didn't pick up on the hint, though, and he lapsed into a broody silence.

'So, how are you doing, after, you know . . .'

He sighed. 'Well, the Balfours haven't sacked me – they can't, over a rumour, so that's something, I guess. But I've no prospects here now. No way to further my ambitions. And nowhere else to go.'

Think positive. For Kit. 'Oh, I'm sure there are lots of—'

'No smoke without fire,' he said sharply, cutting her off. 'Who else in the horse world would employ me after this? Or my parents. It's a disaster. I feel so guilty. I should have thought about how it would look. But how could I possibly have known something like this would happen, with Willow and Hugo?'

Luella dropped the fake positivity and got real. 'It wasn't your fault,' she said gently, but he wasn't listening.

'How am I supposed to make something of myself now?' he said angrily, kicking at the ground.

'I know. It's awful.' She reached out to touch his arm, but he pulled back sharply. The jagged silence between them lengthened.

For a long time, he stared out at the distant treeline. Eventually, he cleared his throat. 'Look, Lu, I've been thinking. I've got so much to deal with, and now we're talking about moving away. It's not certain, but that's the way things are going. I need to spend my time looking for a new job outside this area, and hope the rumours haven't spread too far. It's a lot. Maybe you and I should . . .'

She froze. 'What? *Stop training?*' she cried, then told herself firmly not to be selfish. This was about a roof over his family's head and food on the table. 'I understand,' she said. 'You have to prioritise . . .'

'No. Well, yes. But . . . I mean . . .'

She braced. *Oh God, don't say it. Don't say it.*

'Let things cool off between *us*.'

Her stomach twisted. Tears sprang into her eyes. 'But *why?*'

'It's . . . It's . . .' He faltered. 'It's too complicated now.'

She felt the devastation of rejection, and then it was overtaken by spilling tears. 'Well, obviously you don't feel the same about me as I do about you, if you can just let it go that easily.' Her voice cracked with emotion.

'Lu . . .' He reached out and took her hand but she pulled away sharply. 'No. You're not going to comfort me, when you're the one who's hurting me!'

'It's better this way.'

She was pulling Charlie along then, into her stable. The mare protested at the suddenness and she saw Kit wince, but she hurried her on. She slipped off her head collar, closed the stable door and headed for her house, tears blurring her eyes.

'Lu!'

She didn't look back. It was over. Before it had even really started.

She'd made it halfway up the lane when she heard footsteps behind her.

He grabbed her hand and she whirled around and banged hard into his chest. His arms encircled her and his lips crushed against hers. She pushed herself hard against him and opened her mouth. For a moment, neither of them moved. And then they were kissing, frantic and wild, and she could taste him, mixed with the salt of her tears. She gasped as waves of energy flowed up her body. He slid his hands down to her waist and she pressed her hips into his. He groaned with desire and broke away from the kiss, pushing her hair back from her face. 'Oh God, Lu, I'm so sorry,' he said, his voice thick with emotion. 'I *do* want to be with you. There's nothing I want more. I was trying to do what I thought was right. To protect you – from the rumours, from me leaving. I mean, you could be with some amazing guy who—'

She kissed him quiet and then stroked his face and kissed him again and again. 'I don't care what anyone says. And I don't care if I have to follow you to the ends of the earth, Kit. You *are* that amazing guy. I want *you*, OK? *You.*'

He smiled a gorgeous, sultry smile, right from the heart, and rested his forehead on hers. 'Good. Because I want you too.'

She pulled him close again and they fell into a deep, passionate kiss. It was everything she'd ever dreamed of, and more.

Chapter Eighteen

Bex

'Well, I think we've got everything we need?'

The photographer looked up from flicking through his shots and nodded. 'All good.' Bex had ridden both Gordo and Bomba for the shoot, wearing a different outfit for each set of pictures, of course, and then they'd done a glamorous look with her sipping champagne in a Saint Laurent summer evening dress, looking out over the glorious estate. Maybe if some people just skim-read or flicked through the magazine, they'd assume it was hers. The thought made her feel very happy indeed, and, yes, one day she would have an estate like this, all from her own efforts.

'And . . .' He checked through his notebook too. 'Yep, we're done. Thanks so much, Bex. And the very best of luck with it all. You're a talented young lady, and your charity work is inspiring.'

The journalist from *Surrey Style* magazine shook her hand firmly, matching her robust grip.

No, it wasn't *Tatler*. Not yet. But it was a start. She'd had the stable hands at the yard an hour early that morning to get everything looking extra spick and span for her. And the grooms – she'd roped them in as well, fibbing that Jasper had told her to. *Just a little white lie to help things along.*

In fact, Jasper, Delia and that plank of wood Eric didn't even know about the photo shoot. She didn't want the awful Balfours getting involved, stealing the spotlight. But she knew that they'd be thrilled when they saw the article, and the pictures of their estate looking so fantastic. She'd say she'd wanted it to be a surprise, and they'd be thanking her.

Next job – Alfonso. She knew he was out in the arena, giving a masterclass to some other clients. As in, the ones who were actually interested in learning and didn't just chuck money at the estate so they could turn up a few times a year and ride in a game.

She did a quick change in the tack room, back into one of the riding outfits from the shoot, and made her way up to the main arena. Alfonso had just finished up the lesson, and everyone was thanking him profusely as they rode out of the gate and on to the dirt track.

'Sounds like it was a great class.'

'It was.' Huh! So, none of that Great British modesty, then. Or fake modesty, at least. But then Alfonso was a great trainer, and he knew it, and he said it. What was wrong with that?

She was mounted on Bomba, leading Gordo, whom she now let loose in the training arena. Alfonso was on a stunning grey called Trueno, which meant thunder. He threw her a mallet and she caught it in her left hand. 'Right, let's see what you've got.'

She looked at him coolly. 'Let's see what *you've* got.'

Alfonso worked them hard, but Bex didn't complain. When Bomba got tired, she swapped on to Gordo and the hard work continued. After coming full pelt at her to challenge for the ball, again and again, he finally signalled for her to come into the middle. She came in, Gordo doing an impressive canter to halt and she let him have a long rein and waited for Alfonso's praise.

'Your lines are good. Your action with the mallet is good. Your position is . . . acceptable.'

Bex baulked at that. *Good? Acceptable?* She tried to think of the last time a trainer had said she was less than fantastic and amazing and she couldn't. Still, she wouldn't show him she was riled. 'Fine. Let me try again. Challenge me, no mercy.' She gathered up the reins so suddenly that Gordo was startled and leaped into action a little wildly. She thought Alfonso might call her back and say that *he* ran the class, thank you. But he didn't, and she smiled to herself when she heard hooves thundering behind her.

She'd show *him*.

She threw her heart and soul and all of her anger and pain at losing Estrella and Blanca into her plays. She hooked his mallet, dodged his challenges and scored, one, two, three times – smacking the ball hard against the painted goal at the end of the arena. Gordo gave it everything he had, emboldened by her strong focus and high confidence.

Bex could feel the Guillards Cup in her hands. The sponsorship deals in the bag. Her social media profile in the stratosphere. She felt good, like she hadn't done in a long time.

'OK, time!' shouted Alfonso. She ignored him and whacked the ball toward the goal, challenging him to stop her scoring again. 'Hey!' He urged Trueno on and the powerful mare sprang into a canter and then a full-on gallop. He hooked Bex's mallet on the nearside backhand stroke. 'Foul!' she yelled. 'Ref!'

He laughed and they came to a halt, both breathing hard.

'I thought you were a pro!' she gasped. 'Don't you even know the rules?'

He moved Trueno towards her, pulling on her mallet with his.

'Hey!' she cried, but she let herself be pulled closer.

'Yes, I do know the rules,' he said. His eyes burned into hers. 'But I wanted to break them.' And with that, he leaned across and kissed her.

She pulled away and glared at him. *What the hell?!*

The cheek. The arrogance. The presumption.

How incredibly hot.

She jumped down from Gordo and turned him loose.

Alfonso did the same with Trueno. And then he pulled Bex into his arms and kissed her hard, pressing her body up against his.

He smelled so good. And tasted divine. He groaned as she pushed her thigh in between his legs. She gasped as he reached under her shirt. He tugged at the button on his white jeans as they kissed furiously.

Alfonso may have been happy to get it on there in the arena, but she wasn't. 'There's a groundsman's shed.'

'Show me,' he breathed.

She led him by the hand through the couple of minutes' stumble over rough ground behind the arena, and then into the shed. It smelled of grass cuttings and creosote. She kicked the door shut, kissing him again, taking control and pushing him down on to the broken garden sofa. Then, she let go, forgetting everything that had happened and focusing only on the moment. On him. On this wild unbridled chemistry between them.

And, Bex being Bex, she had the time of her life.

Bex returned to the yard half an hour later with a telltale glow, leading Bomba and Gordo and feeling like a queen. Alfonso walked behind her with Trueno, annoyingly on his phone when he should have been admiring her ass and swishing ponytail.

It had been over in minutes – fast, furious and full on, just like the training – but she'd completely lost herself in it. In him. And she'd got enough of a taste of how things could be between them to want more.

She found a quiet corner of the yard and tied her ponies up, then went to fill a bucket of water. When she returned, Alfonso had tied Trueno up next to them. She was quietly pleased. She was planning to play it cool and not mention what had just happened at all. But as they sponged the horses down and scraped off the excess water, he said, 'You have spirit. In the game and in the bedroom.'

She laughed. 'It was hardly a bedroom!' If he was waiting for a compliment in return, he didn't get one. Instead, she raised an eyebrow and said, 'If you say I was *good* or *acceptable* in that shed I'll kick your ass.'

She was testing the water, speaking to him like that. Breaking the formal boundary between trainer and student. But then, they'd kind of smashed through that already and trampled it into the dust.

He looked put out for a moment, but then he smiled at her, slow and flirty. *Good teeth.* 'There are some areas for improvement. I think we may need some more sessions.'

She dropped the sponge in the bucket and stepped up close to him, tilting her chin, their lips a whisper away from each other's. 'Oh, do you now?'

Sexual energy pulsed between them. A group of clients glanced their way. Bex didn't step back. Publicly kissing the hottest, most high-profile guy on the yard would be a great way to establish her Queen Bee status. Well, *Queen Bex*.

But Alfonso was the one who stepped back and busied himself with scraping Trueno down.

Oh well. Later. Meanwhile, she could get the next best thing. She pulled her phone out of the back pocket of her tight white jeans. Time to get polo's hottest pro all over her social media, in a way that strongly suggested he was her boyfriend. She had to think of her personal brand at all times, and it would boost her profile nicely.

In one fluid motion, she turned, tucked herself under Alfonso's arm and held up the camera. His stunningly handsome face lit up – he loved a lens as much as she did, clearly. 'Smile!' She beamed, pulling a few different poses, putting her hand up on to his cheek. She'd look great with the hot sex afterglow, too. She put a track on the video, a highly suggestive one, and uploaded it everywhere. *Something tells me I'm into something good.*

The likes and comments were flooding in before she'd even put Gordo and Bomba back in their new stables. *I'm on the rise again*, Bex thought, *and nothing will stop me this time.*

Chapter Nineteen

Carrie

'You know, with all this talk about polo, I think it's time you played some,' Luella announced to Carrie, as they had coffee in the empty Langdon yard office.

That's how Carrie had come to find herself in her current situation. Well, predicament. She was seeing another side to Bounty, for sure. Forget happy hacker – she was more like a racehorse when she got on the polo pitch. The four of them were in one of the practice arenas far from the main yard: her, Luella, Sims and Freddie. So – double bonus – she was getting to watch Freddie galloping around at full pelt in his white jeans and polo shirt, his beautiful shoulders rippling as he swung the mallet and whacked the ball.

She'd seen a deeper, and no less sexy, side to him in the office that day, after she'd loaded Bex's horses. They still hadn't kissed, though. Every time she'd caught herself daydreaming about it she'd cracked on with yard work, or coursework, or housework. After one particularly steamy mind-montage, she'd even shocked her parents by offering to deep clean their cottage and had blitzed the whole thing, insides of the windows and kitchen cupboards and all.

Luella had pulled a decent polo helmet out of her jeep for her to wear, thank goodness, so at least she didn't have the bloody Cinderella riding hat on. She knew her ass looked good in Luella's white Zara jeans too, partly because Lu had told her so, and partly because Freddie kept getting distracted by it. He'd only got a handle on himself after Sims had yelled out, 'Stop lusting over Carrie and focus, Langdon!'

She trotted Bounty over to the fence-line to grab her water bottle and take a swig – polo was thirsty work, especially on such a hot July afternoon. She watched her friends laughing and joking as they raced to beat one another to the ball. Luella had explained to her how to hold the mallet and swing it, from the line of her pony's hindquarters all the way to his shoulder. One long, relaxed, swing allowing the mallet to hit the ball as it connected, brushing the old shredded-tyres surface of the arena as it went.

If only it were that easy. She balanced the water bottle back on the fence and cantered over to join in the fun again, determined to hit one bloody ball, at least. After loads of misses and once almost whacking poor Bounty in the face, Freddie trotted over, explaining that it helped to twist in the saddle a little bit, putting more weight into her right stirrup, so she was more over the ball. Suddenly it all fell into place and she was connecting, time after time. She felt Freddie's eyes on her as he watched her body twist, too, and she revelled in it.

After that it was like *Wacky Races*, galloping at top speed, smashing balls and almost crashing into one another, while laughing and arguing about whose ball it was. Carrie took another swing and smiled as Luella cheekily hooked Sims's stick. 'Hey, woman, this isn't a game, it's a practice and anyway, your knee wasn't forward of mine!'

She stole the ball from him, hitting it forward, shouting, 'I think you'll find it was, smart-arse!'

Carrie snorted with laughter. She'd never heard Luella call anyone that before. Just then, Freddie galloped towards the goal with Sims by his side, marking him. Freddie whacked the ball – it hit the area inside the painted lines and bounced off, hard. 'Goal!'

It was time for Carrie to put her natural horsemanship training into practice. She connected with Bounty, as she did on their rides, moving the reins up her neck. Bounty leaped into a trot and then a canter, excited to join in the fun. She shot past Sims on the inside of a corner and they both went for the same ball. She was absolutely thrilled, flowing with the moment, and her friends, Bounty, the focus . . . and *whack*! She whooped with joy.

'Good shot!' cried Freddie. 'Right, let's end it there, shall we?'

Carrie was a little disappointed – now she had a taste for polo she thought it might be the most exciting thing in the world. And it was great to see Luella connect with her old friends again. Maybe she could be part of the gang now too. And Kit. Though they'd have to clear his name first.

Back on the yard, Luella took Charlie down to one of the empty stables to get her into the shade, and Sims handed Rico to Heather and went to see Terrence about something, up at Far Field, leaving Freddie and Carrie to sponge down their horses.

Cool water splashed from the bucket as she smoothed the sponge over Bounty's withers. She would have rubbed the sponge all over herself too, if it hadn't been covered in horsehair. She shook her head again and ran her hand across her forehead, trying to get rid of the hat hair and unsexy red pressure mark across her forehead. Freddie had Willow tied up on to some baling twine a couple of strides away and was sponging her neck. '*Hot*, isn't it?' he said.

She registered the cheeky tone in his voice too late and looked up as he pulled the nearby hosepipe from where it was filling a bucket and unleashed it on her. She screamed as it soaked her shirt and Willow shot backwards in a clatter of hooves.

Icy cold water trickled down the inside of her shirt, making her gasp. She wiped the wet tendrils of hair from her face. 'That was not very professional!'

'Well, I–I—' Freddie stuttered, looking uncertain. She took advantage and grabbed the hose. He smiled, shaking his head. 'Carrie. Carrie, no. Come on. Carrie . . .'

She gave him a full-on flirty smile and flicked her eyebrows. 'You started it.' *Game on.* She turned the hose on Freddie.

'You witch!' he yelled.

She laughed and soaked him more. The arcs of water sparkled in the sunshine then hit the ground with a satisfying *splat*. 'Let's get him, Bounty!'

He wrestled the hose from her and she resisted for long enough to get them both soaked and then let him take it. He put it back into an empty bucket close by and turned back to her. His checked shirt looked even better dripping wet and stuck to his muscly shoulders. 'I can't believe you did that. Prepare to be sorry.'

He strode towards her, flicking his dripping hair out of his face. She stepped away from Bounty, ready, taking a stance. Her body coursed with fiery energy and it looked very much like he felt the same. 'OK, Freddie Langdon, let's have it.'

As he came towards her, she shrieked and turned to run away, but he grabbed her by the waist and lifted her right off the ground. She shrieked again and struggled, feeling like she'd explode from the feeling of her bum pressed into his groin, his hands round her waist. 'Put me down!'

He bent forward, so that her feet touched the ground again, and she turned in his arms. They both breathed in sharply. Then, suddenly, they were kissing. Long and slow and deep. Carrie was lost in it, in him. He wrapped his arms around her and crushed her tight to his chest, as her body flooded with desire.

Finally they broke apart, both flushed and beaming. 'Well, that was a long time coming,' he said. 'I've been wanting to do that since the first day I saw you, you boots thief.'

She kissed him again – full on, bodies pressed up against each other, heat building between them. It made her gasp when they stopped.

He kissed her lightly then – one, two, three times. 'And that,' he said. 'And that, and that.'

A disgruntled whinny interrupted them. They turned to Willow and Bounty, who did not look impressed with their behaviour.

Carrie laughed. 'I think we're in trouble.'

Freddie smiled down at her. 'It's hot. We'd best get these guys back in their stables.'

She offered him her hand and they linked fingers as they walked down the yard, heat sizzling between them. *We kissed, we kissed, we kissed*, she thought, over and over, to the rhythm of hoofbeats.

Chapter Twenty

Luella

Of course, Carrie told Luella about the kiss right away. Luella felt bad for Bex but happy for her, and for Freddie. They were so great together and the sexual tension between them during the polo mini game had been ridiculous. You couldn't fight that kind of chemistry.

Things were pretty hot between her and Kit too. She thought about their first kiss as she bumped the Suzuki down a dirt track on the Balfour Estate. She'd seen him again that evening, and there had been a second kiss, a third kiss, a fourth . . . they were now firmly in the double digits.

She was intoxicated with the feeling she had when she was with him. She'd never felt *sexy* before. Not like Bex.

Now she did.

Kit had unleashed something in her. Something she hadn't been expecting. Something wild and primal. She couldn't wait to explore it more. And to see him again.

Not long now.

He hadn't asked her on another date yet, but what they were doing today was even better. Even more intimate. Kit had invited her up to the cottage to meet his family.

She'd seen his mum and dad around Yetbourne and at the polo over the years, of course. But it wasn't the same as *meeting* them, meeting them. Like, as Kit's . . . Was she his girlfriend? Would he introduce her like that?

They hadn't said they were together, but maybe they didn't need to. There was no way she could even think about getting with anyone else, and she thought – hoped – that Kit felt the same. *Of course he does*, she told herself firmly. *We're so good together.* But would he think she was super keen and a total loser if she brought it up?

She put a stop to the merry-go-round in her mind by pulling her Suzuki up into the gravel driveway of Kit's family cottage. She hadn't seen it before and she was wowed. It was big, old, thatched and stunning, with yellow roses in full bloom.

Kit came bounding out of the front door with a huge grin on his face, as if he'd been looking out of the window, waiting for her to arrive. Her heart leaped and she smiled to herself as she got out, feeling sexy as her bare legs moved over each other under her pretty sky-blue skater dress. Maybe she didn't need to worry about acting cool if he wasn't. Maybe she could just relax and be herself and they could be super keen total losers together.

'Wow! Gorgeous!' she said, gesturing at the cottage. He reached her and swept her up in his arms, lifting her feet off the ground.

'That's what I was thinking,' he said. Then he kissed her hard and she kissed him back, intense, like they'd been separated for weeks and not just overnight.

'Put the poor girl down and bring her inside!'

Kit broke away and blushed cutely. 'I'll just apologise for my mum now,' he said. 'She's got zero filter.'

Luella laughed. 'Neither has mine.'

His hand found hers and their fingers intertwined, having a secret conversation, as they walked up to the cottage. They grabbed another quick kiss before they went through the door. It opened straight into a large, cosy sitting room with a huge inglenook fireplace, an ancient boxy stereo playing Radio Two and about ten of Kit's closest relatives.

Luella didn't know whether to laugh or die of embarrassment, but she managed to smile and hold it together.

'So, my auntie Helena *just happened* to pop round,' said Kit, gesturing towards a kind-looking lady who was like an older version of his mum.

'Total coincidence,' said Helena, with a wink at Kit's mum.

Luella smiled at her and held out her hand. 'It's a pleasure to meet you. I'm—'

'Oh, tsh!' Helena enveloped her in a huge, warm hug. 'We don't stand on ceremony here!'

'Oh, OK!' Luella hugged her back, catching Kit's expression over her shoulder. He made her giggle by rolling his eyes dramatically.

She was about to introduce herself to Kit's grandfather, who was sitting in a big chair by the window, but Kit's young nieces launched themselves at her legs. 'I done you a friendship bracelet,' said one, holding it out.

'Mine's better. I done it blue and it matches your dress.'

The older girl did a little curtsey as she handed the bracelet over and Luella felt like some kind of visiting royal. 'Oh, gosh, thank you! They're both lovely, and look.' She put them on, next to her loaded Pandora charm bracelet. 'One goes with my dress, and the other goes with my lipstick.' She held her wrist up to her face and pouted, making them both laugh.

She shook hands with his grandfather, who introduced himself as Toby, and then Kit's mum enveloped her in another huge hug. 'I'm Jackie, dear,' she said. 'Right, tea!' She bustled out of the room, looking giddy with excitement. Then Luella met his older cousins and his Uncle Tom, and dad, Daniel.

Kit leaned into Luella as she sat down beside him at what was clearly the sofa end of honour, beside Toby's chair. It had its own little side table for teacups, and a plate of biscuits laid out already.

'Muuuuuum,' shouted Kayla, one of the little girls, 'now we've had a look at Kit's new girlfriend, like you said, can we go out and play Ninja Warrior round the orchard?'

'She's not my girlfriend,' Kit muttered, flushing.

Oh, aren't I? thought Luella, keeping her face carefully neutral. Well, it was the truth, she supposed. For a moment, she questioned what she was *actually doing* there. Had she misunderstood what this visit was all about? But then she reminded herself of all the kissing, and the look on his face as he'd rushed out to greet her. No, it was OK. It didn't matter what they were calling the thing between them. They were solid.

'Yes, you may,' Helena was saying. She looked to Kit's older cousins, boys, who were about fourteen and twelve. 'You go with them – make sure we don't end up in Minor Injuries like last time. There's good lads.' She smiled at Luella, shaking her head. 'And, by the way, I did not say we were coming over to *have a look* at you.'

'But you diiiiiiid,' protested the other girl, and Helena stood and shooed the four kids out of the room, looking a little embarrassed.

Jackie came back with the tea and Luella leaped up to help, handing the filled cups and saucers round and offering biscuits. She'd rather be busy than sitting there on display trying to think of things to say. Kit seemed to relax a bit then, giving her a warm smile, and she did too.

'So, I hear the dressage is going well?' That was Kit's grandfather, Toby. His cup shook a little as he lifted it to his lips. Luella guessed that he was about eighty.

'Yes, it is, thank you for asking. It's all down to your grandson, really. Charlie and I were technically pretty good, but we were struggling with connection and flow.'

'He's got a way with horses, that's for sure,' said Toby. 'Just like my father did, and his father before him.'

Luella smiled. 'He does indeed,' she said. Kit looked super awkward, which she found adorable.

'He has a bright future ahead of him,' Toby continued. 'A brilliant horse trainer, or a fine polo player, although that's a tough game.'

There was a painful silence. Luella knew they were all thinking the same thing.

'Dad, you know there's some trouble for Kit at the moment,' said Kit's dad. 'Some trouble for us all.'

Jackie glanced anxiously out of the window, presumably to make sure the kids were playing and not listening in.

Toby waved this away with a shaking hand. 'Troubles blow over. Sometimes as quickly as they blow up. There have been Pearces working on this estate for nigh on three hundred years and we'll be here for another three hundred.'

'We really might not be,' said Jackie.

Toby ignored this and gave Luella a piercing look. 'Take it from one who's been around a few years,' he said. 'Lots of things change. But some stay the same, because that's the way they're meant to be. Destined.'

She smiled at him, and from the corner of her eye she saw an anxious glance pass between Kit's mum and dad. 'Some of us can be mystical, and some of us need to be practical,' said Kit's dad sternly. 'This is a bad business. Our Kit's done nothing wrong, but folk round here aren't interested in giving the benefit of the doubt. It may be better for us to jump before we're pushed. Jasper was round here yesterday, sleazy little toerag that he is.'

'Not a patch on his father,' Kit's uncle muttered.

'Laying it on thick. Profits in the farm shop are way down. If people lose trust in the Balfour Estate, and if they lose their reputation as a top-quality polo yard, our friends and neighbours' jobs will be at stake, and that's all on us.'

Luella had kept quiet that far, but she found herself protesting, 'But it's *not* on you! Kit didn't do anything wrong. This is so unfair! Jasper should be standing up for him, not coming round here putting pressure on you all. And if I hear anyone else round the village say "*no smoke without fire*", I'm going to bloody kill them!' She came to a sudden stop and glanced around the room at the stunned faces. 'Well, that's what I think, anyway,' she mumbled, and sat down again.

There was a moment's silence and then, the tension broken, they all smiled and laughed. 'You tell 'em, lass!' said Kit's dad approvingly.

'She's a keeper,' said Jackie to Kit, making him blush again.

As chat broke out around her, about this year's wheat and barley harvest, and farm tariffs, and the football, Kit caught her eye and they shared a deep, intense look, full of connection and understanding. She wanted to slide across, sit on his lap and kiss his face off. But instead she let her arm push against his as she sipped her tea and vowed to do whatever she could to clear his name. They *had* to find out who had really poisoned Willow, they just *had* to.

The Pearces couldn't be forced to leave.

It wasn't fair, and it wasn't right. And it was happening over her dead body.

Chapter Twenty-One

Bex

Lunch with the Balfours. Bex would rather have had her fingernails pulled out, slowly, one by one, obviously (the food, the company, the ugly garden furniture . . .) but, on the other hand, it was a huge opportunity to further her plans for her shiny new future. And a great chance to take her red halter-neck sundress out for a spin, too, and show off her tanned, toned shoulders.

She was sitting next to Alfonso – it wasn't a date as such, and there hadn't been a repeat of the shed incident, but they'd been flirting on the yard over the previous few days, and he'd invited her to come. Bex had been waiting in her car until she'd seen him cross the driveway. She'd wanted them to walk in together and look as couply as possible, really get her foot in the door. Get some more material for social media as well – the stills and video she'd posted of them together on the yard had got the most likes and comments she'd ever had, a lot of which were asking her about whether they were an item.

There was a lot to be said for Alfonso. For one thing, he was a great trainer. For another, he was hot AF. He was helping her profile. Plus, he was her best bet for a seat at the Balfour table (in this case, *literally*). Barnaby hated her, after all – even as she'd sat down the loathing had been rolling off him in waves. It would have put her off her roast vegetables, if she hadn't been put off already – they were swimming in olive oil and had the texture of slugs. And she barely knew Felicity. The girl seemed to be eating at the kids' table anyway, playing with the annoying offspring of some distant Balfour cousins who were visiting. There were fourteen for lunch, in all, including dour Eric.

As Jasper launched into another anecdote about his heroics on the polo field back in the day, Bex stopped herself from rolling her eyes and arranged her face into a mask of rapt attention. *Networking*, she told herself. *Keep your eyes on the prize and just wash down the sluggy veg with lots of Pimm's.*

She hadn't had any offers to play as a pro, basically a gun for hire, on any teams so far. She was considered too young and inexperienced for that. But she was planning to take several giant leaps up the ladder in the coming weeks. The season ran until late September, so there was plenty of time to turn her fortunes around – and she was sure she'd be the hot ticket once she wowed everyone by playing for the Balfour team in the prestigious Guillards Cup. After that, when the offers started pouring in, she'd get a few grand whenever she played. It was pocket money really and hardly going to make a dent in the family situation but, still, it was a step in the right direction. More importantly, she'd be building her reputation as the new, young face of British polo. That road was paved with riches – sponsorship, networking and business opportunities, as well as celebrity status.

She flashed a smile at Eric as Jasper finally finished his skull-crushingly boring anecdote. She'd had no luck building rapport with the staid business manager. It was like trying to build a relationship with a jump stand. She planned to win favour with Ronan Blake, who was choosing between the Balfour and Langdon Estates to host huge business conferences, which would mean the building of a dedicated centre, and accommodation, so lots of guaranteed, year-round income. That was a big enough pie to turn things around for her family. A building contract for one of her father's property companies would be a nice slice, for a start. Jasper stopped hogging the floor for a moment to stuff his face with more garlic bread, and conversation broke out around the table.

Alfonso rested his leg against hers under the table and she didn't move it. Her heart pounded in her chest and her lips curved into a genuine smile. She had been hoping he'd make a move like that, in the direction of another make-out session. Although they'd flirted, she hadn't wanted to look desperate, and she'd left it to him to follow that up. Which he hadn't, until that moment. But now, it was *game on*.

'You look lovely today,' he said.

Bex gave him a demure smile. 'Thank you.' She paused. *Go on, you know he's waiting to hear it.* 'You look very nice, too. I love your shirt. Givenchy is always a good choice for summer chic.'

He was pleased. Why were men so easy to manipulate? 'I have one in each fabric,' he said.

Her smile flickered. Still *off the peg* then. Not bespoke.

Barnaby leaned back in his chair and snorted, amused, pushing his dark brown curls back from his eyes. 'I've *been there*, mate. I wouldn't recommend it,' he said to Alfonso.

'You *wish*,' said Bex smoothly. Obviously she'd never admit that she got with him the year before, when trying to make Freddie jealous.

Delia turned in their direction suddenly, breaking off her conversation with Eric and a Balfour cousin mid flow. 'Barnaby, be civil to our guest, please.'

He bristled, being told off like that in front of everyone, like he was a kid. Felicity flicked her head up from the game of snakes and ladders she was playing with the three little brats at the add-on table. Bex noticed her quiet delight at her brother being embarrassed by their mum. Seemed like there was no love lost between them.

When she put her glass down, Alfonso held her hand, right there on the table for everyone to see. She flicked a smile at him and drew his fingers to her lips and kissed them. The lunch was going very well indeed.

'When are you going to bring a date to lunch, son?' roared Jasper suddenly, making everyone turn in his direction.

Delia reached over Eric and patted Barnaby on the arm. 'Yes, when? When are you going to find yourself a nice boy or girl?'

Barnaby just shrugged and returned his focus to Bex. 'You know, we can't get enough staff for my bash, Bex . . . Well, we have Clarissa, obviously, and some bods from the catering company, but I want everyone to be well catered for and we need a couple more. It would be awful if anyone had to wait for champagne – if I see a glass empty, I'll die of embarrassment.'

She braced. What was he up to?

'Horrendous,' agreed a Balfour cousin, and Delia added, 'Unthinkable. We want everything to be perfect for your special night, darling. Even though us oldies won't be there cramping your style, of course.'

'Maybe *Bex* knows someone?' Barnaby said pointedly.

Her breath caught in her throat. He was sniffing round the money thing, letting her know he suspected something. Suggesting she needed work.

Don't crack.

Just then, her phone buzzed discreetly, the perfect distraction.

'Excuse me.' She picked it up and looked at it, right there at the table. She'd never have done that at the Langdons' but the Balfours were all on their phones at the table half the time. Freddie had sent her a funny snap of Willow shaking her head, tongue flying about. *We miss you over here, mate*, it read. *No hard feelings.*

She felt a pang of pain in her heart but shoved it down. He was only being nice – she'd been far too rude to everyone there for any of them to miss her, and the way she'd left had been appalling, she knew. She'd meant to speak to Freddie, and Lord and Lady L, and thank them properly for everything they'd done for her over the years. But when it had come to it, she just couldn't. She'd convinced herself at the time that she was like some city big shot, getting headhunted and having to jump ship without warning. But she knew deep down that that wasn't true. She'd just been cowardly and at a loss for what to tell them. Going to their worst rivals. And so publicly. It was unthinkable, and yet she'd done it.

She put her phone face down. Suddenly, she missed the whole Langdon world terribly. She hated being at the Balfours. A stabbing fury shot right through her. How dare Carrie Brent just walk right into their lives and ruin everything?

Before she could stop herself, she glanced up, met Barnaby's gaze and said, 'Actually, I know a girl who might be interested – she certainly needs the cash. Carrie Brent.' She was interested to see Barnaby look up sharply at the name, blush a bit and then try to look neutral. So, he liked Carrie? *Interesting.*

Delia and Jasper missed it completely. They laughed, catching eyes across the table. 'Oh, darling Bex, we thought you meant *you* for a moment!' Delia giggled.

Everyone laughed then, Bex the loudest, to show she was a good sport. She felt raw, though, and deep in her chest there was an undercurrent of panic. She *did* need the cash. If only they knew.

'I've seen that Carrie at the polo a couple of times,' Barnaby said, trying to sound casual. 'Good-looking girl.'

Chavvy-looking girl, Bex corrected, in her mind. She'd enjoy watching Carrie working hard, running round serving them all, while they partied. That would take her down a peg or two.

'Does she have waitressing experience?' asked a Balfour cousin.

'Oh, yes,' Bex fibbed.

'I have exacting standards,' said Barnaby, 'but she looks good and that's a start.'

'Oh, have you got your eye on her, darling?' asked Delia, finally catching on, and looking ridiculously hopeful.

'As if,' said Barnaby. 'She's not on our level, socially, and she hasn't got a penny to her name.'

Delia beamed and squeezed his arm, leaning right across Eric's Eton mess. Bex saw him hide a grimace. 'Fall in love with whomever you like, darling,' she said. 'Boy or girl, we don't care, so long as they're rich, high status and useful to the family.'

At that moment, Bex felt like she was in a viper's nest. If only they knew her true situation. It wasn't about breeding or family history with them, which could never be taken from her by 'bad deals' or incompetent parents. It was about cold hard cash. And 'high status' didn't mean titles and a falling-down manor house. It meant business contacts and opportunities.

Alfonso squeezing her hand brought her back to the present – she'd all but forgotten he was there. She forced herself to smile at him, then rested her knee against his under the table again and tried to choke back the Eton mess, which felt claggy and rancid in her mouth.

Chapter Twenty-Two

Carrie

The next morning, a sunny Saturday, Carrie was up and out on the yard bright and early for her shift. Then, after a quick break, she tacked up Bounty, chatting with Beatrice and Heather as they got Hombre and Blaze ready to take out for exercise. She was going with them up to First Field and then meeting Luella at the gate by the lane. Lu had messaged and suggested a picnic ride together, saying she'd bring everything in a backpack. Carrie had been looking forward to it all through the long, hot morning shift – riding was absolute paradise to her, and it would be good to spend some time with Luella. They'd both been so busy lately – her on the yard and Lu with Charlie's dressage training.

Just as Beatrice had given her a leg up to swing into the saddle, Freddie came riding up from the back stables on Willow. Her stomach tightened. They still hadn't talked about the kiss. And he still hadn't asked her out on a date. She wondered if he planned to just act like the whole thing had never happened. He was bothered about the rules, after all.

You should be too, she told herself sternly. And yes, she was. She really felt that her future horsey career was at the Langdon Estate. But she couldn't stop thinking about him. She fiddled with the chinstrap of the embarrassing Disney princess hat, pretending it needed adjusting, and wished she was invisible.

'All good?' he called.

'Hay's coming at three,' said Heather. 'And yep, all good.'

'You off out?' asked Beatrice.

'Riding out with a friend,' he told her, and then trotted Willow away. 'Catch you later!'

Carrie's stomach twisted. She still didn't look at him or speak. What, a *girl* friend? Maybe he'd hated their kiss. Maybe he'd realised in that moment that he wasn't actually attracted to her.

Heather mounted and they all headed off out of the yard, Freddie already way ahead of them. She focused on looking forward to seeing Luella – they always had fun, and they could take out their frustrations on some fallen logs. Lu was teaching her a bit of jumping now, when they rode out, and Bounty loved it.

At the top of the track she peeled off and headed to the far gate of First Field, where it joined a country lane and gave on to a bridleway. It was the perfect route for their Saturday afternoon ride with a shady wood along the way and a pond where the horses could get a drink and they could eat and chill. She spotted a horse and rider in the far distance, right at the gate. 'Oh, I can see her.'

'Great! See you later then,' said Heather.

Carrie smiled warmly at her and then at Beatrice. They'd both been so good to her. She told herself sternly to start counting her blessings and stop moping over Freddie. 'Thanks, you guys, I really do appreciate everything you do for me.'

They beamed at each other. 'You're welcome,' said Heather. 'You've got a real talent with horses, Carrie.'

'Yeah, we love having you on the team,' said Beatrice.

She said goodbye to the grooms and trotted Bounty over the field, but as she neared the figure, she was confused. Taller than Lu, and broader, and the horse was the wrong colour . . .

Not Luella.

Freddie freaking Langdon.

As she reached him, he looked just as surprised to see her. Suddenly, he laughed out loud. 'Luella!' he roared.

Carrie finally understood, and a shocked smile spread over her face. 'She's set us up, hasn't she?'

'The cheeky mare,' he said, shaking his head and smiling. 'I'll have words with her about this later.'

At that moment Carrie's phone buzzed.

Luella

Lovely day for a ride ☺

Luella

PS. There's a note on the gate showing you where to find the picnic basket x

Carrie looked at Freddie, her cheeks feeling suddenly warm. 'She's made us a picnic, but it's OK if you don't want to go . . .' She tried to sound like she didn't care either way, but her breath caught in her throat. She'd actually roll off Bounty and have a tantrum if he said no.

He shrugged. 'Why not? It's that or a pasty from the yard fridge – and I'm not sure how long it's been there, to be honest. This could be saving me from a serious case of the shits.'

Carrie cackled in surprise. 'Oh my God, gross! So unromantic!'

He caught her gaze and held it for a moment. 'Am I *meant* to be being romantic, then?'

She blushed. *Damn! How had that slipped out?* He expertly leg-yielded Willow right up to the gate and pulled off Luella's note. 'According to this, all manner of luxury is waiting for us at this location in the woods.' He held up the map and instructions.

Carrie's heart melted for her friend. 'Aw, she's put a little X to mark the spot and everything!'

'And five massive red arrows, in felt tip,' Freddie pointed out, scrunching the map into his jeans pocket. 'She obviously thinks we're complete morons. Come on then, tally ho.' And with that he opened the gate and held it for her while she walked Bounty out into the lane.

Freddie was riding beside her, relaxed, Willow's reins in one hand and his legs hanging down, the stirrups crossed over the saddle. *Don't look*, she told herself sternly. *Or at least, don't stare. Definitely do not drool.* 'Luella's so much happier without Bex in her life, you know.'

Shit, where had that come from? Why had she mentioned Bex? *Total buzzkill.* Now she was flustered, imagining the many times he'd hooked up with her, and clearly he was too. He cleared his throat. 'You should know, there's nothing going on between us,' he said briskly, then he suddenly became very interested in the bushes beside them. 'And I was clear with her that nothing would happen ever again.'

Carrie's heart did backflips of celebration. Why was he saying this now? Yes, she and Freddie had kissed. But they weren't a couple. They hadn't even been on a proper date. Luella setting them up didn't count. 'We're not a thing,' Carrie pushed, taking a risk. 'So, if you wanted you could see other people.'

She held her breath.

'I *don't* want to,' said Freddie firmly.

She breathed out, her shoulders dropped about two inches down from around her ears and Bounty relaxed too. OK, so he hadn't said, 'I only want to see *you*,' but as good as.

He glanced at her. Was that almost . . . shyly? 'Do *you* want to see other people?' he asked.

She smiled, deliberately training her gaze on the grassy slope ahead of her. 'No.'

'Well, that's good then,' he said. She risked a glance at him and their eyes locked, intense.

After a heartbeat, they both looked away, and Carrie tried to calm the intensity in her stomach and the buzz in her head. 'Yes, very good,' she said.

They rode on in silence, Carrie enjoying the chemistry between them and stealing glances at Freddie's sexy hips swaying with Willow's walking rhythm. They neared the brow of the hill and the woods came into view. 'Bingo, we have trees,' said Freddie.

They brought the horses to a halt. She smiled at him and the smile turned a little flirty, and he shot one back. She was hungry and looking forward to seeing what was in Luella's picnic. And she couldn't help wondering if anything would happen between her and Freddie.

Soon they had followed their map to a Fortnum's wicker hamper, sitting elegantly on a tree-stump. They dismounted, gave their horses a long drink at the pond nearby and then tied them up with enough room to snuffle about on the ground.

Carrie gasped as Freddie opened the hamper. She was all too aware of how close to her he was standing. He was warm from the ride and he looked and smelled delicious. So did the dainty sandwiches, posh sausage rolls, grapes, blinis and tiny strawberry tarts. There was even cream, in a little ice box, and plates, and a red checked cloth to sit on. 'Oh, cute! Carrots for Willow and Bounty too!'

'Full marks, Luella!' said Freddie. 'No champagne, of course.' He gestured at the horses. 'We're driving. But still – some bubbly, and glasses.'

He poured them each a glass of the sparkling elderflower, which had stayed chilled in a special sleeve, and they clinked their glasses together. 'To friendship,' he said. 'Cheers.'

Carrie felt bold. 'To more than that, I hope,' she said, getting her flirt on and turning it up to eleven.

Freddie smiled. 'I meant, to our good friend Luella, but there we go.'

She blushed furiously and wished that the ground would open and swallow her up. 'Oh! Yes, of course! To Luella, cheers!' She tried to style it out and take an elegant sip of her fizz. But she was so flustered it turned into a glug and she choked a bit and had to concentrate very hard not to spit it out while coughing with her mouth clamped shut. Freddie looked concerned but she waved him away, managing to swallow the drink. *Way to go, Carrie*, she thought to herself. *I bet he thinks you're the height of sophistication now.*

But Freddie didn't seem to mind. He swept her up in his strong arms and kissed her hard, crushing her lips to his. She kissed him back, and soon they were moving together, his hands round her waist and hers squeezing his shoulders, running down his spine, pushing into the waistband of his jeans. They fell to the woodland floor, on to soft moss and ferns.

It was lucky the cream was chilled, because they didn't get up again for a very, very long time . . .

'Urgh! Make it end already! Just pick one!'

Kit sighed dramatically and threw himself on to the pile of discarded dresses on Luella's bed. Carrie was sitting on what must have been the world's most expensive beanbag – who knew Bottega Veneta made them? A month or so ago she wouldn't even have known who Bottega Veneta *were*. She'd learned a lot from being friends with Luella. And had a lot of laughs too. And with Kit.

She smiled to herself as Kit thrashed about like he was trying to swim his way to freedom through Luella's clothes. Luella clearly wasn't impressed. She handed Carrie the cobalt silk evening gown she was holding up and pulled him upright by the back of his shirt. 'Hey, careful! Those are my favourite dresses!'

He groaned but let her hands linger on his waist, Carrie noticed. 'Oh, right – except that they're all too long or too short or too busty or too prim or too yellow or too tight or too floaty or . . .'

Lu glared at him and wrestled him backwards on to the bed. 'Yes, they are, you cheeky sod!' she shrieked. 'They're all wrong for the party! Aren't they, Carrie?'

Oh, you've remembered I exist then? thought Carrie wryly, but she didn't mind. She was happy for her friends. Although, as Kit fought back and pinned Luella down on the pile of clothes, crying, 'Submit, submit!' she couldn't help saying, 'Guys, get a room already!'

'We have, and you're in it,' grunted Kit, as Luella fought back, giggling.

Eventually, they both sat up, and then Luella pushed him back down again and laughed. 'OK, no, Carrie's right. Time for some girl time.'

Kit sat up, grinned and folded his arms. 'Excellent. I'll watch. Is there popcorn?'

Luella swept up the cobalt dress from Carrie's lap and threw it at him. 'Not that kind of girl time. Perv.' She heaved him up off the bed. 'Go on, off you go. You weren't helping anyway.'

Kit laughed. 'Thank God! Freedom! And as for the party, I'm looking forward to Operation Expose The Balfours As The Crims They Are.'

Luella snorted. 'That's a longwinded name for it!'

Carrie recapped their plan. 'Get access to the study in the Balfour house – try to find out about this conference centre business deal, or anything that proves any one of them is linked to poisoning Willow, including Eric.'

'Yep, like I said, there should be some files in there,' said Kit. 'Maybe on the laptop, although I don't know the password so let's hope not. Jasper's old-fashioned – there should be papers.' Luella and Carrie had told him about the apple core, of course, and their thoughts had turned to the Balfours. Jasper, Delia and Barnaby were all prime suspects – and Eric, of course. Seeing what they could find out about the property deal made sense too, given that the Langdons and the Balfours were going head to head for it.

'Freddie's going to die when he sees you as a hot waitress,' said Luella.

'He won't, because he won't be coming,' Carrie said. 'He's the last person Barnaby would invite. Which is sad for me, but good in a way – we don't need him working out what we're up to and blowing our cover. He's so straightforward, if he thought Barnaby had anything to do with poisoning Willow he'd want to have it out man to man. I haven't even told him I'm going to be there.'

'It's good that Freddie's kept his distance from *me*,' said Kit, his jaw set. 'If he'd come up mouthing off about the rumours . . .'

'He's angry that it happened, but he doesn't believe you could have done it,' said Carrie.

'Then he's a good guy,' said Kit, relaxing. 'Carrie, you have my blessing to marry him and have many, many children.'

She gasped in mock horror and made a swipe for him. He ducked out of the way and said, 'See you later, girls, I'll see myself out.' He pulled Luella into his arms and kissed her full on the lips.

When he'd gone, she was left standing there hugging herself, blushing, which Carrie thought was kind of sweet. '*Oh, I wish Kit was my boyfriend,*' she said, copying Luella's stance.

Luella looked even more flustered. 'How do you know?'

Carrie grinned. 'It's blatantly obvious.'

Luella threw herself down on to the pile of dresses. 'We're on kissing terms, now, and we're not seeing anyone else. So I guess we're dating, kind of. But yes, I want us to be boyfriend and girlfriend. Coupled up. Kuella. Lit. And I don't care how old-fashioned that is.'

'I think it's sweet,' said Carrie.

'And you?' asked Luella, fixing her with a knowing glare. 'Picnic went well, I gather? Now Kit's gone you can spill the details.'

'The strawberry tarts were very nice, thank you,' Carrie said evasively. She felt close to Luella but she'd never been one to talk about the actual details of making out with someone. She forced herself to open up a bit more. 'And so was the kissing and ... more ...'

Luella sat bolt upright and shrieked in delight. Carrie felt a sudden rush of love for her and hugged her tight. 'Thank you, again, Lady Cupid!'

'So, do you want to *be* with Freddie?' Luella asked. 'As a couple?'

Carrie wouldn't let herself think about that. Going down the boyfriend–girlfriend road, with how tricky the work situation was, would only lead to hurt and heartache. Who knew if Freddie even wanted that anyway? 'We're just having fun,' she said. 'And neither of us is going to see anyone else. So . . . we'll see where it goes.'

'Well, that's good enough for Lady Cupid today,' said Luella, with satisfaction. 'Now, we might be able to think without the cloud of testosterone in the room.' She surveyed the pile on the bed and pulled out a red satin evening dress and a light, floral sundress. 'This one or this one?'

Carrie popped some Candy Kittens from the packet on Luella's desk into her mouth and chewed slowly, considering. She pointed at one dress then the other. 'Shagging him senseless or meeting his mother.'

'Carrie!' Luella cried and Carrie snorted with laughter and almost swallowed a sweet whole. Luella gave her a stern look and held up the cobalt evening gown. 'Middle ground?'

Carrie nodded. 'Gorgeous.' Even though Freddie wasn't going to the party, she had a feeling that it would be a night to remember.

Chapter Twenty-Three
Luella

'The polo set don't muck about when it comes to parties,' said Luella, as she sipped at the champagne she'd just taken from Carrie's tray.

'You're not kidding,' Carrie replied. Barnaby's birthday party was like a movie set. There was an ice sculpture, a huge tower of vodka shots, a table groaning with food, including a whole lobster, huge sides of smoked salmon, caviar and a big bubbling cheese fondue, strangely.

Luella saw her peering at it. 'He wanted all his favourite foods, apparently, and he's spent a lot of time après-ski all over the world.'

Carrie rolled her eyes. 'Course he has. Hey, lucky I got on champagne duty.' She snuck a glass for herself with a cheeky smile. Many of the other waiting staff were going round with trays of delicate canapés. 'I didn't fancy trying to keep those tiny roast beef things on the tray. You look amazing, by the way.'

Luella swished the cobalt dress a little. 'Why, thank you. And thanks for doing my make-up – I love it.'

'You're welcome. It's a shame I look so gross, but never mind, all in service of clearing Kit's name.'

Luella didn't bother to protest. Bex had had Carrie sent the vilest, most hideous, scratchiest waitress uniform ever, far worse than the other girls' ones. But it was cool that Carrie didn't care. Carrie was cool, full stop. 'She'll be sorry when it's so damn itchy I pull the whole thing off and just serve the drinks in my hot-pink lace underwear and this little white apron.'

Luella laughed and they smiled at each other. Kit had asked her to the party as a date after Carrie had gone home. But she'd said no. She'd known Bex would be here – guaranteed. She was the new darling of the Balfour family, apparently, and dating that vain plank of wood, their star pro, Alfonso. As much as she hated to admit it, she still really cared what Bex thought.

She hoped once again that Kit had bought the fact that they were digging into the Balfours as the reason she'd said no to being his date. She'd got a thumbs up emoji as a reply. What did that mean?

'Oops, the boss is watching.' Barnaby was gesturing at Carrie, so she put her empty glass down on a side table and got back to work. A moment later, there were whispers and furtive glances towards the ballroom doors.

Kit had walked in. On his own. With those awful rumours flying about. Urgh. That must have been horrible for him. Why had she only thought of herself and what Bex would say if they arrived together? How selfish *was* she exactly?

While she was still berating herself, he made a beeline for her. He looked pissed off. *Very* pissed off. 'So, you want to be with me in private, and even meet my family, but you can't be seen with me in public.'

It wasn't a question. It was a statement. A challenge. She narrowed her eyes at him, friendly, trying to keep it light, but her heart was pounding. 'It's just, we're not really here to party, we're here as a team with Carrie, to snoop.' She stepped forward to hug him, but he stepped back. She hated to be at odds with him, it felt awful. She sighed. 'OK, I admit it. I do still care what Bex thinks about me seeing you. A bit. She's been my best friend for years. For most of my life. We've been through so much together. I can't just . . .' She trailed off and stared hard at the food table.

Kit said nothing. *Well, this was fun.*

She gestured to where Sims and Hugo were getting stuck into the fondue. Hugo had a wheelchair by the door, and was on crutches, his leg pinned into the external fixator. 'Good to see Hugo out and about again.' Then she felt cringingly tactless, but she couldn't act like Hugo didn't exist. They were friends, after all.

'You don't have to be awkward,' said Kit, giving her a stony look. 'I didn't *do anything* to him.'

She waffled on to move away from the subject. 'I hadn't thought they'd be invited – like me, they're Team Langdon through and through. But I guess Barnaby wanted a crowd, and to rub it in Freddie's face that all his friends were here and not him.'

'I guess,' said Kit flatly, as if he couldn't care less. 'Anyway, I'm going to the bar.'

Luella threw her hands up as he walked off. 'Great! Glad this is going so well – and yeah, I'd love a Dark and Stormy, thanks for asking! The drink, I mean – not *you*!' He hadn't even said she looked nice. She knew she didn't have a leg to stand on, though, really. It was fair enough that he was upset with her. She saw Carrie over by the food, chatting with Sims and Hugo. She could go and join them, but then Kit would have to hang out on his own.

Just then Bex made a fabulous entrance on the arm of Alfonso, with Venetia and Aurelia flanking her like bridesmaids, or covert security guards. There was another ripple around the room, but this time of admiration and excitement. Bex Chapman-Foster was here – now the party could really get started.

Bex pointedly looked the other way as she swept past Luella in something both classy and incredibly sexy, Yves Saint Laurent, she guessed. A public snub. She tried to shrink into the wall behind her – she felt even more of a lemon standing by herself now that most heads were turned in her direction. Fortunately Carrie was beside her moments later, and she gratefully took another glass of champagne. Bex swept Carrie over with a disparaging gaze and smirked. Carrie gripped the tray and managed not to hurl it at her. Kit returned with a coke, as he was driving, looking slightly less furious with Luella – but only slightly.

'Right,' said Carrie, sneaking some more champagne, 'you need to find a way to get upstairs and have a snoop around Barnaby's room without it looking suspicious. Then do the Balfours' room if you have time, but I doubt they keep anything in there.'

Luella snorted. 'Just some dodgy porn and a load of horrible sex toys probably.'

Carrie shuddered. 'Urgh, don't!' and Kit smiled – a little, at least. 'I'll get the key for the study somehow – probably via Barnaby,' Carrie continued. 'No idea how yet but I'll think of something.' She glanced at him, dancing in a lairy way, arms round two of his schoolmates. 'It's helpful that he's getting hammered.'

'What excuse is there for me going upstairs and disappearing for ages with *her*?' Kit drawled, giving Luella a contemptuous look.

Carrie winked at him, clearly not reading the current vibe. 'You'll think of something.' Her eyes flicked upwards, indicating the bedrooms.

Kit didn't look keen and neither did Luella. 'I could throw a drink over him and he'd have to go and find the bathroom, rinse his shirt out,' she offered, her voice edgy. '*If* he'd bought me one.'

'If I'd come here as her date, I might have done,' Kit replied, coldly.

Carrie sighed and emptied her glass. 'Come on, guys, take one for the team. And Willow, and Hugo. Get your flirt on and draw everyone's attention.'

Luella sighed deeply and Kit glared at her.

'Fine.'

'Fine.'

Carrie hurried off again and Kit and Luella grudgingly made a pretence of flirting. Softening and leaning towards each other. Nudging arms. Laughing loudly together. Whispering into each other's ears. Luella felt a shiver of desire run up her spine as her lips brushed the skin of Kit's neck. His warmth, his smell, his solid, sexy body beside her. She let herself revel in it for a moment, before pulling away, doing another big fake laugh and batting at his chest. 'Ow!' he cried. It was meant to be flirtatious, but she'd done it a little too hard, in her annoyance.

People were looking, and nudging, nodding and whispering. If there was one thing that the Yetbourne young polo set loved, it was a bit of gossip and a bit of romance – and this one had the extra bonus of being tainted by a whiff of scandal too.

Kit made a big show of whispering something in Luella's ear and began to pull her by the hand from the room. She made a thing of looking all coy and then followed him. Together they cut a swathe through the guests, causing a ripple of interest as they went.

They walked up the stairs together in silence, more people clocking them along the way. Then, in full view of a group of Barnaby's rugby mates, Kit threw his arm around her and ushered her into one of the bedrooms.

'Don't think you're coming anywhere near me!' said Luella vehemently, as soon as the door was shut.

Kit snorted. 'It must have just about killed you to pretend-flirt in front of your precious Bex. *Oh, what must everyone think!*'

His impression of her was so mean that the words just popped out of her mouth. 'Fuck you!'

Kit looked startled. 'If anyone's saying *fuck you*, I should be saying *fuck you*!'

'Well, I should be saying *fuck you* more,' she replied, incensed. '*Fuck you, fuck you, fuck you!*'

'Well, I say *fuck you* to your *fuck you* and I raise you a *fuck you*!' he snarled.

It was almost funny. *If* she'd allow herself to let go of her fury for a moment. Kit had a smile playing at the corners of his lips.

Luella couldn't help herself – she laughed and shook her head. 'You know, they all think we're kissing in here. We'll have to pretend that's what we've been doing when we come out.'

Suddenly Kit was sweeping her up into his powerful arms and crushing her body to his. And just before the deepest, sexiest, hottest, most connected kiss of her life, he said, 'Why pretend?'

Chapter Twenty-Four

Bex

Well, *that gave them all something to look at.* It was only a local Yetbourne crowd, but some of Barnaby's set were influencers. Bex had also invited a few people herself – signing it off with Delia, of course, rather than the birthday boy, who detested her.

She'd got bloggers Jen and Anton, socialite Jemima and Finn, formerly Carl, who had the style insider thing on Insta because they worked as a fashion PR. She'd made clear to them that the only reason they were there was to take pictures and social media the shit out of how amazing she looked. And she'd brought Venetia and Aurelia along too, for her big entrance. They did nothing useful but were pretty, rich and connected enough to make her look good, but not pretty, rich and connected enough to overshadow her. In fact, they were the perfect amount of pretty, rich and connected, and they weren't shy with the credit cards either, which was a bonus until her save-the-future plan started to yield results.

It was also gratifying that Carrie looked so hideous in the waitress uniform. *I really ought to go and compliment her on it*, Bex thought, with a wicked grin. She swished across the room, turning heads. 'Good evening, Cinders,' she said acidly, arriving at Carrie's side. 'You got to go to the ball. Looks like your Fairy Godmother forgot your dress, though.'

'Good, practical gear,' Carrie said cheerfully.

Annoying.

'Nothing wrong with honest, hard work. Champagne, madam?'

'*God*, no. I've sent my friends off to the bar to find me something interesting – I'm not drinking nasty, lukewarm Balfour champagne for anyone, especially not from *your* tray. You do hang out with a suspected poisoner, after all.'

'Oh, I wouldn't bother poisoning you, Bex.' Her tone was edgy.

Ha, I've riled her, thought Bex.

'I'd just wrap this tray round your head.' Carrie stepped closer, right into her face.

Bex refused to let herself step back this time, holding her ground. 'If you'll excuse me, I need to get back to my date.'

Carrie smirked, locating Alfonso across the room. He was holding court in a small group of hot young women. They were hanging on his every word. 'Looks like he's doing fine without you.'

Bex followed her gaze, felt a sharp sting of embarrassment, and went on the attack. 'Scuttle back to your scullery,' she sneered. 'And enjoy the high life while you can – or serving champagne to it, anyway. You won't last long in Yetbourne.'

Carrie looked intensely at her. 'Is that a threat?'

Bex smiled sweetly. The kind of 'sweetly' that could put a person into a diabetic coma and was potentially fatal. 'Just an observation.'

She took a glass from the tray, sipped at the champagne and grimaced. 'Throw this swill away and open something decent, for God's sake, would you? And make sure it's properly chilled.' With that she swayed off, putting on a smile as she did – it was a much-needed skill round here – the emotional U-turn. She was glad to see that Carrie, a total amateur at it, still looked furious. Even better, the girl turned round and banged straight into Barnaby, who started drunkenly telling her off for slacking. *Excellent.* Bex just had to rescue poor Alfonso from that pit of boring hangers-on and it would be a perfect evening.

However, half an hour later, Bex wasn't smiling, despite Venetia's excellent choice of a pomegranate martini followed by a strawberry no-jito. She was pacing herself – she was here to further her plans, network and see if any opportunities arose. And to watch Carrie make a mess of things.

Unfortunately, Carrie was whipping the other young staff into shape and getting the service moving. She'd taken the telling-off from Barnaby well and was now in turbo mode. She was here, there and everywhere, being charming and attentive to all the guests, but not unprofessional. She'd changed the music to something cool and street, which had taken the party up another level. Even Bex's own friends were up and dancing – traitors – and the vibe was getting higher and higher with each track.

The bitch. She hated that Carrie knew about her family's financial situation too, and about two of her horses being sold. The fact that Carrie hadn't used it against her yet didn't mean anything. That she'd promised not to tell anyone, and specifically not Luella, didn't mean anything either. *She could bring my world crashing down at any moment*, Bex thought, her stomach lurching. *She's probably just enjoying the power she has over me.*

Another half an hour later, Barnaby was whirling Carrie round the dance floor, while she drank straight from a bottle of champagne, something totally rock and roll that Bex had always wanted to do but knew she couldn't pull off. And she was still directing the staff, her hawk-eye trained on what was coming out of the kitchen.

Then Hugo and Sims parted the crowd to join her. She'd heard on the grapevine that Luella and Carrie had visited Hugo in hospital and played polo with Freddie and Sims. There was still no sign of Luella and Kit. *Having sex at a party – tacky*. Not that she hadn't done it herself, but that was different – she'd been *subtle*. Her stomach twisted. Was the old gang getting back together, but with Carrie in *her* place? That would be the last straw.

Alfonso appeared back in the circle with the Moscow Mule she'd asked for, and she snapped that it didn't have enough lime and made him return it. It was the worst evening ever. The absolute worst.

But just then, very unexpectedly, things got much better. Freddie Langdon walked in and saw his darling Carrie being spun around on the dancefloor by Barnaby Balfour, champagne bottle still in her hand and head thrown back, laughing.

Bex smiled wickedly. Now *this* was a party.

Chapter Twenty-Five

Carrie

Luella and Kit certainly looked a lot perkier when they came back into the ballroom, to a ripple of whispers and turning heads. Carrie spotted them and her heart leaped. She untangled herself from Barnaby and his mates on the dance floor, grabbed a full tray of mini Passionfruit Palomas, which smelled divine, and wound her way over to her friends.

'Drink, sir, madam?' she said, putting on a posh accent. 'You're looking a little in need of refreshment, if I may say so.' She winked.

'Thank you,' said Kit, taking a drink, 'and less chat from the staff would be good.'

Luella drained her glass in one go while still managing to look elegant. Carrie signalled to Paula, another of the waitresses, to bring over the tray of chilled mineral water she was carrying. Kit and Luella took a glass each and downed them too. Carrie raised an eyebrow. 'Productive time up there, was it?'

Luella giggled. 'Oh my God! I just realised – everyone probably thinks we're all hot and bothered because we've been having sex!'

'Well, *obviously*,' said Carrie.

Kit laughed. 'They most definitely *are* thinking that. No one opened the door for forty minutes, *because* they were thinking that. At least that's done my reputation some good. I may be a dangerous criminal, but I know how to show a woman a good time.'

Luella slapped him on the arm. 'Kit, stop it!' But she was beaming – and blushing.

Ah, so something did happen. She knew that Luella would tell her all the juicy details when they were alone together. For now, she smiled and said, 'At least you guys aren't mad at each other any more.'

They didn't respond, but a smile passed between them. 'Speaking of which, thanks to the scandalous sex rumours going round about us, we had time to go through Barnaby's room with a fine-tooth comb,' said Luella. 'We couldn't get into his laptop but we did find three very interesting items. They might be something – they might not. We took photos, so he wouldn't know anything had been disturbed.'

'Good work,' said Carrie. They went out on to the terrace, where they could actually hear one another without shouting. Also, there was a bit more privacy and she could cool down a bit. The viscose-tastic hot, itchy waitress uniform was slowly roasting her alive. She put the tray down and helped herself to a Paloma. 'Hmm, as delicious as it smells.'

Luella held up her phone and she peered at it. 'So, we found a Post-it note with a name and number in his wallet.'

'Dudley,' Carrie read, from the phone screen.

'We don't know anyone of that name in Barnaby's circles,' said Kit, 'either from school or the polo scene. But we thought it was weird that he wouldn't just have put the number in his phone, but kept it on a bit of paper.'

Carrie smiled to herself. There was a lot of use of the word *we* going on. *Cute.*

'And then this . . .'

She peered at the screen. It was from the Scottish National Gallery. The postmark was Edinburgh EH4 so looked like it was sent from there too. It wasn't signed by the sender. The message said, *Remembering Venice* in scrawly handwriting, and there were two kisses.

'Sounds romantic,' she said.

'We thought it could be something because it was tucked in behind a photo frame by his bed,' said Lu. She shivered and Kit took off his jacket and put it round her shoulders. She smiled and pulled it round herself, then leaned into him. *Even cuter.*

'Good thinking,' said Carrie, letting the cool evening air wash over her. 'I wish I could just rip this bloody dress off.' She groaned. 'Although, given how stuck to me it is, you might have to cut me out of it with some kitchen scissors. Anyway, it seems like Barnaby may actually care about someone other than himself. Interesting.'

Luella laughed. 'The photo it was hidden behind was of Barnaby on Speech Day, with a huge trophy next to his giant head, you won't be surprised to hear.'

Carrie laughed too. 'He's so full of himself,' she agreed. 'Maybe it's from this Dudley. Like, perhaps he's seeing someone that no one round here knows? But what could that have to do with trying to hurt Willow, or Freddie? We know he was the real target, after all. What else did you find?'

'A paying-in slip stub, for a deposit he made into his bank, for *ten grand*,' said Kit. 'It was inside a book so we thought he'd maybe used it as a marker and then forgotten to dispose of it.'

'Ten grand!' Carrie gasped. 'Oh my God! I'd have to shovel a whole lot of horse poo to make that kind of money! I wonder what it was for?'

'Yeah, and who it was from,' added Kit. 'The stub just says "cheque". Who writes cheques now anyway? There was no name, and just the last four digits of an account number. We were thinking maybe someone elderly, someone who doesn't bank online? Or a trust or company? They send out cheques still.'

Carrie's eyes gleamed. 'Intriguing. Barnaby could have taken a bribe from someone to sabotage the Langdon team, or he could be blackmailing the person who did.'

'Or Mummy just threw him a few grand for a nice holiday,' Luella reasoned.

Carrie shook her head. 'Nope. I think we're on to something here. I feel it in my bones.' Just then she felt a presence, as if someone were right behind her. And electricity. She turned her head to find the last person in the world she expected to see, storming towards them. And he did *not* look happy. She stared at Luella and Kit in panic.

'Freddie!' cried Luella, taking charge, waving. He came over and air-kissed her stiffly. He shook Kit's outstretched hand. He glowered at Carrie and said, 'Why didn't you tell me you'd be here?'

'Because I didn't think you'd find out.' She cringed inwardly. That was true, but it sounded awful. He didn't know they were secretly looking into the Balfours, to try and help Kit.

He glanced at Barnaby and sneered. 'Anything else you didn't think I'd find out?'

She threw Luella a panicked look. 'We'll leave you to it,' Lu said hurriedly, and she and Kit headed back inside.

'I didn't know you were working here,' Freddie said curtly. 'Well, you're not really *working*, are you? You're just hanging out and getting pissed, making a show of yourself with Barnaby Balfour.'

Carrie blushed furiously, which was annoying, as it made her look like she'd done something wrong. She didn't want to tell Freddie about them sneaking around checking out the Balfours. It was too risky. The mood he was in, he'd blow their cover in seconds. Then Kit would be in an even worse situation than he was already. 'He's drunk,' she said. 'We were just dancing. And anyway, I didn't think you were coming.' She cringed. *Shit!* Why couldn't she stop saying incriminating things?! 'Who invited you? Not Barnaby, I'm guessing.'

'He did, actually,' he said coolly. 'About an hour ago. Sims asked him if it was OK, and he was so drunk he said yes, or he didn't hear properly. If you'd checked your phone, you'd have seen I messaged you, to ask if you wanted to come with me. But' – he gestured angrily at her – 'here you are already – apparently.'

Carrie sighed. What could she say to that? The awkward silence and the miles and miles of distance between the two of them was agonising. 'I have to get back to work,' she said, after what seemed like an eternity.

Back on waitress duty, she passed by Barnaby skulking in a corner, his back turned to her, having an intense conversation. She slowed, leaned in and listened. 'You know I love you. Course I do, idiot. And I love that you're here.'

She hurried on, before he turned and saw her. What?! His lover was *here*? She looked around the room. Of course, there were people all over the house and some in the gardens, but . . . maybe this Dudley *was* a secret lover. She scanned the crowd. Or . . . Hugo was on his phone. He ended the call and stuffed it into his pocket angrily. She thought back to what Luella had brought up at the hospital. Sims and Hugo fell out when Hugo came out.

I wonder...

Just then, Kit messaged for them to meet in the alcove with the knock-off Botticelli statue in it. She found it easily, as the statue was wearing ski goggles, underwear on its head and a large green bra for the occasion.

'Is everything OK between you and Freddie?' Luella asked her, the second she got there. Carrie shook her head and then, to avoid more questions about it, said briskly, 'I'll get the study key from Barnaby, so you two can go and have a poke around.'

'You're confident,' Kit said.

'He's so wasted he'd sell me his own grandmother at the moment.' She turned to Luella. 'Oh, and I overheard something and had a thought. It sounds mad, but . . .' She leaned in close and told them her theory.

Kit baulked and Luella raised her eyebrows. 'Seriously?'

'Yeah. Can you check it out, Lu?'

Luella nodded, and Carrie said, 'Let's both meet Kit back here in a few, yeah?' With that, she wove her way through the crowd to Barnaby. He was back on the dance floor and she whispered – well, yelled – into his ear. 'Catering messed up! The best champers, for your birthday toast, was locked in the bloody study for safety! We need to get it out and in ice buckets asap or people will be talking about toasting you with Appletiser for the rest of the season!'

She didn't think he quite understood it all, but he got the gist that she needed the key or he'd look like a dick. He pulled her close, danced her about and almost knocked her off balance. She grabbed on to him and leaned in to hear what the hell he was saying, about the spare key being on top of the study door but no one knows that so *shhhhhhhh*, and spitting all over her.

Just as Freddie spotted them and gave them a gut-wrenching glare. *Great.*

Barnaby glared back at him. 'What the hell is that dickhead Langdon doing here?' So he didn't remember inviting him, then. His happy drunk turned into savage drunk in a second. ''S'my faacking birthday party!'

Freddie was holding two drinks – no-jitos, like he and Carrie sometimes made at the end of her shift on the yard to chill out together for a bit on the bench by the paddock. He glared at her and held one up, in a sarcastic *'Cheers'*. She gathered that the drinks had been a peace offering. Not any more. He shook his head and stalked away.

Damn. They'd better find some dirt on the bloody Balfours, because she was risking Freddie over it.

Chapter Twenty-Six

Luella

Luella did that awkward walk-dancing thing across the dance floor, over to Hugo. He was sitting with Sims and a couple of the artsy girls from school by the bar, away from the main crowd. He still looked very pale and fragile. He greeted her warmly with a wave and smile. Sims did too, then stood up and busted out some silly dance moves, wiggling his eyebrows, to try and get her out on the floor to dance, but she shook her head. She leaned in. 'Just hoping to borrow Hugo for a moment.' Time to see whether Carrie's theory held any weight.

Sims grinned. 'He's all yours. We'll show you kids how it's done.' With that, he pulled both the artsy girls up and they all danced away, drunkenly laughing.

Hugo patted the chair beside him. 'Come, sit.'

Remembering that Kit was waiting for her, probably on his own, she got down to business. The best approach was to be confident, act like she knew already. If she was completely off beam Hugo would laugh and think she was joking, and she could just say she'd had one too many Passionfruit Palomas or something. Chinking glasses with him, she said, 'It's great to see you recovering so well. Great to see you in general.'

'Great to see you too.'

She leaned in. 'So, any gossip? How's your love life?' He looked a little taken aback. 'Sorry, I'm a bit merry, less inhibited,' she said, as an excuse. 'But still, do tell. Are you seeing anyone at the moment?'

Hugo looked super awkward. 'I could ask you the same thing. There's been a little rumour flying round here on gilded wings tonight. About you upstairs with a certain stable hand for half an hour.'

'Forty minutes, actually.' She grinned. 'We did it twice.'

Hugo gasped in pretend shock. 'You harlot!'

'Joke!' she cried. 'Kidding!' Then she wickedly added, 'It was three times.'

That broke the ice a bit more. But she couldn't get off track. 'I heard a rumour too,' she said smoothly. *Act casual.* 'That you're seeing Barnaby Balfour.'

The look on his face told her instantly that Carrie had been right. *Huh.* She'd never in a million years have put them together.

'That's crazy,' Hugo was saying. 'That drunken idiot mummy's boy? Oh my God, Loops, you must think I have really low standards!' But it all just washed over her. She knew the truth.

'You so are. Come on, you can talk to me. We're old friends.'

'OK, fine, I am. But where did you hear that? Shit!' He sighed and gulped at his drink. 'It's very up and down. I think he's a massive twat half the time and the best guy on earth the other half.

I didn't want to announce it, but he did, and now I do and he doesn't. I didn't want to lose Freddie as a friend, and there's my place on the Langdon team, but I'm willing to risk it now, for us to go public. But Barnaby – sometimes he's proud to be with me and sometimes he seems scared of what his father would actually say if he brought a guy home, and a Langdon guy at that. Jasper seems supportive, but . . . it's different, actually dating someone in front of his face.'

She suddenly had a thought. 'Does Sims know?'

Hugo nodded. 'Yeah. He's been amazing. That's why we fell out – because he didn't trust Barnaby and he thought him seeing me was some kind of trick, to get Langdon information. And he felt betrayed, too, like Freddie would if he knew.'

Ah, it all made sense now. She squeezed his arm gently. 'Don't worry. There is no rumour. Carrie overheard him talking to you on the phone and worked it out. So you'll be able to do whatever you choose, and to only tell people when you're ready, if you want to.'

Hugo smiled. 'That's a relief.' Some guys from school came over to see him then, so she took the chance to head back to the fake Botticelli.

Carrie was there with Kit. 'Yep, Barnaby's secret boyfriend is Hugo,' she told them. Carrie's eyes widened. 'So, we'd assumed he hated Hugo and was jealous of his superior ability in polo, but he'd never have risked hurting him, however awful he is. He would have known that him subbing in for Freddie would be a possibility – he was there ready, and the Langdons' first reserve.'

'So, Barnaby didn't poison Willow,' said Carrie. 'But . . . how bad of a boyfriend is he?'

'Yeah,' said Kit. 'Who's Dudley?'

Luella grimaced, worried for Hugo. 'Maybe he's cheating, the scumbag,' she said. 'Maybe that's the real reason he wants to keep the relationship secret now. He's probably telling this Dudley the same thing, to make sure they don't find out about each other.'

Carrie blinked at her. 'Wow! That's devious! How did you come up with that?'

Kit pulled a nervous face. 'That *is* a little scary actually.'

'Hanging around with Bex too much, I guess,' said Luella. 'Not my style, obviously, but it's the sort of thing she'd do – has done, in fact – and I wouldn't put it past Barnaby either.'

'Hang on, hang on,' said Carrie. 'Let's rein ourselves in a bit here. We don't *know* who Dudley is. Let's keep open minds or we won't be able to see clearly what's in front of us. Time to get into the Balfour study, guys. The key is on top of the door, OK? I've got work to do – finding a load of top-notch champagne for Barnaby's toast from somewhere. God, why the hell did I say that?' She pulled at her neckline, adjusting the scratchy dress, then swished off. 'Good luck!' she called, and then, over her shoulder, with a wink, 'And don't get distracted.'

Kit and Luella acted drunk while checking for security cameras, including opening the French doors to the balcony and stumbling out there too. When they were sure there were none, they got down to business and slipped in unseen.

There were a lot of staff and supplier contracts, tenancy agreements and land boundary documents in the files on the shelves, but nothing of interest. Luella had a quick flick through each one while Kit went through the desk drawers.

A while later, 'Oh, Jasper, mate – that's not nice,' he groaned.

Luella looked up. 'What, a gross porno?'

'Half a mouldy cheese baguette, actually.' He shut the drawer – nothing of interest in there. But then he paused for a moment and opened it again. He rummaged inside and pulled out a cheque book. 'Hey, Lu, come and look at this.'

Luella was just finishing with the last file. She put it back carefully and clicked over to his side in her strappy high heels. 'It doesn't look like it's been used for years, though.'

Kit flicked through. 'It hasn't, except for this last one.'

'Bingo,' muttered Luella. The cheque stub had a scribbled figure on it. £10K. The note just said '*Fees*'.

'It's dated the day before the paying-in stub we found,' said Kit. 'And the last four digits of the account number match.'

'Interesting.' She took a few pictures of it and then he put it carefully back where he'd found it, behind the mouldy baguette.

Luella held up her hand, he high-fived it and then they locked fingers. They were caught in each other's gaze for a moment before they both looked away, bashful. Luella guessed Kit was probably thinking of their kiss in Barnaby's bedroom, as she was. Was he hoping it would happen again? she wondered. *As she was.* 'What now?' she said.

'This dinosaur.'

Unbelievably, the password for Jasper's computer, a big, heavy desktop thing that did indeed have a Jurassic look about it, was 'password'. Luella finished with the files and came to look over Kit's shoulder. 'It's surprisingly common, apparently,' he said. 'That's why I tried it.'

'Makes me think there won't be much of anything secret on there,' she said.

They searched in 'recent files' and then for the bank name, the account number, 'Dudley', 'Ronan Blake', 'conference centre', 'Willow', 'magnesium', 'Langdon' and 'Freddie'. Nothing. Then, finally, 'private' and 'confidential'.

But nothing still. As Kit wiped their search history, Luella checked through the random papers left on the desk, but there was nothing of interest there either. She looked at her phone. 'Time's getting on. We should go back.'

He shut the computer down and stood, close to her. 'I know. But maybe, a few more minutes . . .' Their eyes met. This time *she* pulled *him* close and they had another long, slow, delicious kiss. Luella felt like she was swimming in bright gold energy, flowing with everything. Strong heat flooded up her body – she was full of desire for him. And from the way he pressed himself against her and held her tight, running his hands up her spine and down to her hips, he felt the same.

They pulled apart, gasping. Smiled deep into each other's eyes. And fell into another incredible kiss. Then, suddenly, they were on the desk, kissing passionately, scrabbling with each other's clothes. His hand was on the bare skin of her thighs, pushing up her dress. She gasped and threw her head back with pleasure as she pulled him close to kiss her neck and buried her hands in his hair. He grabbed her waist and pulled it hard against him and a wave of hot desire shot up through her. She groaned and pushed back, arching her body to press against his and turning her head to the side. 'Kit?' she breathed.

'Uh-huh?' His voice was groggy with want. For her. She could hear it, and she could feel it with every pulse of his body.

'Look – there's a safe.'

Chapter Twenty-Seven

Bex

Thanks to Finn's great photos of her, Venetia's credit card and the arrival of Freddie Langdon, the evening hadn't been a complete disaster, Bex decided. She was leaning against a gaudy ornate pillar, drinking a vodka martini from the bar. It was borderline criminal that the drinks weren't free. All three of Bex's credit cards, on her parents' accounts, had been frozen and her personal account had dwindled to a trickle. The sum from the perfume ambassadorship had seemed like a lot at the time but hadn't lasted long without her parents' backup.

If she won the Guillards Cup, perhaps she could start offering training. That would be a money-spinner without looking like one. She'd have to keep in with Delia and Jasper so she could use the Balfour facilities – of course, the stables at home were falling down and full of old junk and her father's half-finished classic car restorations. They were no good for Bomba and Gordo and most certainly wouldn't do for wealthy, connected polo clients. The stable doors needed to be replaced, with decent oak — that alone could run into thousands — and the arena needed a resurface. She felt that sting again — of resentment, betrayal. If her father had spent more time saving their sinking ship, and less with his head under a bonnet, they might not be in the position they were in now.

Urgh. Alfonso was coming over again. Checking himself out in the big rococo wall mirror on the way. Smoothing down his eyebrows. Who actually *did* that in real life? They hadn't hooked up again since the shed incident, and without the thrill of illicit sex, she'd felt the full force of how boring he was.

She watched him stride over, not even bothering to stop at the bar and buy a drink for her on the way, and she felt suddenly very bleak and very lonely. She looked like she was having a fabulous time, with her fabulous star polo player and fabulous friends. *Looked like.*

Suddenly her traitorous heart twisted in her chest, making her gasp. For a moment, she just wanted everything back the way it was. Not just the money and, of course, her beloved horses. But the old gang back together, hanging out. She'd been able to be herself, back then. *Damn, damn, damn. Shut up, heart.*

Alfonso reached her and there were shouts from the middle of the dance floor. She saw a space clearing and heard a ripple of shocked gasps around the room. She went to look, not caring whether Alfonso followed or not.

'It's my party, you arsehole!' Barnaby was shouting — well, slurring — at Freddie. He had a bloody nose. If he'd thrown the first punch, Freddie had dodged it. Bex felt a frisson of attraction, *desire* for Freddie. A proper *guy* guy, who had principles, sexy broad shoulders, a good right hook and a truckload of old money.

'*You* invited me,' Freddie retorted. 'Probably just so you could gloat about getting it on with *my girlfriend*.'

'He wasn't! There was nothing like that!' screeched Carrie, in ear-splitting tones. 'And anyway, I'm not your girlfriend!'

Not his girlfriend? Well, that was interesting.

Barnaby was having to be held back, while Freddie stood calmly. The Balfour heir finally thrashed his way out of the grip of his rugby mates and launched himself like a missile at the gorgeous future Lord L. Freddie did some kind of martial arts using-your-balance-against-you thing and Barnaby landed hard on the floor.

Kit and Luella came rushing in then, holding hands, and cut through the crowd. Bex stared at them in shock. How many times were they going to hook up at this party?! It was depraved.

Barnaby scrabbled to his feet. It was interesting that no one helped him. Blood dripped from his nose on to the floor. *Disgusting.* He fixed Freddie with a contemptuous glare. 'Get out of my house.'

Freddie didn't give him the satisfaction of a direct reply. Instead, he looked straight at Carrie, piercing, angry and hurt at once. *Poor darling Freddie.* He did not deserve to be treated like that. 'Don't worry, I'm gone,' he said.

Carrie instantly started crying – like anyone believed she really meant it. 'Freddie, don't, please!' She tried to catch hold of his arm, but he pulled it roughly away. The enthralled crowd parted as he made for the main doors.

Bex made a split-second decision. Suddenly, life felt thrilling and wild and dangerous again. She swished over and linked arms with Freddie. Loyalty mattered to him, she knew, more than anything. To Bex's delight and Carrie's obvious horror, Freddie didn't protest.

As they passed close by Kit and Luella, Bex fixed them with a steely glare, challenging her to drop his hand. But Luella held it tighter, pressing her fingers against his, and stared Bex down.

Then Kit said loudly, 'They're already all talking about us, so let's give them something good, at least.' Luella threw her arms around his neck and kissed him long and slow as the music came back on, and the lights went down again.

Bex wanted to scream, cry, and be sick, all at once. But she kept her composure. 'Come on, Freddie, this party is full of traitors.'

She left Alfonso to infer that he'd been dumped and swished out of the ballroom on Freddie's arm, cutting a swathe through the crowd.

She could still get it all back – Freddie, a Langdon team place, the top-notch facilities there for Gordo and Bomba. Maybe even Estrella and Blanca. She enjoyed the moment – all eyes on them, her hips swaying, the dress moving seductively, her long, glossy dark hair swinging, and Finn catching it all to post online.

She and Freddie had walked right out of the Balfour house and got into his car without a word. He hadn't let go of her arm the whole way. He opened the door of his vintage Landy for her and slammed it hard once she'd climbed in, but not as hard as he slammed his own.

'I'm sorry,' said Bex. 'I've had a feeling there was something going on between Carrie and Barnaby for a while. I should have told you, but I wasn't sure . . . until tonight.'

Freddie sighed and gripped the steering wheel, the muscles in his arms flexing in a way that made her breathe in sharply at the heat rising in her body. He turned and fixed her with his green eyes. There wasn't a hint of smoulder or flirt in them – not yet. But the night was young. 'What do we do now?' he asked her.

She sat back in her seat and threw her head back, to show off her profile in the moonlight. 'Let's just go somewhere and have fun,' she said. 'You know, like when we were kids. Just fun.'

Obviously, she'd wanted to say, *Let's go back to yours and run a huge bubble bath in your en suite and get it on all night.* But it was more important to remind him of their long history and to reignite their deeper connection. Hot sex would come. But it could wait – for now.

He thought for a moment. Looked at the old-fashioned dashboard clock. 'Hmm, what is fun to do at quarter past midnight in Yetbourne, the world's most boring village?' He managed a smile, which hit her right in the stomach with desire, then he said, 'Oh, I know,' started the car and screeched off up the gravel drive, throwing her back against her seat. *How the hell did I take my eye off the ball so badly that he slipped away?* She had to stop herself from putting her hand on his thigh. It would be so easy . . .

They drove back and forth through the ford at top speed, spraying water up to the roof, laughing, Bex screeching with delight. After the ninth go, Freddie drove on, deeper into the countryside. Down a narrow lane, he pulled over into a layby, climbed into the back and sat on one of the long benches. He pulled the dripping canvas roof down and there, revealed as if by magic, were the bright, full moon and a sky full of stars.

Bex forgot her schemes and plans. It was just so nice, being with someone she actually liked, who actually knew her, out under the stunning night sky. He pulled a bottle of Langdon Estate cold-pressed organic apple juice from a crate on the Landy's floor and they took turns to drink from it, looking up at the full moon, listening to the owls and the rustling in the bushes nearby. 'What was that?' she asked Freddie.

He shrugged and swigged from the bottle. 'Foxes, maybe. Or badgers.'

'If a massive one tries to get in here, will you defend me?' she asked, only half joking.

He laughed. 'I think you'll be safe.'

She did feel very safe with him. Like she could finally relax. 'This reminds me of night walks with my father,' she told him.

'Yeah?'

'Yeah, we used to do them a lot, from when I was about eight, or nine, right up to when I was twelve, and then we stopped, for some reason. I'd forgotten all about those. It was one of our things, and then we'd go in and get warm by the fire, if it was winter. The housekeeper would have gone off duty, so Mummy would make us all hot chocolate.'

He shifted on the bench, stretching his arms out wide for a moment. God, it was all she could do not to sneak into the space between his chest and his arm before he put them down. 'You know, I thought our friendship was over,' he said, after they'd watched the stars for a while longer. She risked leaning her head on his shoulder and he let her – he didn't pull away. 'The way you left our place, taking your horses with no notice, and then showing up to the charity game to play for the Balfours . . .'

'I'm sorry,' she said. 'Really. That was awful of me. With my parents, the money thing . . . and . . .' Her voice cracked. 'Having to let Estrella and Blanca go. It was a tough time. Still is . . .' She fought hard to hold it together. Finally having a safe space to let go in – it was all she could do not to dissolve into floods of tears. But that wouldn't do. 'Thanks for sending me that message the other day, and the funny snap of Willow,' she said, casting off the worst of the pain. 'I was going to reply, but I didn't know what to say.'

''S'OK,' he said. 'And I get it, that you've had a hard time.' He put his arm around her – or maybe it was along the back of the bench. Her heart began to pound with thrill and excitement.

'I heard you and Carrie had gone exclusive,' she said. 'This is the first time you've been serious about someone other than me. I didn't expect to care, but . . .' She breathed in sharply and forced herself to say something nice about Carrie, so she'd look kind and decent to Freddie. 'I always thought she seemed like a lovely girl.'

'*Seemed*, past tense, is right,' he snarled. 'She was completely out of order, being like that with Barnaby. It's like she was *trying* to hurt me and make me look like an idiot.'

Bex smiled to herself and pressed on. 'I'm glad I left your yard, in a way. I wouldn't have been able to stand seeing you with her every single day.'

He pulled away and turned to face her, and their eyes locked. He looked surprised, questioning, and, yes, he wanted her – she was sure of it. *Time to take another big risk.* 'I know how I feel, now,' she said. 'I want you, Freddie. You and only you.' Slowly, deliciously, making the moment last, she leaned in to kiss him.

Chapter Twenty-Eight

Carrie

Carrie was in a cosy corner table in the back garden of the King's Arms, sipping peppermint tea under a beautiful shady canopy of scented jasmine. She was wearing huge sunglasses and a simple stretchy black sundress that she loved, nursing a pretty bad hangover.

Luella came out of the pub with a lime and soda and equally big sunglasses. She was one of those people who did *hungover* really glamorously. She glowed. Carrie just felt like a sweaty, bilious, knackered mess. Or maybe Lu's glow was to do with spending the night with Kit...

Kit himself appeared a moment later, carrying a pint of orange juice and a wooden spoon with a number on, which indicated a giant breakfast on the way. She smiled and waved, and they made their way over, through the buzzy late-morning crowd. Sunday brunch at the King's Arms was a *thing*. Luckily no one from the party was there, though.

She got up and hugged Luella and then Kit. 'Oh, you two! I haven't heard all the juicy details, yet, Lu!'

Kit groaned and slid on to the bench opposite Luella, next to Carrie. 'Lu, promise you won't tell her the juicy details,' he said.

Luella shrugged and lifted her sunglasses to wink at Carrie. 'Kit, I've got to break some news to you. *Girls talk.*'

Carrie beamed. 'Well, I know you're together – right?'

Kit gave a slight nod and took a sip of orange juice. 'Yep.' He was acting casual but clearly glowing with pride and happiness to be by Luella's side.

'So does all of Yetbourne, after that very public kiss,' said Carrie, loving the subject.

'I just felt brave,' said Luella. 'I'm sure the alcohol helped, but mostly I just wanted to show the world that Kit and I are together, and sod anyone who doesn't like it.'

'Bex, you mean.'

'Mainly, yep,' said Luella. 'If she's any kind of friend—'

'Which she isn't,' Carrie cut in.

'If she's any kind of friend, she'll just have to accept that we're together,' Luella finished.

'Which she won't,' said Kit, and shared a conspiratorial look with Carrie. She didn't feel bad about it – whatever Bex was going through, she'd left with Freddie, so Carrie couldn't access much empathy for her right then. She hated keeping Bex's secret from Luella too. But still, she'd promised, and she'd honour that.

'I know what you guys think of her,' Luella said, sipping her lime and soda delicately. 'But honestly, she really did used to be OK, underneath. Maybe this is just a phase.' She looked sad and Kit leaned in and kissed her again, passionately, but still appropriately for a Sunday morning, public place.

Carrie was pleased for them, of course she was. But her stomach dropped, thinking of the mess between her and Freddie. Luella picked up on the vibe and grew serious, putting her sunglasses on the table and reaching over to squeeze Carrie's arm, concern in her eyes. 'But, anyway, how are you holding up?'

Carrie made herself smile. 'Don't say it like that! Like I've got something terminal!' She sighed. 'We haven't spoken yet, or messaged. But it's just a silly misunderstanding. It's so annoying that he left with Bex – now everyone will be talking about that and thinking something happened between them.'

'That's bad,' said Luella. 'Worse, Freddie now thinks something's going on between you and Barnaby.'

They all did a big dramatic shudder at once and then fell about laughing, which lightened the mood. 'Don't!' Carrie protested. 'I feel sick enough already!' Then, 'Right, let's get down to business. Did you find anything when you were rooting around in the study?'

Kit blushed and Luella suddenly got very interested in poking her lime around with her straw. Carrie laughed. 'Oh right! Like *that*, was it?'

'Maybe a little like that . . .' Luella admitted, 'but we were on the case. Nothing in the files or on the computer.'

Carrie looked disappointed. 'Oh well, you tried . . .'

'We did find something in the desk drawer, though,' said Luella. 'A cheque stub for ten grand, with an account number that matched the paying-in stub we found in Barnaby's room. In the name of one of Jasper's companies – Shaftesbury Group.'

'And a mouldy cheese baguette,' added Kit, with a grimace, 'but that's not important right now.'

Carrie leaned back and sipped her tea. 'That's interesting. Why would Jasper pay his own son ten grand? And why from a company account rather than a personal one?'

'Who knows?' said Luella. 'We came up with slinging him a few grand for a holiday or tax fraud or a bribe maybe? The stub said "Fees", so not very specific.'

'Maybe Barnaby paid for something – training clinics, polo coaches or whatever – and Jasper's company paid him back,' Kit reasoned.

'Could be,' Carrie agreed. She held her cold drink against her forehead. 'Oh, curse you, Passionfruit Palomas!'

'We found a safe as well,' said Luella.

'A safe? OK, wow! Where was it?'

Why was Luella stirring her drink again, looking bashful? And was Kit just hot in the sun, or blushing still? It was a simple enough question. 'On the wall hidden behind some shelving,' said Luella. Then she flicked her eyes up at Carrie. 'I happened to be at a particular angle . . .'

Carrie's eyes lit up, with double excitement. *A safe and some juicy romance details to hear later.* 'So, we know the cheque was from Jasper and the scribble on the cheque stub was "Fees".' Luella handed her phone over to Carrie, so she could look at the picture they'd taken of it.

'As for Dudley, we've no idea who he is,' said Kit. A waitress appeared with a huge Full English and he leaned back and said 'Cheers' as she set it down. Carrie couldn't help grimacing at the smell of bacon, but she beamed at the waitress. 'Thank you so much,' she said. When she'd gone in, she added, 'I am going to appreciate waiting staff so much more after last night!'

Kit slathered the whole plateful of food in ketchup. Luella groaned. 'Urgh! How can you do that after last night?'

'How can you *not*, after last night?' replied Kit, giving her a cheeky smile. With that, he dived in, filled his face and sat back, in heaven. 'Mmmm, ahhh, oh my God, so good.' He picked up a hash brown and wiggled it at Luella. 'Want some?'

'Urgh! No thank you!'

Carrie was thinking aloud. 'It's definitely not Barnaby who poisoned Willow as he wouldn't have risked hurting Hugo, but he may be cheating on him. Which means maybe this *Dudley* could have a motive.'

'Or they're both being cheated on and they don't know it, hence the secrecy thing. The old Bex double bluff,' said Luella.

Carrie had a sudden, sharp desire to call Freddie and make sure that Bex hadn't started playing him again too. He wouldn't go there, would be? This was a silly blip. They were meant to be together in the end, right? He wouldn't get with someone while he was hanging out with *her*, surely? They'd both said they didn't want to see anyone else, and she, for one, had meant it. And *Bex* – that would be the absolute *worst*. Carrie didn't like hearing about how manipulative and ruthless she was with guys. Just hearing the name *Bex* made her feel kind of . . .

'Are you OK?'

She came to, to find Kit looking at her with concern. She pulled on a smile. 'Yeah, fine, just . . . the bacon smell is kind of making me want to vomit.'

Luella and Kit shared a look. Neither of them believed her, clearly. They must have known it was about Freddie. But they very kindly left it alone.

'You know – I just feel like I saw something in that study but I don't know what,' said Luella, changing the subject. 'It's really nagging at me. I can't put my finger on it though.'

Carrie picked up her phone. 'No time like the present.'

'What?' asked Kit, through a mouthful of fry-up.

'Are you calling Freddie? Good idea,' said Luella.

'No way, he can call me first, if he's got something to say,' she said, feistily. 'I'm calling this Dudley person.'

Luella's eyes opened wide. 'What?! But what are you going to say?'

Carrie smiled. 'Not sure,' she said. 'Just anything to get him talking – and to confirm he exists. Get a surname if we're lucky.' Then she put on a French accent. 'Maybe he left something in one of our chalets.' She switched to a businesslike tone. 'Or perhaps his car was spotted parked illegally by one of our cameras, and we haven't received the fine payment yet.'

They laughed. 'You know, you do that a little too well,' said Luella. She held up the photo on her phone and Carrie tapped the number in. But she didn't have to do any accent. Dudley didn't answer. It didn't even ring.

The number you are calling has not been recognised.

They all stared at the phone. 'Weird,' said Luella. 'So, what now?'

Carrie sighed. 'We're a bit stuck. There's the postcard, but that's no real use until we know more. I can try and find out who Barnaby went to Venice with, maybe. But I think we should focus on finding a way to get into that safe. Go direct to the heart of Balfour operations. I mean, even if we don't find anything to do with Willow and the poisoning, if we found anything dodgy at all we could use it to make them leave Kit and his family alone.'

Kit winced. 'Ooooh, I wouldn't want to try blackmailing the Balfours,' he said. 'They're pretty ruthless.'

'I'd do it,' said Luella firmly. 'For you and your family.'

Kit pulled her close and kissed her. 'That's my girl.' She blushed cutely.

'But how do we get in there?'

'No idea. But where there's a will there's a way.'

Kit finished the last of the breakfast and wiped the plate round with his final bite of toast. 'I've got to get back. There's a surveyor coming to the cottage, to check for damp. And everyone else is working so I said I'd let him in. Later, ladies.' There was a whole big hugging and kissing thing with Luella, of course. But Carrie just wiggled her fingers at him, too exhausted to get up. 'Take that plate in with you,' she told him. 'Those girls work hard enough. Waitressing's not for pussies.'

As soon as he'd wandered back into the pub, plate in hand, Carrie leaned forward, eyes wide. 'So, oh my God, tell me everything! Did you . . . you know? And where and when and how many times and was it good and . . .'

Luella sipped on the last of her drink, making the straw gurgle. 'We're coupled up. He said he wanted me to be his girlfriend,' she said. 'And I feel the same. And we kissed in Barnaby's room . . .' Carrie gasped with delight. '. . . and made out on the desk in the study.'

Carrie laughed. 'Aha, that's how you spotted the safe. You were horizontal!'

'Shhhhh!' Luella's eyes flickered to the nearby tables. No one was listening or cared, obviously.

Carrie wasn't going to let her get away with not answering, though. 'So, after he drove you home, you went inside to your beautiful cream bedroom with all the gorgeous painted furniture and fell into the Egyptian cotton sheets and . . .'

Luella blushed. 'Actually, we had a kiss goodbye in his car and one thing led to another . . . We didn't go all the way, but . . . things got pretty steamy.'

Carrie looked both scandalised and impressed at once. 'Luella!'

She giggled. 'I know, so unlike me! But we couldn't resist each other. He did manage to put me down and drive home eventually, though. I didn't think Mum and Dad needed the shock of him sitting at the breakfast table, or sneaking out the back door. I'll tell them and I'm sure it will be OK for him to stay over, though, now we're officially together.'

Carrie sighed. 'So, was the making out amazing?'

Luella shivered with pleasure at the memory. 'Completely out-of-this-world amazing.'

Carrie beamed, and then – she couldn't help it – she thought of Freddie again, and the whole rubbish situation, and the smile fell right off her face.

'Are you thinking about Freddie?' Luella asked gently.

Carrie nodded. 'I'm thinking, this is just stupid. I didn't get with Barnaby. I'd rather *die*. So, really, it's over nothing. Maybe I should just call him and . . .'

Just then, Luella's phone buzzed on the table. She looked up. 'Bex – she's finally returning my call.'

Bloody Bex again, Carrie thought. But she said, 'Take it.'

'Hi.' Luella's tone was hesitant and she wound a strand of blonde hair round and round her finger. 'No . . .' She glanced at Carrie. 'I'm alone.'

Bex said something. Luella sighed. 'Look, if you've called to have a go at me about being with Kit then I don't want to hear it. We're together, get over it.'

Carrie raised her eyebrows, silently clapping, and signalled that she wanted to listen. Luella put the phone on speaker, but quietly, and they both leaned over it to hear. Bex was stunned silent for a moment, clearly.

Then she said, 'Anyway, I'm not calling about that. I know we're not close at the moment, but we go way back and I still consider you my best friend.'

'Of course – I feel the same,' said Luella. Carrie did a choking mime and Luella swatted at her. *Don't make me laugh*, her look said.

'We've always told each other things like this and, whatever I said last night, I was just angry,' Bex said. 'However many times you betray me I will always be loyal to you.'

Luella frowned. 'Things like *what*?'

There was a pause, then Bex said, 'Last night I slept with Freddie.'

Carrie rode over to the Langdons' at full speed. She bypassed the cycle rack and rode right through the clock archway and up to Freddie. He was on the busy yard with a supplier, surrounded by sacks and boxes, ticking feed supplements off a list. She threw her bike to the ground, shouting, 'We said we wouldn't see other people!'

The yard fell silent. Everyone turned to stare at them. Freddie looked horrified. 'Let's take this into the office.'

What Carrie heard was, *Yes, I slept with Bex*. She didn't move. Her whole body was shaking. 'You slept with Bex!'

Now *he* looked angry. 'Excuse me,' he said to the astonished supplier. He grabbed her arm and pulled her into the office. 'You can't just march into our workplace and shout at me, Carrie!'

She snorted, hands on hips. 'Ha! Yeah, because that's what matters.' She fixed him with a steely glare and cursed the tears brimming in her eyes. 'You fucked Bex.'

He glared back at her. 'I did not.' But she watched his eyes slide away from her gaze. Shifty.

A huge wave of fury broke over her. 'You're lying!' she screamed, the tears coming fast.

'I don't have to prove anything to you!' he shouted back, then looked surprised at himself. They glared at each other.

She still felt it – that he was holding something back. 'If you're not even going to man up and admit it, then you've got no respect for me at all,' she said, trembling with rage. 'And this *thing* between us, whatever it was, it's over.'

Even so angry, she desperately hoped he'd sweep her up in his arms and tell her how wrong she was. Tell her he wanted her and only her. Tell her he didn't get with Bex. That he could never. Not when the only girl he cared about was her.

But – *nothing*.

The painful silence drew out, every second stabbing her deeper in the heart. And then he said, 'Fine! We're done. Go and get with Barnaby Balfour, see if I care! You already have anyway!'

Carrie almost yelled that she hadn't but stopped herself. Her heart was breaking in half in her chest and she could hardly breathe. If that's what he really thought of her, he didn't know her at all. She didn't have to defend herself. Not to him, not to anyone. *He* was the one who'd done something wrong. He'd slept with Bex. She just knew it. She could feel that something was off, and she trusted her gut.

Which meant that that was it. There was nothing more to say.

She dared herself to look deep into his eyes, despite the pain wrenching her heart in half. She held his gaze.

He cleared his throat. 'I . . .'

Yes? For one stupid second, she'd thought he was about to say he loved her. But he just shook his head and in a low, choked voice said, 'Doesn't matter.'

She turned, stormed out, still shaking, and grabbed her bike. As she rode away, she sobbed hard. Hot tears, ugly crying. It felt like she was riding away from her whole future. She didn't want to see Freddie or set foot on the bloody Langdon Estate ever again.

Chapter Twenty-Nine
Luella

'Oh, Lu, I feel such an idiot!'

'*He's* the idiot,' Luella said firmly. Carrie had told her everything, and she felt furious and protective – like a lioness with her cubs.

'I thought we had something special!' she wailed now. 'I feel so used and like he just strung me along. Breaking the rules at work is a big deal, and I thought we were risking it because we had real feelings for each other. That's how *I* felt, anyway. And I really believed him when he said he wasn't going to get with anyone else.'

'Are you sure he actually did it?' asked Luella gently. 'It doesn't sound like Freddie.'

'He denied it, yeah – but I could tell he was lying,' Carrie insisted. Luella didn't push it. Carrie sighed and collapsed in a heap on to the mounting block, head in her hands. 'Everyone heard, Lu. It'll be all round the yard by now. How can I ever go back?'

'You will,' Luella said firmly. 'Your future is there. You'll just have to face it and get on with being an amazing stable hand and horse whisperer.' Luella squeezed her hand. 'It'll be OK.'

Carrie just shrugged and then glanced at Luella's phone. 'Shit! I'm supposed to be home by now!'

The girls had a long hug and when they broke apart, Luella said, 'You two would have been so good together. Are you sure it's not worth talking to him again? He did deny it, after all. And Bex could easily be lying.'

Luella watched as Carrie thought about it, but then she shook her head. 'No. I want out of whatever weird thing he has going on with Bex. Maybe this was a lucky escape, before I got in deeper and got even more hurt.'

Right then, Carrie didn't look like she could be any more hurt. Luella could feel the pain coming off her in waves. She winced. Heartbreak. '*I* could talk to Freddie . . .'

'Thanks, but don't. I'm going to leave it,' said Carrie. 'I know I need to step away. I felt so jealous, seeing him with Bex at the party, like *crazy jealous*. And just now, when I confronted him, I was *furious*. Like, raging. I can't get in that state at work again. I just can't. And now, I'm in freaking *agony*. It's all too much.'

They hugged again and Carrie headed home, with promises to message Luella when she got there. Luella planned to call her again later. And she planned to talk to Freddie, too, whatever Carrie had said.

Freddie looked up and blinked at her. 'Oh God, not you as well. Come to roast me, have you?'

'You tell me. Do I have a reason to?' Luella looked at Freddie sternly. She'd found him in a dark corner of the tack room, unusually actually cleaning some tack himself.

He shoved a bridle at her. 'Here. Make yourself useful.'

She huffed and sat down on a hay bale next to him, reaching for a sponge. *'Fine.'*

'Carrie said I slept with Bex. Came round here, ranting, accusing me. She's so jealous and possessive, jumping to conclusions and throwing around accusations just because we left together.' He glanced up. 'Anyway, it's over now, whatever it was. She said so. Given how unhinged she acted, I probably had a lucky escape.'

'For God's sake! She didn't just decide that for herself! Bex *said* you did, you idiot!' Luella swung the bridle and slapped him with the reins.

'Ow!' He rubbed his arm and stared at her. 'What, actually *told* Carrie that?'

'Well, told me and Carrie was listening, not that it matters. The point is – *did you*?'

Freddie looked like revving up to be angry again, but then he just sighed and shook his head. 'No, I did not. She's lying.'

Luella felt stung. Here was another awful thing she was being forced to see about Bex. Where was the girl she knew? The best friend she'd had since primary school? She pushed the thoughts away – this wasn't about her. It was about Carrie.

'Anyway, Carrie got with Barnaby,' Freddie said, 'so it doesn't really matter now what—'

Luella gaped at him and whacked him with the reins again. 'No, she didn't!'

He stared at her. 'But . . . the party! And Bex said . . . You're sure?'

She whopped him again. 'Of course I'm sure!'

'Ow! Stop hitting me, you sadist!'

She sighed. Relaxed. 'OK, well, there you go. It's all sorted.' For a moment, she felt like Lady Cupid again – the master of all things love and romance. She'd fixed it, and now they could be together in bliss, love, joy and hot sex, just like her and Kit.

Only Freddie didn't look relieved. He looked awkward, shifting around on the hay bale and not meeting her eyes. 'What?' she asked. 'You should be happy, right?'

He sighed deeply and put his head in his hands. 'Oh God, Lu. I've really messed up. I didn't sleep with Bex. But I kissed her.'

Luella's stomach lurched and she gasped. It was like she could feel how devastated Carrie would be, in her own body. 'No . . .'

'Well, half-kissed,' said Freddie. 'She came on to me, and I pulled away, when I got a hold of myself. But . . . we kissed.'

Luella glared at him. 'You are an absolute bloody idiot,' she said. 'And Carrie is going to be so upset.'

'What, Carrie who didn't tell me she was going to the party? Carrie who was dancing drunk with my worst enemy in front of everyone?' His voice had a hard defensive edge. 'No offence, Lu, but I think I'm better off without her.'

Luella wanted to tell him why Carrie hadn't told him she'd be at the party, but she couldn't. She wanted to say that Barnaby was with Hugo, but she couldn't. She wanted to say that nothing Carrie had done warranted his behaviour and he was pathetic for coming up with excuses to try and defend himself. But she didn't say any of it. She just put the bridle down, turned around and walked out. Freddie Langdon could wait. Right then, she had bigger fish to fry.

Bex.

Luella called Carrie immediately on the hands-free in her car and told her everything. 'Don't worry, I made it clear there are *no* excuses,' she finished. There was a heavy silence on the other end of the phone. 'Look, on the plus side, Bex lied. And yes, there was a kiss – but just half a kiss, and he pulled away, remember. I got the impression he regretted it. So, you could—'

'No way. It's over,' said Carrie firmly. 'I *am* going back to work at the Langdons', I've decided. Why should I give up my whole future there when I've done nothing wrong? But—' Luella heard her take a deep breath. 'I can't risk getting into anything with Freddie again.'

The romantic in Luella felt crushed. 'But, Carrie, you—'

'Lu, really, I mean it. I don't want there being any problems at work over it, when I've got this amazing opportunity to train as a groom, and a whole future career path with the Langdons if I want it. Lord and Lady L and Terrence are really pleased with my work. Thank God none of them were on the yard to see me kicking off at Freddie! I've been lucky, Lu, and I can't risk that again.'

Luella knew she was putting a brave face on it, and that really her friend was very, very hurt. She and Freddie had been good together and, yes, she believed that they were meant for each other. 'Carrie, it's OK to be upset.'

'I'm not. I'm fine. It's best I know now.' She sighed. 'Gotta go, Mum's calling me. Love you, bye.' She hung up before Luella could respond. She hit the car stereo button in frustration, whacked up the music and stepped on the gas. Her little Suzuki four by four clanked along with stirrups, feed bags, hats and water bottles rolling about, but she didn't slow down. In fifteen minutes she was at Bex's front door, ringing the bell in long bursts and banging the knocker hard.

Bex eventually answered, still in a cerise silk dressing gown. She looked a mess, quite frankly. 'All right, all right! For goodness' sake!'

Luella strode straight in and through to the kitchen. 'You and I need to talk.'

Bex was clearly alarmed. 'My darling Lulu! Whatever is the matter? Would you like coffee? The Harrods order hasn't come yet, so I've only got this Waitrose stuff but it's—'

Luella turned to face her, fierce, and the fury coming off her made Bex step back. 'You lied about Freddie. Admit it.'

That caught her off guard. 'Well, I—It's just that—' Luella watched her get control of herself. 'No, I didn't. I most certainly did *not lie* and, actually, I resent the—'

Luella glared at her. 'Freddie says he only half kissed you, then pulled away. And I believe him. So, admit it.'

'I slept with him,' said Bex, her face like stone.

Luella clicked her fingers in front of Bex's eyes. 'Don't check out, Bex. This is me. I know you. I was there for you when they had to put your darling Shelka down.' Tears sprung to Bex's eyes. 'And when you got your period in Year Seven in Geography and you stood up and blood gushed everywhere and I pulled a moony to get the attention off you while you ran to the bathrooms and I got sent to the head. *Me!* And I almost got suspended!'

Bex snorted with laughter, tears running down her face at the same time. 'Yes. Of course. But, Lulu, I swear, I didn't lie, not this time.'

Luella almost crumbled and believed her. Deep down, she still loved her so much. But then she thought of Carrie, and the world of pain she was in. She fixed her with a deep, soulful stare. 'Swear on Bomba's life, and I'll believe you.'

Sobs choked in Bex's throat and she leaned back against the kitchen counter, gripping it tight.

Luella held firm. 'Swear.'

'You don't know what's been going on for me, Lulu. It's all fallen apart. Everything. And it's pretty harmless, what I said. I just wanted to get Carrie out of the way. I could see that she wasn't good for Freddie – I mean, look at the way she was acting with Barnaby. I was just watching his back. And I do have real feelings for him.' She reached out to hug Luella, who stepped back.

'You've gone too far, Bex,' she said, her voice choking with emotion. 'Carrie hasn't done anything wrong.'

Bex wiped her eyes and stared into space, checking out again. Luella didn't want to lose her behind the hard, shiny mask, so she gripped her arm and shook her present. 'Look at what you've become. You've always been ambitious, yes, and there's nothing wrong with that. But now you're just using people to get what you want. I don't believe you really like Freddie. You went straight from him to Alfonso, then back to him again. Well, you tried.'

'That awful Carrie has come in and ruined everything!' Bex protested.

Luella wasn't a violent person, but she could happily have slapped Bex at that moment. She resisted, though. She couldn't be dragged down too. 'No, Bex, *you* have! *You've* ruined everything! We could have all been friends – me, you, Carrie and Kit, but no. You had to be scheming and jealous and manipulative!'

Bex began to cry again, loud, ugly sobs. 'They've taken you away from me! *Everything's* been taken away from me. You don't know what it's been like . . .'

Luella couldn't believe that she was still only crying for *herself*. That was it – she was done. She walked out, noticing the little clay pig she'd made for Bex in Year Five sitting on top of the mantle over the Aga. She reached up, pulled it down and smashed it on the slate floor tiles. Then she turned around and walked out.

If she never saw Rebecca Chapman-Foster again it would be too soon.

Chapter Thirty

Bex

Bex was dressed to the nines, on her way to the train, for an event in London. The perfect moment to meet Freddie for a drink at Brown's. She picked a good table out front, as she had with Alfonso, so that everyone could see them. It would be great for word to get round. Obviously, he might be a little bit upset about her lying to Carrie, now that Luella had come charging in and messed that up for her. But she'd only done it to protect him, and once they'd smoothed that over . . .

Suddenly he was looming over her.

'Freddie, darling!' She stood and leaned forward to kiss him on the cheek.

He stepped back. 'What the hell are you playing at now, Bex?'

Her heart started to pound and she glanced around, wishing she hadn't chosen such a public table now. 'Let's sit down and get a drink.'

'I'm not staying,' he said stiffly. Beneath his composure, she could see he was furious. 'Why did you lie to Luella, knowing it would get back to Carrie? Were you just trying to get her out of the way? Nothing is going to happen between me and you again, Bex. Ever.'

Heads were turning at the tables around them. Her heart banged in her chest. 'Shhh! Sit down.' She pulled at his shirt sleeve. This just seemed to make him angrier and his jaw worked, his fist clenched.

'You lied.'

His look was so cold, and the contemptuous tone of his voice stung. The words crawled under her skin. Her own anger rose. 'Don't act so self-righteous! You're not innocent in this – you know you aren't!'

He didn't take the bait. 'That's it,' he said flatly. 'I'm sorry about your family situation, I really am. And about Estrella and Blanca. But none of it is any excuse for behaving like this. Our friendship was on thin ice after you left our yard the way you did. But now, it's over.'

'Fine by me.' She gave him a stone-hard stare, and then raised her eyebrows and looked beyond him out into the busy street.

'What's happened to you, Bex? I don't even recognise you these days.'

She gazed past him impassively. To Freddie, she was unreachable. But deep down inside herself, as she got up and walked away, her heart broke just a little.

Bex looked out of the train window, dressed to kill, doused in the unholy Boudoir perfume she was being paid to wear, already half-cut. The event staff wouldn't serve her, of course, knowing she was underage – the last thing they'd want was bad PR. But she'd bought a few cocktail cans for the train with her fake ID then topped herself up with sips from her hip flask.

She had a sudden image in her mind of the pottery pig smashing on the floor and winced. She'd had to clear it up herself, of course, now that there was no Carlotta. She'd cut her hand on a shard, badly enough to need a dressing and bandage.

Real friends could hurt you.

She wouldn't let anyone get close to her again. She didn't give a toss about Finn or their crew, or Venetia and Aurelia – God, they were boring – and that was perfect. She didn't need emotional shit. She needed to drink and party and feel amazing.

She tottered off the train in her sky-high strappy heels, which looked great with her Ralph Lauren satin charmeuse halter gown. She got into a black cab – there was a red carpet and she needed to arrive in cool London style. A frenzy of photographers flashing their cameras and journos shouting her name later and she was in the event, the sparkling cranberry juice in her hand improved by a slug of vodka from her hip flask, ready to get her show back on the road.

Urgh, God, the *Balfours* were there. Obviously Delia looked hideous, in something scratchy and floral that had probably crawled out of her wardrobe on its own. And Jasper – when would he learn that one can always tell when a suit hasn't been tailored to fit? They were with that businessman, Ronan Blake. The one who was in talks with them and the Langdons over the conference centre project. No Eric, though, thank goodness. No Lord and Lady L, or Freddie, either. It wasn't a Langdon kind of event. Hugo and Sims were sitting in a booth, however, and somehow they'd managed to get champagne. She almost went over to join them and was struck with sudden doubt – had Luella told them she'd lied about Freddie?

Sims noticed her and waved and she waved back, but she didn't dare risk going over, just in case it was a trap and they planned to give her a bollocking.

And then, striding in to another flash of cameras, was Alfonso.

She'd jumped the wrong way at the party, with Freddie, and now she had to try and get things back on track with the great big vain plank of wood. She'd managed to avoid him around the yard, but now he was striding towards her, and he did not look happy. She flashed him a dazzling smile as he reached her. 'Sorry about Saturday. Freddie's a very dear old friend, even if the Balfours and Langdons don't get on. He was so upset, bless him, about his awful, cheating girlfriend. I had to make sure he called an Uber – he was really drunk.'

'He didn't *seem* drunk at all,' said Alfonso brusquely.

'He doesn't show it, he's one of those guys, but he was. I could tell.'

'You could have messaged me, or come back in, instead of going home.'

'It seemed sensible to jump in the cab with him, see him home and then go home myself.'

Damn. He wasn't softening at all. She played for sympathy. 'I was upset, too. That Carrie was an awful bitch to me, saying really nasty things about me, *and about you*.' Might as well throw that in. But he didn't flinch. 'I'm not interested in the childish squabbles of teenagers,' he said loftily. 'It was good to spend some time with you, Bex. But now it is over.'

She breathed in sharply and resisted the urge to double over with shock. What?! He was just freezing her out? Rejecting her? *How dare he!* 'OK, if that's how you feel, that's fine,' she managed to say. 'We can just be friends. That's better for me anyway. I look forward to our training session in the morning.'

He stared at her, eyebrows raised. 'No, no more extra training sessions. No one-to-ones. No using my grooms or my ponies. If you want my time and expertise, you pay the standard rate, and book through Eric, the same as everyone else.'

As she was staring at him, in absolute shock, he added, 'Oh, and speaking of Eric, he was looking for you on the yard today. He wishes to talk about unpaid bills, I believe.'

Bex choked back her fury. How dare that jumped-up little office boy discuss her private business with this arrogant tosspot! She forced herself to smile and said smoothly, 'He's mistaken. Delia, Jasper and I have a friendly agreement.'

He gave her a withering look. 'Not any more, it seems. Remember this, Rebecca. The sharks you swim with have to eat.'

He walked away and she stared after him. Ridiculous man! He wasn't from round here and he obviously didn't know how much influence she and her family had, otherwise he would never have dared speak to her like that.

A moment of panic overwhelmed her. She saw the Balfours moving across the room and quickly strode off in the other direction, her heart pounding. And there was the journo from *Surrey Style* magazine. What the hell was his name? He thought she was on their Guillards Cup team, in the patron's place – well, when she'd done the interview, she'd thought she would be too. She hoped to God that he wouldn't talk to the Balfours about it. The article was due out the following week, in the August edition, ready for the start of the Guillards Cup. She was the official face of young British polo – but . . . she wasn't . . .

The bar was too hot, the music too loud, and she suddenly just wanted to be at home, in her pyjamas, eating chocolate and watching Netflix while they still had it. A headache was buzzing at her temples and her vision was blurring. She should glug some water – but that was for amateurs. What she needed was more booze to pep her up, and for Finn and Co. to get there, so the party could really get started. She went to the bar and tried to get a vodka martini, but the stupid girl gave her a cranberry juice and a patronising smile. She dumped the rest of her hip-flask vodka in, and then the ultimate disaster unfolded.

With his photographer by his side, the journo from *Surrey Style* was talking to the Balfours and Ronan Blake. They were gesturing to her and they didn't look happy. A lairy group of lads behind her were messing about, and one knocked into her, sending her flying. As she hit the floor, Bex's drink drenched a well-known supermodel. She tried to get up, spreadeagled, her dress up round her thighs, her heels sliding. The bar fell silent and all eyes were on her. She could hear it all around – smirking, whispering, mocking. Phone cameras flashed. 'Hey, bad form!' cried Hugo, and Sims was on his feet and wrestling a phone from a society blogger who Bex followed religiously.

Oh my God, the dress – the silk was ruined, and the bloody cranberry juice would never come out. Before Sims could get to her, one of the lads offered her a hand up, and she took it. He was smiling, open, easy – 'Sorry, love. David and his huge rugby body . . . Let me get you another drink.'

The boy who'd just virtually assaulted her turned too. 'Yeah, sorry, love. No harm done, eh?'

She rounded on him. 'Course there's bloody harm done!' she screamed.

He leaned backwards and pulled a face. 'All right, sweetheart, calm down!'

'Don't call me sweetheart, you moron! You've wrecked my dress, and I could have broken my neck!' She whirled around, scanning the shocked collection of guests, searching for some kind of manager. 'Who the hell's in charge here?! This floor is so slippery – it's lethal! I could sue!'

'Now, come on, Bex . . .' Sims was beside her now. She turned on him, out of control. 'And screw you, Sims! You're only on the Langdon team because your dad bankrolls half the costs!'

Sims just gaped at her.

'Fuck you, Bex!' called Hugo, so good-naturedly that a lot of people laughed.

She hated them all, and that pretentious cow Finn, and those boring sheep Venetia and Aurelia, who hadn't even turned up. 'I am the face of young British polo,' she announced, holding up her empty glass. 'As you'll see next month in *Surrey Style*. Cheers, and fuck you all!' If she was going out, she was going out with a bang.

Oh, the horror – Delia was stalking over to her from one side, and a burly security guard was heaving his bulky frame across the lethal shiny floor from the other. Time to leave. But she wasn't quite quick enough. Delia reached her first.

'Don't think you'll ever play polo in this country again,' she hissed.

Bex wrinkled up her nose and leaned backwards away from her hot breath, which smelled like spicy tuna rolls and yeasty champagne. *Gross.*

'And we know about your father's business.'

Bex didn't let herself flinch, even though she wanted to puke. The Balfours knew. Soon everyone would.

What about Bomba and Gordo?

Her worst nightmare was coming true. 'And we *will* take your father to court for the money you owe us.' She smiled nastily. 'Let me know where to send your ponies – if you have any friends left who'll take them.'

That did it – the thought of Bomba and Gordo having nowhere to go. She'd let them down. They were innocent animals. They had no part in the crazy circus her life had turned into. The security guard put a hand on her shoulder. He squeezed it kindly, which was worse than if he'd been rough with her.

'It's OK, I'm going.' Bex lurched to the door, broken, defeated, to another wave of whispers and phone flashes, and staggered out on her sky-high heels.

Chapter Thirty-One

Carrie

Carrie wondered if things could actually *get* any more awkward between her and Freddie around the yard. They hadn't had a proper talk since their screaming row – which, as an added bonus, all the staff had heard. Whenever they found themselves alone together in the office, it was so brain-meltingly awful that one or the other made an excuse to leave.

Carrie had started timing her afternoon hay run so that she missed Terrence's staff briefing, and no one had said anything about her not being there. She just couldn't stand the thought of everyone watching them, seeing how they were together, and probably talking about them afterwards.

That's silly, she told herself firmly. *These guys work hard and they've got their own lives. They're not interested in gossiping about me and Freddie.*

But if that was true, why did conversations end when she came round the corner? And why did Beatrice and Heather keep shooting her sad looks and asking if she was OK?

She was thinking about this as she spread out some lovely new wood shavings in Kerala's stable. It smelled so good, and so did Kerala – Carrie was working round her rather than tying her up outside, so they could hang out. The sound of the door catch made her glance up and she found herself eye to eye with Freddie.

'Oh, sorry. I didn't know you were in here.'

'Yes. Here I am.' She cringed. *Urgh, what a weird thing to say*.

She expected him to mumble some excuse and leave right away, but he stayed there, watching her, a sad smile on his lips. 'Remember the second time we met, when I took you to see Kerala?'

Carrie couldn't help smiling too. 'Yes. She was still really injured then. She melted my heart in a second. I couldn't believe I was so close to a horse. Touching her and connecting with her. It was all my dreams come true. Now it seems so normal to be around them – but no less magical.' She stroked Kerala's mane lovingly as she spoke.

'I'm sorry about Bex.'

She glanced up sharply. *Whoa*. That had come out of nowhere. But she knew they had to deal with it sometime. She braced herself, expecting fury to overtake her, but there were only small ripples of frustration.

'Honestly, Carrie. It took me by surprise and I should have reacted more quickly, but I did get a hold of myself and pull away. I don't want to be with Bex, and any feelings I had for her have long gone. I promise you.'

'Thanks,' she managed to say, through the intense feeling in her chest and throat. 'And I'm sorry I riled you up, dancing with Barnaby. Nothing's happened with him though,' she added quickly. 'I swear.' She didn't say anything about him and Hugo. She'd promised Lu.

'That's good to know,' Freddie said. He cleared his throat and swayed from foot to foot awkwardly. He came closer, stood beside her and stroked Kerala's glossy neck. The beautiful pony snickered softly. 'Carrie, do you think we could start again?'

Feeling for him surged through her heart. Here they were. No drama. No chaos. No pain. Just them, and Kerala. She could take one step and be swept up into his arms. She could be kissing him, running her hands down his body. It would be so easy . . .

'You know we can't,' she said, although the words almost choked her. 'It could get messy again so quickly. We're . . . I get crazy, when it comes to you.'

Freddie smiled at that. 'I'm the same. I was so angry and jealous.'

'And there's the work thing,' Carrie said. 'I want a future here. I can't risk losing my job.' It nearly killed her saying it, but she knew it was the truth. She had to choose herself and her future over romance, however painful.

He grimaced. 'I have to respect that,' he said. 'It's breaking my heart, but I understand. My place here is a given, whatever I do. That's not the case for you.'

'Thank you for understanding,' she said, and almost reached for his hand, instinctively, but stopped herself.

'So, friends?' he asked.

She knew he meant to be kind, but he might as well have stabbed her through the heart. Tears surged up, from deep in her chest. *Dammit.* When would this stop being so agonising, so awful? 'Maybe, in time.'

She saw the pain in Freddie's eyes too. *Why did they keep hurting each other?*

This was for the best. She still felt so much for him, though, and she still worried. 'Please will you change horses for the final chukka?' she blurted out. It had been on her mind for days. The first match in the Guillards Cup was the following day, and they still had no idea who'd poisoned Willow.

'No,' he said firmly. 'I won't be intimidated. I always pull Willow out for the final chukka.'

Carrie wanted to slap him in exasperation, then kiss his face off, he was so brave and sexy. 'God! Polo players!' she cried. 'Stubborn, daredevil idiots!'

Freddie laughed. The painful tension between them broke. 'Come on,' he said. 'I want to show you something.' He turned and went out through the door, just expecting her to follow. *Entitled jerk*, she thought. She watched his body move as he strode across the yard in front of her. *Sexy entitled jerk*. Looking wasn't against the rules, at least.

A minute later, Freddie was showing her the security camera he'd had set up in the feed room. 'OK, so, it's up there, in the eaves.'

'You wouldn't spot that even if you were looking for cameras,' she said, impressed.

'If anyone comes in here we'll have it all recorded. I've even left the magnesium tub where it was, in case the poisoner strikes again.'

Carrie thought for a moment. 'The fact that the jar was wiped and obviously used suggests it was opportune the first time. If whoever it was does it again they'll probably bring it themselves. Premeditated now, you see.'

'True. Still, we've replaced it with harmless glucosamine just in case. Unlikely, but . . .'

She was impressed. 'You've thought of everything.'

He shrugged. 'Tried. Well, it's for Willow. If someone tries this again, she might not be so lucky. She could be seriously injured or have a heart attack. We'll have security staff checking everyone's bags tomorrow too. Whoever did it, they won't strike twice – we'll make sure of that.'

She felt a rush of admiration for him and suddenly knew she could trust him with everything. 'Kit, Lu and I have been trying to find out if the Balfours had anything to do with it.'

'The Balfours?' Freddie repeated.

'Yeah. We thought maybe Barnaby was trying to get you injured and out of the season, or that it had something to do with this property deal that's on the table with both estates. I can't see how but it is a weird coincidence. We checked out the Balfour study but couldn't find anything. We did find out they have a safe, though – so there might be something in that, if not about Willow and the poisoning, then maybe something on their dodgy deals so we could blackmail them to leave Kit and his family alone. They're pressurising them to leave.'

Freddie looked impressed. 'Wow, Carrie.' Then he sighed. 'I'm sorry. You've had a lot on your plate, with your friends. I hadn't really thought . . .'

'It's OK.' She smiled. 'Our next move is to try and find out the safe code. We were at the party to do some digging on the Balfours. That's why I couldn't tell you why I was really there. I was worried you'd punch Barnaby in the face if you thought he had anything to do with poisoning Willow,' she said. 'But then, you punched Barnaby in the face anyway, so . . .'

'I actually didn't.' Freddie grinned. 'He took a swing at me, slipped in some spilt beer and landed on his nose.'

'Oh! Sorry, I just assumed . . .'

'That's OK. I might have done, if he'd kept on coming at me, the jumped-up little twat.' He fixed her with an intense stare. 'And I know you were trying to help Kit, but thanks for looking out for me and Willow too.'

'Of course – I'm worried about you. That's why, if you'd just not ride Willow in the—'

He grinned and put his hands over his ears. 'Not listening!' Then he thought for a moment, looking serious. 'About that conference centre deal – there could be something in that. It was all going well for us, looking like our bid was in favour and then, suddenly, Dad's meetings with Ronan Blake were being postponed, on flimsy excuses. And we knew from our contacts that he and his team were having extra talks with the Balfours. That was just a couple of days after the poisoning, now I think about it.'

'Interesting,' said Carrie. 'Oh!' She remembered something. 'Kit told us that someone was going round to do a damp survey on their cottage. I didn't think anything of it at the time, but now, I wonder . . . What if it wasn't a survey for damp, but secretly for renovations? Or a valuation?'

'You think Kit's home could be part of it? That the Balfours saw a way to get the edge in the deal, by forcing the Pearces out and throwing in the cottage?' He was incensed. 'That's illegal.'

Carrie gaped at him. 'I hadn't, but I do now!' she cried. 'It's not illegal if the Pearces leave of their own accord. Kit's parents are already talking about moving because of all the rumours.'

'So, one of them saw an opportunity when Kit went into the feed room, gave Willow the magnesium themselves and framed their own stable hand?' Freddie shook his head. 'I wouldn't put it past them. Any of them. Keep me posted if you do find anything. I know Mum and Dad would stand behind us if we had solid evidence.'

Carrie breathed out, and she didn't even know she'd been holding her breath. Having Freddie on their side could make all the difference. 'Look, just be really careful tomorrow, won't you?'

'For you, anything.'

Carrie had to turn and leave, before she torched her future and fell into his arms.

Chapter Thirty-Two

Luella

'We've made a decision, as a family,' said Kit. He looked torn in half, and Luella flinched at the pain in his eyes and the brimming tears. 'We're leaving the Balfour Estate.'

'No.' She tried to pull him close, but he resisted. 'There's no evidence you did anything wrong, Kit. The rumours will die down.'

'My mum's embarrassed to go into the village and Dad's had enough of warnings from the other ground staff about how badly it reflects on the Balfour Estate. It's already affecting revenue at the farm shop, and the polo school, and it could start costing jobs.'

'That's crazy!' Luella gasped. 'And so unfair.' Her eyes were brimming with tears now too. 'We'll find out who did it and—'

'We tried, Lu,' Kit cut in. 'We failed. There's no more time. Dad says we need to accept the situation.' He sighed and looked at his boots. 'He's been offered a job with an old friend.'

She glared at him. 'Where?' she demanded.

He flicked a glance up at her and then looked down again. 'Northumbria.'

She felt all the breath leave her body. 'But that's hours away!'

'It's a good offer. And we need to go now, Lu, before it gets worse.'

She couldn't say anything else. She tried but the words choked in her throat. Instead, she threw her arms around his neck and lost herself in his deep, passionate kiss.

When they finally broke apart, gasping with heat and desire, she whispered, 'I'd best make the most of you while you're here then and finish what we started in your car.' She led him by the hand up the stairs to her bedroom, where they stumbled through the door and on to the bed, kissing hard, like the world was ending.

Kit and Luella woke up late, tangled around each other. They came to slowly, cuddling and falling in and out of sleep. Eventually Luella managed to pull herself upright. 'OK, coffee,' she said groggily. She was tired. *Well, we were up half the night . . .*

'I'll make it,' Kit offered.

She laughed a little, stroked his face and leaned over to kiss him gently on the lips, careful to keep her mouth closed and not subject him to morning breath. 'I'll go. My dad's cool with us being together, but he might club you to death with his nine iron if he finds you in your boxers standing over his precious espresso machine.' She laughed. 'It's the only thing he loves more than me and mum.'

'Fair enough. And bring toast. Lots and lots of toast. I could eat a horse after last night.'

'Hey, stay *away* from Charlie!' She raised her eyebrows and gave him a flirty smile. '*Good*, wasn't it?'

'Spectacular.' He pulled himself up on to one elbow and met her gaze with sparkling eyes. 'You are amazing – mind, heart, soul, legs, the lot.'

She giggled and threw the duvet over him. 'Keep warm for me.' She got up, pulled on a silk dressing gown and trotted downstairs, feeling like an angel floating on fluffy clouds. Then, 'Jesus!' she cried, as she reached the hall. A blurry face loomed up against the glass of the front door.

'Luella! It's me, it's Bex.'

Luella breathed in sharply. *Bex?!* She'd assumed she'd never hear from her again, especially after she'd smashed the pig. She did feel bad about that now, but she stood by everything she'd said.

She opened the door. Bex looked a hell of a state. She stood there in a simple summer dress and sneakers, no make-up, her face puffy and tear-stained. For a moment, Luella's heart went out to her, but she didn't let it show. She gathered herself and said, 'What do you want?'

'I need to talk to you. Can I come in?'

'No.'

Bex sobbed and leaned against the door-frame. 'Please, Lulu.'

'No one calls me that any more.' Pause. She sighed. 'Look, just go. There is nothing you could possibly have to say to me that I'm interested in hearing.'

Bex looked up, tears running down her cheeks. 'It's all fallen apart, Luella. It's all online. Everyone knows.'

'Knows what?'

'That we're finished. Done. My family is broke. We've got nothing.' With that, she burst into fresh sobs. 'That's why Estrella and Blanca were really sold, and why I had to move Bomba and Gordo to the awful Balfours' place.'

Luella stared at her. *Bloody hell.* So much for coffee and toast and hot morning sex with Kit. 'Stay here. Don't move. We'll be down in five minutes.'

'We?'

'Me and Kit.' Bex looked like she was about to protest, but Luella wasn't having it. 'Anything you can say to me you can say to him.'

Ten minutes later, they were all down in the beautiful, rose-clad summerhouse at the end of the garden, where they wouldn't be overheard. Luella had grabbed a bottle of water on their way out, but Kit was grumbling about coffee, probably to take his mind off wanting to shout at Bex for ruining their first, precious morning waking up together. Her phone pinged. 'Carrie says she'll be here in five – her dad's driving her over,' she told Kit.

'Tell her to bring coffee,' he said.

'Urgh!' Bex complained. 'Carrie? Is this not humiliating enough for me? Why is that girl *everywhere*?'

'She's our friend,' said Luella firmly. 'And you owe her an apology, for lying about Freddie.'

Bex rolled her eyes, but she didn't protest.

When Carrie arrived, Kit gratefully sipped on a double-shot macchiato from the Costa in the village, looking much happier, while Bex mumbled a grudging apology. 'What you've got to understand is, I got carried away and wasn't *entirely* honest about what happened between me and Freddie.'

Kit snorted into his paper cup. 'That was the *worst* apology I've ever heard. I mean, for a start it didn't even include the word "sorry".' Luella felt a huge wave of love for him. His life was falling apart too, but here he was, still laughing, still smiling. Her beautiful, brave, very, very sexy boyfriend.

'Fine, accepted,' grumped Carrie, arms crossed. 'But I don't have to like you.'

Bex looked down her nose at her. 'The feeling is mutual.'

Luella gave Bex a warning glare and she sighed petulantly. 'Fine. I'm *really sorry*, Carrie. What can I do to make it up to you?'

Carrie did crack a smile then. 'You can stop trying to seduce Freddie, for a start.'

'Why? Are you guys still together, even though he cheated on you?' said Bex. 'Because, otherwise, he's free and single.'

Carrie looked like she was about to thump her, but Kit leaned over and tipped her coffee cup up to her face. 'Here. Drink coffee. Nom nom.' Carrie glared at him, but at least she didn't lunge for Bex.

Bex turned to Luella. 'And, by the way, Carrie knew about my parents' financial situation. She agreed not to tell you, so maybe you two aren't as close as you think, Lu.'

Carrie snorted in disbelief. 'Wow, you're on fire this morning,' she said to Bex. Then, to Luella, 'I'm sorry. I wanted to tell you, but I promised not to. So I had to honour it.'

'I respect that,' said Luella, giving her a genuine, warm smile.

Bex looked pissed off that she hadn't driven a wedge between them, and then Carrie said, 'Anyway, in other news, I've been online this morning. It's not pretty. Total social destruction.'

Bex gave her a death stare. 'I'm going now,' she said. She flashed her red-rimmed eyes at Luella. 'So much for any support from my so-called best friend!'

No one stopped her. When they'd watched her go all the way up the garden path, Carrie filled them in on what she'd discussed with Freddie about the property deal and Kit's cottage. Of course, they were outraged, and Kit got to his feet, pacing in fury. 'You think one of them did the poisoning just to frame me and force us out? I wouldn't put it past them,' he fumed. 'I really wouldn't.'

'Me neither,' said Luella. 'But it's only one theory. What if the poisoning was something to do with trying to sabotage the Langdon team, by hurting Willow or Freddie? What if someone tries something again at the game tomorrow?'

'If only we could get into that bloody safe,' said Carrie.

'Oh my God,' said Luella suddenly, sitting up tall. She picked up her phone and pulled up the photos of the things they'd found in Barnaby's room – the paying-in stub, the postcard and the Post-it note. 'Look.'

Carrie and Kit stared at the photo. 'Don't you see?' said Luella.

'See what, babe?' asked Kit. 'The number wasn't recognised, and we couldn't find anyone called Dudley in Barnaby's circles . . .'

'And if Dudley was the one he went to Venice with, we'll never find out,' added Carrie.

Luella laughed and shook her head. 'No. There *is* no Dudley. Well, there *is*, but it's not a person. I knew there was something nagging me about when we were in that study.'

'Oh my God, Lu, what?!' cried Carrie.

'We've got the safe code. It's disguised as the phone number. The *make of the safe* is Dudley.'

'Seriously?' gasped Kit.

Luella laughed. 'Haven't you ever done it with a PIN? Written the last four digits as the end of a phone number?'

Carrie stared at her. 'No – I don't have as many to remember as you. But that's brilliant! You figured it out!'

Luella beamed at her then raised an eyebrow at Kit. 'Thank goodness we got it on on that desk.'

Chapter Thirty-Three

Bex

Saturday was the day of the first game in the Guillards Cup. And this year, it was the Langdons versus the Balfours.

Bex had got a summons from Luella and her annoying Scooby gang. It was the crack of bloody dawn, and she hadn't planned to go anywhere near the Langdon Estate that day, when everyone who was anyone in the polo world would be milling around, sipping Pimm's and judging her after her social implosion.

For once, she wasn't interested in being the talk of the event. Not since the photos of her had ended up online. And not just in posts – there were whole blogs about the sad self-destruction of the could-have-been face of young British polo, Bex Chapman-Foster. She hadn't replied to *any* of her fake friends who had swarmed her inbox after realising they'd missed the scoop of the year. And she hadn't had any messages from the ones who'd been real, back in the day.

Hugo, Sims, Freddie.

A pang of pain shot through her heart and she gasped and pedalled harder. As she reached the Langdon yard on her old mountain bike from the back of the garage (there was no money to MOT the Lotus) she felt increasingly nervous. If they'd called her in here for another dressing down, they could all F off.

Was she a little bit pleased, though, deep down, that Lulu – sorry, *Lu* – had got in touch?

Maybe a tiny bit. But mostly she saw opportunity: a toehold back into the world that now shunned her. And a chance to get into the Langdons' good graces – through *Carrie*, annoyingly.

Gordo and Bomba still had nowhere to go, and the Balfours were sending them in a lorry to her front door on Monday. They'd have to live out in the tiny paddock, with only trees for shelter, until she could somehow make the old stables safe. Which, with no budget, might never happen. The thought of it just about broke her heart. They deserved better, and she'd let them down.

The last stable in the furthest block from the office, Luella's message had said. Bex guessed that was so they wouldn't be overheard. She strode through the yard, quickly, head down. She didn't want to be seen – or, worse, spoken to – by anyone.

'You're ten minutes late,' said Carrie. 'We've all got jobs to go to, you know.'

'Not that you *would* know,' said Kit, but fairly good-naturedly.

'It's a huge day here. I've been on the yard for two hours already, helping out,' added Luella. 'Thanks for coming.'

Bex smiled grimly. 'Well, I suppose the good thing about social annihilation, abject poverty and the end of my polo career is that I'm free at short notice on the first day of the Guillards Cup.' She thought she'd get in there first, take a jab at herself before they did and make it seem like she didn't care.

But, 'We are sorry you're dealing with all those things,' said Luella, with a tiny trace of warmth in her voice.

'Yes, we really are, even me,' said Carrie. 'That's not the point though.' She looked to Kit.

'We need your help today,' he said.

For a moment, Bex thought that they were going to ask her to help out on the yard. Her betraying heart leaped – *part of the team*. But no, of course not. 'We need you to do something at the Balfours',' said Carrie. 'See it as a chance to prove that you're sorry for lying to me and being such a cow to Lu.'

Bex folded her arms and sighed. 'What is it?'

Kit gave her a serious look. 'We think Jasper dropped a flash drive in the septic tank to get rid of evidence of their crimes and we need you to go in and look for it.'

Bex gasped. 'What? No! I—' *Quel horreur.*

The three *amigos* – no, *stooges* – no, *idiots* – all laughed.

'Hilarious,' she said flatly.

'We need you to wear this.' Carrie handed her a flat, rectangular box, with a sweet smile.

Bex took off the lid and pulled out the disgusting waitress uniform.

'Sorry, I didn't have time to wash it,' said Carrie.

Bex had a strong urge to tell her where to shove it, and it wasn't in the washing machine. She shook the dress up and down, then wrinkled her nose at the smell. And God, the texture – it virtually crackled.

'The Balfours are having an *after* the after-party tonight at their house and there'll be staff from the catering company going in and out all day,' Kit said. 'You'll need to wear that and go in with wine boxes or something. Make sure you're not being watched and then go up to the study, take the spare key off the door-frame—'

'Who the hell keeps the key to a locked room on the door-frame?!' cried Bex.

'The kind of person who has *password* as a password,' said Luella.

'And get into the safe,' Kit continued.

'I'll text you the code,' Luella added.

'But how do you—' Bex began.

'None of your business,' said Luella crisply. Bex noticed that she glanced at Kit and looked a little flustered.

'Get in there and see what you can find,' said Carrie bossily. 'Anything dodgy looking, or that you're not sure of, take pictures, and then send them to Lu.'

'*Oh sure.* Is that all?'

'Yes,' said Carrie. 'Off you go. You might need to hide in the grounds for a few hours, so you can pick the right moment.'

Bex couldn't be bothered to think of a smart reply. She just said, 'Fine,' and sighed, turned and stalked off. It wasn't like she had other plans, after all.

So, that was how she came to be crouching in a bush only just less prickly than the bloody waitress costume – sorry, *uniform* – watching trucks and vans come and go. Cleaners. Extra chairs. Flowers. Caterers. An ice sculpture, for crying out loud. And waitresses with wine boxes, setting up tables with cloths and champagne glasses outside the front of the house.

She watched carefully. She had to get this right. If only to prove to that awful Carrie that she was quite capable of doing a simple task. And maybe to win Luella over just a tiny bit. Did she want that? She hardly dared to hope. So, she guessed that meant yes, she did.

Things went quiet as one o'clock approached, and people seemed to be taking time off for lunch or heading back to their businesses. About ten past, she saw her chance. A wine box had been left beside the front door. She was nervous, but excited too. If there was one thing Bex loved, it was a challenge. And a challenge that involved possibly taking down the hideous Balfour family – well, even better.

She strode up to the house, acting like she was meant to be there, but then stooped a little and made herself more uncertain, like the gawky teenage waitresses she was always having to put up with in Yetbourne. They simply didn't have that London polish. She paused when she reached the box and looked around, pretending to question it. She was really getting into the role, now. Then she heaved it into her arms and went through the open door.

She was taking the wine box upstairs, half hiding herself behind it, when a shrill voice said, 'Where are you going with that?'

She improvised. 'It was left on the steps, and John said to take it up to the first-floor sitting room.' She peeked over the box to find a stern woman in a housekeeper's uniform glaring at her. 'For goodness' sake, why listen to *him*? What does an ice sculptor know about logistics?'

Picking a common name had worked. 'Erm, not much, I guess . . .'

'It was a rhetorical question – I don't require an answer, thank you.' The woman gestured imperiously. 'Through here, to the fridges. Hurry up, you're not paid to stand about. There were complaints that the champagne wasn't chilled enough at Barnaby's party, for Delia's precious baby boy. If the white's warm tonight, she'll have a bloody cardiac arrest.'

Bex was getting to like the feisty woman. She clearly had about as much respect for the Balfours as she did, i.e. none.

She went through to the huge kitchens, put the wine in the fridge as directed by a harassed older man who clearly spent all day being bossed about by the housekeeper and then slipped out of the open back door. She went round to the ballroom. The doors were open too, on to the terrace, where yet more wine glasses were set out on linen-clothed tables. She hurried past the stupid statue, which was no longer wearing its ski goggles and knickers, and with a quick glance around her to check the coast was clear this time, slipped up the main staircase.

The spare key was supposed to be on top of the door-frame. She felt about, all the way along. But it wasn't there. Damn. Maybe they'd sussed that someone had been snooping around at Barnaby's party. Or perhaps one of them had used it and forgotten to put it back.

She wasn't one to give up, though. She remembered something, from that dreadful lunch with the vile Balfours and that tedious Alfonso. The drainpipe, which went all the way up to the study window, and then up to the roof. When one was desperately bored at a God-awful event, one noticed things like that. She went back downstairs and found the one she'd been thinking of. The Balfours may not have taste but, fortunately, with the old country house, they had inherited quality. The drainpipe was sturdy – it looked like cast iron. Anyway, not flimsy plastic rubbish.

She checked that no one was around. The lunch break was still in full force, happily, so she stepped through the flowerbed and shinned up the drainpipe. She had powerful thighs from all the riding she did. She made it most of the way up and then had to use some of the wisteria to clamber up on to the balcony. The strict housekeeper came out into the garden at that moment, chewing out two of the gawky teenage-waitress brigade for setting out the glasses wrongly. Bex threw herself over the balcony as quietly as possible, rolled up on to her feet like a stuntwoman (years of falling off while riding helped too) and examined the French doors. She was just working out how to force them open when she tried the handle and found them unlocked.

Voilà. She was in.

The safe was right where Luella had said it was. Though how she'd spotted it in the first place she didn't know. She opened it with the code she'd texted her and riffled through the papers inside. There wasn't too much, only three paper files of documents and a few loose sheets inside an envelope. She took pictures of everything, rather than trying to work out what they were looking for, and pinged them off to Luella right away.

Oh, yes, here, *interesting*. Plans and contracts about Berrymead Cottage, where Kit's family lived. A long-term rental agreement, for an exorbitant amount, even by Bex's standards, signed in advance by Jasper and Delia, and by Ronan Blake for Blake Enterprises. There were designs for a high-end, luxury refit of the cottage, too, which definitely wasn't going to be for a labouring family. And the minutes from a meeting during which the inclusion of the cottage in the deal was discussed.

When she was finished, she put everything back exactly as she'd found it – she'd been riffling through her parents' personal files since she was about six because it was the only way to find out what was going on in a household where no one actually *spoke* to one another. She closed the safe, reset the lock as it was, gave it a good wipe and headed out. As she slipped out through the French doors again, her phone vibrated silently by her hip. She pulled it out.

Luella.

Three words.

We were right.

Chapter Thirty-Four

Carrie

Meanwhile, over at the Langdons', the Guillards Cup season opener was about to get started. Kit, Carrie and Luella had worked flat out all morning since they'd met with Bex, and had only just managed to catch up with one another. They hadn't even *seen* Freddie to get an update from him, he'd been so busy.

Carrie was kind of relieved – although they were moving towards being friends, they were awkward enough around each other on the yard. It would be ten times worse with all these people watching. She hadn't changed her mind, though. They couldn't be together. She was still coming to terms with it but, for now, she'd have to put her heartbreak to one side – they had a job to do.

Kit, Luella and Carrie were now pitch-side, close to the Langdon pony lines, which were being vigilantly watched over by Lord L and

Terrence this time, as well as the grooms and security staff. They gathered round Luella's phone, looking over the pictures from Bex again. Even with all the noise and bustle around them, at that moment it felt to Carrie as if they were the only three people in the world – a tight team, completely focused on what they'd just discovered.

Reading the text in the photos, Carrie had felt elated and awful at once. They had evidence, yes – but it was evidence that the Balfours had calculatedly planned to force Kit's family out of their home and off the estate. That was terrible. Just terrible.

Luella entwined her fingers with Kit's and squeezed his hand. 'This must be a lot to take in.'

He shrugged his shoulders, waves of unexpressed emotion rolling off him. 'I'm . . . I don't *know* how I am. I feel . . . I'm upset for my family, and shocked that the Balfours could actually try pulling this shit, after the decades of service we've given. I mean, even knowing what they're like, that's . . .' He blew out his breath. His voice took on an angry edge. '. . . fucking unbelievable. I'm torn between getting Mum and Dad to take them to court and punching Jasper in the face.'

Luella gripped his fingers. 'Don't. You're better than that.'

Kit smiled grimly. 'Don't worry, I won't. I'd never give him the satisfaction of handing him real grounds to evict us.' He took a deep breath and gathered himself. 'I'll process this later. Let's keep our eyes on the ball. We know the Balfours took advantage of the poisoning, for sure. And we suspect that one of them did it. But we don't *know* that. If it was a Balfour, yeah, they've achieved their aim, or so they think, so there's no reason to do it again. But if it wasn't . . . Willow and Freddie could be in danger today.'

As well as another pang of fear for Freddie's safety, Carrie felt admiration flood through her – Kit always put the horses' welfare first. Bloody hell, if it were her, she'd have punched Jasper in the face on her way to the lawyers while announcing over the tannoy what they'd done and sticking the pictures on social media. For starters.

But that isn't what matters right now. Inspired by Kit, she got a grip on herself. *Freddie* mattered, and Willow. At least Willow wouldn't be playing until the final chukka – and Freddie hadn't messaged Carrie about anything suspicious in the feed room, or from the security checks.

The game got started and she waved to Freddie as he took his position. Things went well for the Langdon team, although she could only half concentrate – her eyes kept straying to Willow. She was keeping an eye on the Balfours too. They were all in the VIP area, drinking champagne and schmoozing Ronan Blake and his cronies, probably thinking they had the conference centre deal in the bag now that Kit's family were leaving. Kit and Luella were hypervigilant too, Carrie saw, and the jovial, thrilled atmosphere around them felt all wrong.

Still, the first chukka went well, with the Langdons one up at 3–2. It had been a heart-poundingly exciting game so far, with Freddie heading up the Langdon team while Alfonso captained the Balfour team.

The second and third chukkas, in which Freddie rode Blaze, put them down at 4–5, but it was an even match and Carrie felt sure Freddie could get it back for them. He'd played brilliantly and scored two of the goals, outdoing even the pros. She felt a wave of longing for him and swallowed it down. He wasn't hers. Never would be. She was just another face in the cheering crowd, now. Just another Langdon staff member. *Just another girl.*

Freddie was on Fly for the fourth chukka, and neither team scored.

The fifth chukka, with Freddie riding Phantom, went badly at first, but then the Langdon team really pulled together and got themselves level at six all.

No one scored in the sixth, either. Soon it was time for the final chukka, and Heather was there ready to hand Freddie Willow and walk Phantom back to the pony lines. Carrie felt a stab of worry in her stomach as he strode over to her.

Luella squeezed her arm. 'He'll be OK. They both will.'

She turned and found a small smile. 'I hope so.'

The riders and horses came back on to the pitch into the line-up. The referee rolled the ball in and it was game on. Freddie and Willow bolted up and down. Soon it was seven all and Orlando, the Balfour number three, was aggressively hooking Freddie as they charged down the field towards goal.

'How is the ref not calling that foul?!' cried Kit. Carrie's heart thumped.

Luella's anxiety had clearly reached crisis point too, and she wasn't even watching the match. She was scrolling through the photos of the Balfour papers from Bex on her phone, hands trembling, zooming in. 'Something's nagging at me,' she explained, to Carrie's questioning look, 'like the name of that bloody Dudley safe did. Something I didn't know I'd seen.' She scrolled and zoomed in and frowned at the screen some more. And then, 'Aha!'

She turned her phone round to show Kit and Carrie. 'Look, here. The minutes of the meeting when the illegal eviction of Kit's family was discussed, a week before Willow was poisoned. Look who took them.'

'It's always Eric,' Kit muttered. But he leaned in, shading the screen from the strong sunshine and trying to see anyway. Carrie took off her sunglasses so that she could read it too.

'Not this time,' said Luella gravely. 'Look – there.'

Carrie gasped, and her stomach flipped over. 'Oh my God! Felicity!'

'No,' muttered Kit, quailing with shock. 'So, she was in on their property scheme, which means she *is* a suspect for the poisoning, same as the rest of them.'

'Technically, she is,' said Luella. 'But she's so sweet. And she's crazy about Kit. Surely she couldn't have done it.'

They all looked across at the VIP area, where the Balfours were watching the match. Felicity was there with the rest of them. She locked eyes with Carrie and raised her glass of sparkling elderflower. Then she blew Kit a kiss. And took a bite of the apple in her hand.

'She's crazy about Kit, yes,' said Carrie. 'But she was rejected by him.'

'And she was keen to prove to her dad she has a business head, like the rest of them,' Luella muttered. 'I remember her saying so.'

Kit blanched. 'Surely not,' he croaked.

'The apple . . .' Carrie said. 'You don't think she was taunting us, taking a bite like that?'

It took Luella a moment to catch her meaning. 'Oh my God! The apple core we found, in the feed room, after Willow was poisoned. Surely, Felicity couldn't have . . .'

They all turned to stare at Willow, just as she started to buck and rear, and spin wildly around.

Carrie stared, wide eyed. Bewildered. 'No . . .'

Her heart was hammering in her chest and she thought she might throw up. Freddie was being thrown all over the place, almost out of his seat. He kept playing though. The teams were still neck and neck. Willow whinnied in distress and plunged at another horse, and they both almost went over. 'Shit, one of them could break a leg at this rate!' growled Kit.

Willow was rearing up, spinning and bolting forward.

'They'll lose the game!'

'Screw the game, I'm worried they're going to lose their lives!'

Heather was arguing with Lord L. She wanted to take Freddie another horse, but he wasn't going to let her on to the pitch and near Willow with her going off like that.

'Come on!' cried Carrie, running, calling back to them. 'You distract Lord L and Terrence! I'll take Blaze to Freddie!'

They didn't have to worry about how to create a distraction. Luella, trying to run in wedges, tripped at the pony lines and virtually bowled Lord L over. Carrie took Blaze's reins from a stunned Heather, and Kit gave her a leg up.

She urged Blaze away, towards the pitch. Freddie was almost thrown off again as she galloped towards them, bouncing about in the saddle, not used to such short stirrups. She jumped over the small board and shouted, 'Freddie!'

He turned and stared in astonishment. 'Carrie, for God's sake! Get out of here!'

Luckily, he was at the side of the pitch by then, as Willow was now trying to bolt off with him, and Carrie cantered Blaze right up to them. 'No! You can still win! Come on!' She leaped to the ground and held out her hand for Willow's rein.

For a moment, she thought he'd refuse. But then he smiled. 'I want to be with you,' he said, as Willow bucked and reared like a bronco. 'We belong together. We both know it.' He half fell, half jumped off and handed her the rein.

Adrenaline pumping through her veins, Carrie pulled him close by the collar of his polo shirt and kissed him hard. Everything else melted away.

Finally, she forced herself to pull back. 'Go!'

With a determined grin, he launched himself up on to Blaze and galloped back into the game. 'Be careful!' he shouted over his shoulder.

Carrie managed to walk Willow to the sideline, heart hammering, dodging her hooves as she reared, one of the reins snapping. Still holding the other, on wobbling legs she made it to Beatrice and Heather, who ran to meet her. Beatrice had a rope and head collar and threw the rope round Willow's neck, so they could lead her from either side.

Off the pitch and away from the action, Willow started to calm down a little. As the grooms walked her up and down the fence-line, she was snorting, shaking her head and pawing at the ground. The vet was soon on hand, too, helping them lead her away. As Carrie stepped over the board, Luella and Kit were suddenly by her side and she fell into their arms, her legs finally giving way.

'Oh my God, you idiot!' Luella roared, hugging her tight.

'Brave, though!' cried Kit. 'And did you just *kiss* Freddie?'

'Yes, she did!' squealed Luella.

Shouts went up from the crowd and they all turned to see Freddie galloping towards the goal, in possession of the ball. He took an edgy slam from Alfonso and cries of 'Foul! Ref!' went up. But there was no call on it and Freddie shook him off and kept going, scoring the golden goal.

The crowd went wild. Kit lifted Luella off her feet and spun her round. Carrie's heart almost burst out of her chest with joy. He'd done it. Her beautiful Freddie. He'd won the game for the Langdon Estate.

Chapter Thirty-Five

Luella

The Langdon team had won! Which meant, deliciously, the Balfours were now out of the running for the Guillards Cup. Things over at their marquee looked pretty dark and stormy.

'Right, time to talk to Felicity,' said Kit. He glanced around, scanning the crowd. 'I don't know if that apple thing was some kind of taunt, but if she did do it, let's find out. And if she didn't, she's been in on Balfour business, and she might know who did.'

'I need to go see Freddie,' said Carrie. 'And find out if Willow's OK.' The vet was with her then, along with the grooms, Terrence and Lord L at the Langdon pony lines.

'Of course you do. And you need some time to calm yourself down, after your heroics,' said Luella, giving her a quick hug. 'We'll handle this.'

As Carrie hurried off to find Freddie, Kit and Luella made their way over to Felicity, hand in hand. All around them people were celebrating the win and talking with concern about Freddie's battle with the wild Willow, no doubt speculating about her being poisoned again.

As they neared Felicity, who was in the VIP marquee, Kit squeezed Luella's hand and leaned close to her ear. 'Keep calm,' he said quietly. 'We've got this.'

Felicity saw them coming and raised her glass. 'Darlings!' she shrilled, turning heads beside her. 'Congratulations – a well-deserved victory. Kitster, although you work for us, I know you're Langdon through and through.'

Luella felt the sharp edge in her voice and Kit's hand tensed in hers. They'd need to be careful – Felicity might only be keeping up appearances because she could be overheard by all the polo-world bigwigs around her, many of them instrumental in keeping the Balfours at the top of the social and financial tree.

Kit put up a mask. 'Fliss!'

They both air-kissed her. A young waiter offered them champagne and they took a glass each. They all looked out at the field, sipping their drinks, watching the happy crowd treading in the divots. Luella subtly manoeuvred to the other side of Felicity, in case she tried to bolt – not that she'd be performing any citizen's arrests in these bloody wedges.

'So, I guess the question is why?' said Kit, calmly.

Straight in there. Brave.

Felicity's fingers flickered on the stem of her glass. She looked uncertain, and *guilty*. But then she smiled. 'I don't know what you're talking about. *Why* what?'

Luella stepped in, thinking quickly. 'I'm guessing the rumours about Kit were an unforeseen consequence of you giving Willow the magnesium. You know, to make sure the Balfours won the charity game? Get the Langdon team on the back foot before the Guillards Cup matches started?' *Slide the accusation in there.* She and Kit both knew that the stuff about the charity game wasn't true, but they didn't want to show their hand about the cottage. All this was communicated in a wave of energy and a look between them, right across Felicity.

That seemed to decide it – the connection between them sent fury flashing in her eyes. 'There were no *unintended consequences*,' she sneered.

Oh my God, so she did do it, Luella thought, keeping her face carefully expressionless. *But she's just a kid.*

'I was perfectly in control of my plan, thank you very much,' she said. 'I *wanted* to frame you, Kit. Who do you think reminded Eric to tell Ginny to get you to take the iodine back? I *intended* to force you and your family out of the cottage.'

Kit must have been using every ounce of his willpower to keep calm, but Luella could feel the tension rolling off him. 'So you took the magnesium from the Langdon tub and wiped it clean, and fed it to Willow in the cored-out apple?' she asked. She kept to the practical, and off the emotional, to help Kit keep it together.

'Yes, that's right. But today I didn't go into the feed room at all – I assume they have cameras up now. Not worth the risk, just in case. And I guessed there would be bag checks, so I cycled over here and tucked a small apple filled with magnesium into one of the struts at the pony lines, at Willow's place, long before anyone arrived here this morning, where I knew she'd find it.' She giggled. 'I didn't even really poison her – she sort of poisoned herself.'

Felicity pouted at Kit. 'Maybe if you hadn't rejected me, none of this would have had to happen,' she said. 'But you hurt me, Kitster.

The best thing was to get you out of my life, away from our estate, so I could find a way to move on.'

Shock passed between Kit and Luella. *Whoa.* The girl was completely unhinged.

Kit lost the battle with everything bubbling under the surface. 'That's total bullshit,' he growled. 'We know about the property deal, and the cottage being included. And that you knew all about it – you took the minutes at a family business meeting with Ronan Blake a week before the first poisoning.'

Felicity spluttered her drink and took a moment to compose herself. Luella got ready to grab her if she made a run for it.

'Fine, I wanted to win my family's respect,' Felicity snapped. 'Prove I have as many business smarts as the rest of them. I'm so sick of being seen as the sappy weakling and left out of everything. I looked for a way to get in on the action. When Eric was too ill to do the minutes for the meeting, I stepped in and saw a golden opportunity to help us win the Blake deal, by including the cottage.'

Kit and Luella exchanged a glance, and more silent communication – he'd got a handle on himself again. 'Do your family know you poisoned Willow, twice?' he asked.

She shook her head. 'No. They suspect, maybe. But I like to keep my cards close to my chest. They taught me well.' She sighed. 'They'll find out now, I suppose.'

'Yes, they will,' said Kit, his fists clenching. He squared up to her, fury flashing in his eyes, and Luella's heart lurched. Felicity would love him to lose control and wreck everything for himself, when they were so close to clearing his name.

Just then, Felicity spotted Freddie and Carrie as they came to join them. 'I think I'll go home now,' she said. 'Headache. Too much sun. Besides, four against one really isn't good form.' And with that she gave them a sly smile and made to leave.

Kit, outraged, stepped in front of her, but Luella hugged him close – partly to stop him grabbing Felicity, and partly so she could whisper in his ear, 'Let her go. I've got it all recorded.' She flashed him the tiny tie-pin mic on the inside of her collar.

He laughed out loud and swept her into his arms, kissing her so passionately she almost fell off her wedges. 'You genius!'

Freddie and Carrie reached them just then, both hot and sweaty.

'How's Willow?' Kit asked Freddie. Luella's face clouded over with concern.

'Rattled, and under observation, because of the danger to her heart, but she should be OK,' he told them.

'I hope so,' said Kit gravely. 'Me too,' said Luella. Then she quickly told them about the recorded confession and relayed what Felicity had said, while Freddie took two glasses of mineral water from a tray and downed them both, one after the other.

'So, it was as we thought?' said Carrie. 'All about the business deal?'

'Yep,' said Luella. 'She tried to make out that her feelings were hurt when Kit turned her down, but clearly that was just a bonus reason to her. She's a steely little snake, like the rest of them, and completely self-absorbed, to a scary degree.'

Kit shook his head in disbelief. 'I thought she was just a sweet kid.'

'We all did,' said Luella, feeling stunned herself.

'What will happen to her?' Carrie asked.

Kit sighed. 'Nothing, probably. Her family will back her up and close ranks.'

Carrie looked bewildered. 'What? No, that's not right. We've got the photos from the safe. Proof.'

'Well, yes, and we can hold those over them, if we need to, but they only show what the Balfours were *going* to do. They hadn't actually *done* anything yet, apart from a fiddle over ten grand, which I'm sure they'd find a way to explain.'

'But we've got a recorded confession! Freddie could have been hurt and Willow . . . Even the police would feel this was enough evidence, surely!'

Luella cringed and made a hand gesture meaning *Keep your voice down*, as Freddie coughed loudly to try and cover her words.

'Carrie, darling, it doesn't work like that,' he said, pulling her close.

She glared at him. 'Yes, it does. It's called *justice*.' No one backed her up. She glared at them in turn. 'What is *wrong* with you three?'

'We'll all get copies of the recording,' Freddie said calmly, in a low voice. Kit and Luella nodded, as Carrie gaped at him. 'Show it to the old man. We have it, and all the property deal evidence, if we need it. It's safe to say that Ronan Blake's deal with the Balfours will be off.'

'Uh-huh,' said Kit.

'Absolutely,' said Luella.

'How can you be so sure?' Carrie demanded.

Freddie leaned close to her ear, taking the chance to kiss her cheek at the same time. 'Dad's people will have words in the right ears and with Ronan Blake. We know he was in on it, and he won't risk that being made public. He'll cut ties with the Balfours in exchange for our silence. They won't tell, because they'd be hanging *themselves* out to dry too.'

'Your dad is like the Mafia don of polo,' said Carrie, finally relaxing a little, knowing the Balfours wouldn't get away with all of it.

Freddie smiled wryly. 'Yeah, but a good don – less arranging murders, more supporting British wildlife.'

'You could get the conference centre deal back, for the Langdon Estate, and do it all above board, how it should be done,' Kit suggested.

'Maybe,' said Freddie, 'but I doubt Dad will want to be in the running for a deal with Ronan Blake, knowing what he was involved in. We have our reputation to think of, and if he's got a relationship with the Balfours, we can't risk some secret plan of theirs going off and all this backfiring in our faces. It's too risky. Like your family, Kit, we're in this for the long term – we think in terms of four, five generations forward, not about making a quick buck tomorrow.'

A waitress appeared with a tray of canapés then – salmon blinis and rare roast beef squares in mini Yorkshire puddings. Freddie helped himself to one of those, then two, and then took the tray from her with a smile. 'Actually, I'll just have this . . .'

'Oh, and with all the drama, I forgot to say – well done, Freddie!' cried Kit, shaking his hand.

'And, wow, well done, Carrie!' Luella said then, hugging her friend close, fiercely, relief flooding her again. She went to hug Freddie, then sprang backwards. 'Urgh! Don't you want to change? Phwoar!'

Freddie laughed. 'The sweet scent of victory!'

'There is nothing sweet about that stink, Langers!' Luella said. Aside to Carrie, she said, 'You know, they go to the pub like that after the games – it's disgusting!'

'I could go for a shower,' Freddie offered. He winked at Carrie. 'You could come with me.'

'In your dreams!' Carrie slapped him playfully.

'Exactly.' He grinned, then turned to Kit. 'Hey, if Jasper and Delia Balfour don't fully reinstate you to your former duties, reopen all your opportunities and back off from your family, then let me know, OK? We can trust my dad to handle that, if it comes to it.'

Kit was absolutely beaming, and Luella felt the weight lift off his shoulders. He looked lighter instantly. 'Thanks, Freddie. I'm still ambitious, and planning to ride on the Balfour team. Keep your friends close but your enemies closer, right? We're *not* being pushed out of our home by those scheming snakes.'

A smile crept over Luella's face as she held up a salmon blini. 'To us four,' she said.

They all toasted one another with blinis and mini Yorkshire puddings. 'To a winning team.'

Chapter Thirty-Six

Bex

There was a bit of an early evening lull between the polo and the after-party at the ground, and while Bex had intended to go to neither, here she was parking her bike in the Langdon yard once again.

She'd changed out of the bloody waitress uniform, of course, and chucked it in the outside bin. This time she didn't hurry through the yard with her head down, hoping not to be seen. No, it was chin up and shoulders back all the way. That's what would get her through the gossip mill, and the social media shitstorm, until things settled down again. As her father always said, life was about going forward, ever forward. Looking back was a waste of time.

Luella had messaged her about Willow, and the Langdon win. She suspected that Lu and her new boyfriend and replacement best friend knew who was behind the poisonings, but she didn't think for a minute that they'd ever tell her. She'd done her bit, anyway. That should help smooth things over with the three of them – enough to make living in Yetbourne bearable, at least. She reached the office, adjusted her smart collared T-shirt, smoothed down her hair and went inside to face the music.

Freddie was still in his polo gear. 'Bex – come in.' He was pouring from that ancient percolator jug thing on the side table. 'Coffee?'

Bex sniffed. 'No thanks. You've had that thing in here since, well, since I first started coming to the kids' Saturday polo club. God knows when it was last washed.'

He smirked and said, 'Oh, yes – you had Shelka, do you remember? That tiny Welsh Section A. She was a right handful.' He smiled wryly. *Highly strung.*

'And you had that old battleaxe, Odin,' she said. 'Who calls a pony after a Norse god?! What was he, anyway? He played like a rhinoceros in a pony costume – and he was as tough too.'

'We never quite knew,' said Freddie, sipping his coffee. 'It was pre-DNA testing kits and he was a rescue. Part pony, part yeti, I think.'

Bex took a deep breath and lifted her chin. Why did she find it so damn hard? 'I'm sorry,' she said. 'About lying to Luella, saying something went on between us, which I knew would get back to Carrie.'

Freddie held her gaze for a long time, until she felt so awkward and uncomfortable she wanted to scream. But she didn't drop eye contact, and she tried with every fibre of her being to get across to him that she actually *was* sorry. Because she was. The whole thing had got completely out of hand.

She thought she was in for a tirade, but Freddie being Freddie just took it in quietly. 'Thank you,' he said eventually. 'I accept. And, well, I wasn't entirely blameless myself.'

A genuine smile of relief broke out like sunshine over her face. 'Thank you. I've come clean to Luella and Carrie, and apologised, of course.'

Freddie laughed softly at that. 'Well done,' he said. 'Not easy, to face things out. My old man says you can always recover from the truth. And I hope you do, Bex – I really do.'

For a moment, her heart flooded with genuine warmth, thinking of them both at five, bombing around on Odin and Shelka like idiots. 'Just so you know, I'll cut ties with the Balfours,' she said then. 'At least they've stopped asking for money, for which, I assume, I have your father to thank?'

Freddie smiled. 'I assume you have my father to thank too.'

Bex suddenly wobbled badly, thinking of Gordo and Bomba being packed into the lorry in two days' time, and coming to a tiny paddock with no stabling and no decent shelter. And no money for hay, let alone supplements, wormer, farriers, dental . . .

'What about your ponies?' Freddie asked, as if reading her mind.

She shrugged, a lump blocked her throat and tears welled up in her eyes. She didn't try to hide it and act tough, for a change. She just let them spill down her cheeks. 'Back to our place. You know, the old stables at the back, where us lot used to hang out and secretly drink and play spin the bottle? They'll have to go there, for now. Well, in the paddock. The actual stables are falling down – they're too dangerous.'

Freddie gave her a long look, obviously thinking something over, and then smiled slowly. 'That's not really the place for budding star polo ponies,' he said. 'We've got room here at the moment, since Moira moved back to Ireland and relocated her string.'

Bex gasped, genuinely surprised. 'What, you'd have me back? After everything I've done?'

'Even then,' said Freddie. 'You're a great polo player. You'd be a welcome addition to the team, if you work hard and make good with the staff.'

She was so moved she almost couldn't speak. Could people really *be* like this? *What was the catch? Maybe it was just decent Freddie being decent Freddie*, she told herself, *simple as that*. She supposed she'd have to think of him as a friend from now on and, worse, as Carrie's boyfriend, to keep the peace. A little part of her had to admit that those two were good together, though.

She sighed. 'I appreciate the offer so much, Freddie,' she said. 'Seriously. But as you know . . . I'm a little . . . under-resourced at the moment.'

Wow. Understatement.

She didn't have to say more.

'I understand.' He didn't get all embarrassingly touchy-feely, or start trying to talk about money and mortify her. 'You can have DIY livery for now and work for their feeds and bedding. Work *hard*, I mean. I'll give you a couple of months' stabling on a tab.'

She smiled. 'Thank you. Very much.' This was no time to get uppity. She'd secured a good home for Gordo and Bomba; that was what mattered.

'And have your dad drop by for a drink with mine. I'll talk to the old man in the meantime. We're going another way – he's not touching that conference centre. We're going back to our original plan, and we'll be putting a tender out for some barn conversions, for eco workshops and retreats.'

Bex nodded. 'Thanks, I will,' she said, her voice breaking with gratitude and tears. Then she grinned at him. 'Eco workshops?'

'Yeah, it's a new initiative of ours . . .'

Bex rolled her eyes dramatically. 'Oh God, please don't start going on about mixed native hedges again!' she groaned. 'I literally used to think I'd die of boredom.'

Freddie laughed heartily. She felt a genuine, sharp pang of grief for what could have been.

'Look, why don't you come to the party this evening? Luella will be there, and the others, plus Hugo and Sims.'

Bex glanced up and met his eyes, and for a moment she let her vulnerability show. 'I'm the last person they'll want to see. And I'm pretty sure Hugo and Sims are planning never to speak to me again.'

'Give them all a chance,' Freddie said. He looked at his old-fashioned wristwatch – his great-grandfather's, she knew. 'Well, I'd better be getting on.'

They didn't hug. They could have done, but Bex thought that wouldn't be right by Carrie, after what had happened. She didn't *like* the girl, but she had to admit that she respected her. And Freddie, of course. She offered her hand and he shook it. 'We part as friends,' she said.

Freddie smiled. 'As friends.'

She swished off, feeling lighter somehow. Freer. And a lot, lot happier.

'Oh, Bex?'

'Yes?'

'I wasn't joking about working hard. Prepare to do a lot of poo picking round here, and to eat a lot of humble pie.' He grinned at her.

'Yeah, yeah, I know,' she groaned. But as she walked away, she was smiling too. Life couldn't keep Bex Chapman-Foster down for long. Shovelling poo at the Langdons' suddenly seemed way better than any photo shoot or PR event she could possibly imagine. It gave her two remaining beloved ponies a home and it was the start of her rise to new, even greater heights.

Epilogue

Carrie

There was still a little light in the sky. The fairy lights strung all around the outside of the clubhouse glowed brighter with each moment as the bruisy blues of the sky muted into a deeper dusk. Carrie felt like the belle of the ball on Freddie's arm, with Kit and Luella happy together, dancing to the classic band, playing the Frank Sinatra hit 'I've Got You Under My Skin'. The band was Kit's kind of thing, and Luella's feet had hardly touched the floor all night.

Carrie and Freddie had been talking to Lord and Lady L, who were now off to do the rounds – *pressing the flesh*, as Lord L had called it, with a grimace. They'd been OK with her about getting together with Freddie, although she suspected he was in for the riot act next week, when the celebrations were over. They'd deal with whatever came, though, *together*.

Hugo swung over to them on his crutches. He shook hands with Freddie and he and Carrie shared a warm hug. 'Looking gorgeous, Miss Brent,' he said.

She smiled and swished from side to side. 'What, this old *extremely expensive designer dress* I borrowed from Luella? Why, thank you!'

She knew she looked good in the floor-length rose gold Kenzo evening gown. It had a slit up one side and a hole cut out at the waist, which showed off the curve of her hip and seemed to give Freddie some trouble breathing. 'You look dapper too,' she told him. 'And well, really well.'

'That's probably because I've broken up with Barnaby,' he said.

'I'd say I'm sorry, but that would be a lie.' *Freddie. Ever candid.*

'Well, *I'm* sorry,' said Carrie. 'Even if Barnaby's a dick – no offence – love is love and break-ups suck.'

Hugo smiled warmly at them both. 'Thanks. I'm getting over it, slowly. I deserve someone who's proud to be seen with me.'

'Good for you,' said Carrie. 'It won't be easy, but in time, with lots of healing, you'll come to see that there are other—'

'Actually, I've got my eye on Dashiel over there,' said Hugo, with a cheeky smile.

Carrie nudged him. 'Naughty! But good. Have fun.' She had a sudden thought. 'Oh, can I ask – did you ever go to Venice with Barnaby?'

Hugo peered at her. 'How did you know about that? It was top secret – we were meant to be on an art trip, for A levels.'

'And you sent him a postcard from the Scottish National Gallery?'

'Yeah, it was a joke – like, I did actually go to the place we'd lied about going to, when I was up there to check out Edinburgh Uni. Barnaby's dad found out and B somehow got him to pay up ten grand not to tell his mum he was dating someone from the Langdon camp.'

Carrie glanced at Freddie. 'Aha! Two mysteries solved!'

'What?!' asked Hugo.

She just shook her head and smiled. 'Never mind, it doesn't matter now.' But she was excited to tell Kit and Luella later, when they finally put each other down and got off the dance floor. Her gaze wandered across the clubhouse and Sims caught her eye. She smiled and he raised his glass to her. She'd go over for a chat soon, and catch up with Heather and Beatrice too, who scrubbed up very well, as it turned out, and were turning heads.

'Aye, aye, trouble at twelve o'clock,' said Hugo, nodding to the door. 'Get security on to it, Freds.'

'It's fine, I invited her,' said Freddie.

Bex had turned up late, of course, and was making a fabulous, dramatic entrance in an Issey Miyake silver flowing dress paired with a punky studded leather collar.

She came straight over to them – well, there wasn't really anyone else who would talk to her, Carrie guessed. But Freddie was soon summoned by his dad, with Hugo in tow, after kissing Carrie long and hard enough that Bex made puking gestures.

As Bex took some champagne from a nearby tray, Carrie raised her own glass. 'Cheers. Nice outfit.'

'Cheers,' said Bex. They sipped at their drinks and watched the happy crowd. 'You know, while the PDAs are disgusting and common, I'm not too gutted you got Freddie in the end.'

Carrie almost spat her drink out. 'Erm, thank you, I think.'

Bex nodded curtly. 'And, much as I hate to say it, you're a good addition to Yetbourne.'

'Well, great, because I'm here to stay,' said Carrie.

'In that case, remind me to introduce you to my cousin, Tabitha. You'd get along,' Bex said wryly.

Carrie decided to take that as a compliment whether it was or not.

Freddie returned then and Kit and Luella came over to join them, their arms round each other, broad smiles on their faces. 'God, Lu, you're literally joined at the hip!' Bex exclaimed, rolling her eyes once more.

'We're happy,' said Luella.

'Yeah, suck it up,' added Kit.

They kissed. Passionately.

'How about you, Bex?' said Freddie. 'See anyone you like? My great-uncle Bernard's *got* to die soon – he's ninety-seven. Fancy being a rich widow?'

She gave him a sharp look, but her eyes were dancing with fun. 'No I'm off men, boys, males, whatever,' she told them. 'I'm already making new plans for how to rise to stardom and remake my family fortune, and it doesn't involve dating at all . . .' She trailed off and Carrie followed her gaze to a young, hot social media blogger who sometimes wrote for *Surrey Style*. 'But then again . . .' They all laughed. 'What?!' she protested and went off to talk to him.

Later, when it was just Carrie and Freddie, he invited her to dance and she swayed slowly in his arms. 'I love this,' she said softly, into his ear.

'Me too,' he said. They danced for a moment more. Then he suddenly pulled away. 'Oh no, I forgot. I'd better go and top up the water in the end stable. I know we don't usually use it, but we've moved Blaze while we repair his door and I forgot to do it. I don't want to ask anyone else, not now.'

'Don't worry, I'll go,' said Carrie. Now she thought about it, she'd love a little bit of fresh air and a walk in the beautiful dusky light. Some time to herself. Let the huge day land.

'If you're sure . . .'

'No problem,' she said. 'Won't be long.'

They kissed again and she left the dance floor and headed out of the open doors on to the terrace, and then over to the yard. She took her shoes off and relished the feel of the cool grass on her bare feet. She reached the stable block and walked down over the concrete. It reminded her of the first time she'd come to the Langdon Estate. Not only had she found a job there, but a boyfriend, new friends and a whole life plan, as it had turned out. *Horses.* The very best thing in the whole world. She was living her dream, and it was just the beginning.

She reached the final stable. 'OK, Blaze, let's get you—Oh!' To her surprise, Blaze wasn't in there. Instead, a stunning chestnut mare she'd never seen was munching hay at the back wall.

And – strange – the water trough was very nearly full.

Carrie went in and the mare snickered softly as she approached. She stroked her soft nose and admired the beautiful white stripe down her face. She had the softest, kindest eyes, but there was a fierceness in them too – like she could take on the world, *fearless*.

'Hey, you. Hey, gorgeous. I'm Carrie,' she said softly. 'You're not Blaze. I guess someone made a mistake, put you in the wrong place . . .'

And then she saw the note, pinned to the wall by the hay net.

This is Spirit Dancer. You can train her and bring her on. Riding on to the pitch like that was brave. I think you'd make an amazing player. I've seen what you can do, and I want to see more.
Freddie
PS. She's yours.

Carrie gasped in delight and her heart melted with love. She looked into Spirit Dancer's kind, fierce eyes and felt an instant connection.

Carrie knew she shouldn't – they'd had no training together, and it would be dark soon, but she'd only had one drink and . . .

Soon she was mounted, bareback, her dress ruched up around her thighs and her bare feet dangling by her beautiful new horse's sides. They walked out of the yard and on to the lane.

The sky was inky blue now, studded with shining stars. With a blissful smile, she lifted her reins, spoke softly with her legs, and together they cantered into the dusk.

Acknowledgements

With huge thanks and appreciation to Lauren and Will Shadbolt for all the polo information and for taking me for a polo lesson . . . during which I realised I am actually quite competitive! Special thanks to Lauren for the kit, Will for spending half his lesson setting up shots for me, and Gordo the polo pony for putting up with my ineptitude. Thanks also to Lauren for the invaluable dressage insights and the lexicon.

Thank you to Tracy Marshall and Clive Hamilton for creating the horse hippies' paradise at Breezy Slopes, where I get so much inspiration, pick up so much poo, and get to hang out with the wonderful Sparks and his pals. And to them and the rest of the Hula Hoops – Jo, Julia, Sienna and Jane – for all the witchy magic, too!

To the fabulous Hachette team – you are all such a pleasure and inspiration to work with. Thank you to Anne Marie Ryan, Lil Chase, Georgina Mitchell and Laura Pritchard in Editorial, Cat Phipps and Adele Brimacombe for the insightful copyedit and sharp proofread respectively, Rosie Bellwood Moyler and Jen Alliston in Design, and Kim Ekdahl for the gorgeous cover. Huge thanks also to Fi Evans (Marketing), Karis Pearson (Publicity), Inka Melson (Production), Annabel El-Karim (Rights), Emma Francini, Katherine Fox, Rachael Jones and Hannah Methuen (Sales) and Sarah Lennon Galavan (Licensing). I'm so excited to be part of this wonderful team, as we get busy sharing *Unbridled* with the world.

With thanks to my brilliant agent, Joanna Devereux, and eagle-eyed beta reader, Jess Butler, too.

K. L. McKain is the UK-based author of over sixty books and has been published in more than twenty languages. She lives in the beautiful Surrey Hills with her awesome teens and spends time in Bristol too with her gorgeous man, loving city life! She's been obsessed with horses since she was a kid and honed her yard work and riding skills by working summers at a pony camp while at Uni. More recently, she's had years of fun doing natural horsemanship with ace ex-eventer Sparks, and she got the polo bug while researching for this book too – discovering her competitive side!

Follow her on Instagram @kellymckain